FLIGHT

When Someone Disappears

FLIGHT

When Someone Disappears

Genevieve Sesto

Britton Road
P R E S S

Britton Road Press
Racine, WI 53402

This book is a work of fiction.
Names, characters, places, and incidents
either are products of the author's imagination
or are used fictitiously.

Any resemblance to actual events or locales
or persons living or dead is entirely coincidental.

Designed by Sari Bogosian, Group 500

Manufactured in the United States of America

First Edition: December, 1999

Library of Congress Catalog Card Number: 99-75473

ISBN 0-9673614-4-3

For my mother

———————————

"Here Cobbet of Cobbs Corner, alone under the monkey puzzle tree, rose and muttered: 'What was in her mind, eh? What idea lay behind, eh? What made her indue the antique with this glamour—this sham lure, and set 'em climbing, climbing, climbing up the monkey puzzle tree?'"

Virginia Woolf, Between the Acts

"If it's any consolation, Sheikie, if it were slightly better it would be very likely to be a still worse lie."

Elizabeth Bowen, The Little Girls

"Sounds are more truthful than meaning, and the word is more powerful than anything."

Khodasevich

"'The way I'm telling it,' replied Sancho, 'is the way all stories are told in my country, and I don't know any other way of telling it. It isn't fair for your worship to ask me to get new habits.'

'Tell it as you like,' replied Don Quiote,' and since it is the Will of Fate that I cannot help listening, go on.'"

Miguel de Cervantes, Don Quiote

1

*She was fourteen, sweaty, smelly, and exhausted,
had recently copped a pregnancy scare,
and was fed-up with the thrill of being young.*

Doubled over on bruised palms and skinned knees, Rosie
Marone scrambled out of the dank ditch weeds, straightened
her spine, and waited on the shoulder of the freeway. When
she sneaked a look back at the cut field, it seemed to narrow
with moving night shades and creeping lines of insipid, man-
planted replacement pines. For a moment the sound of bull
frogs from the river and scrap of forest behind the field
intensified the stillness from which she'd come. A roar of
moving metal burst the silence. Rosie glowered at the blinding
headlights. She was fourteen, sweaty, smelly, and exhausted,
had recently copped a pregnancy scare, and was fed-up with
the thrill of being young.

She didn't want to hitchhike anymore, either. The last ride
had been terrifying. She'd only managed to escape being raped
by jumping out of the jerk's car at the slow-down where the off-
ramp merged. Nevertheless, battered and wary, she gave in to
the need to hitch again. With a mental shrug—nothing else
for it—Rosie stuck out her thumb.

The girl was small for her generation at her age; she looked hardly older than twelve. With dark, straight hair draping her oval face, blunted nose, and piercing, black eyes, she was a walking bitter irony, like a doubtful refugee left over from an internecine war. Case workers had avoided getting involved with her when, everything said and done, there wasn't anything they could do. Damaged goods.

Roberta Branwaithe muttered 'fool' as she pulled over and watched the skinny brown girl in holey jeans and baggy sweater drop onto the car seat. She was wary of giving a ride to this godforsaken-looking hitchhiker. But her fears had their priorities. When she'd braked, the risk to herself had seemed remoter than the danger of this reckless girl being picked up by a vicious nut. However, her foot trembled a little in relief pressing the gas pedal when the girl, who'd sunk into the corner of the passenger seat, didn't pull a knife.

"How far you going?" Roberta wanted her out of the car right now.

A morose stare. "To Chicago." The girl began wiggling the dried, lifted edge of a scab on her elbow.

"Yeah, well, that's a long way...a long way from here. Take a couple hours. I'm not going that far." Roberta measured the sentences out. She had a habit of pausing between words at critical times, as if—even though each word alone had weight—only when cemented in sentences, did they signify. So she spoke with care because even the most trivial words picked up meaning when they bonded together. Listeners who didn't know her would get irritated sometimes, forced to guess what she might be going to say, while Roberta drew her eyebrows up under her heavy, jagged bangs and splayed her nostrils at

them, thinking. People who didn't give her time to finish her
sentences would be casualties of her abstracted response.

"You've got a long trip ahead."

"So?"

"Yeah...so."

Silence. A heated silence. What a strange, inhuman fate,
thought Roberta, that this girl scorched with a blast furnace of
anger should yet be so cold, like a star in absolute zero of
outer space.

"Suppose I wanna listen to the radio?"

"Sure. Okay."

The girl fiddled with the tuner until she found a rapper
station, then clunked back into her apathetic reverie. Roberta
endured, head crushed by the noise, till she thought the girl
was sleeping, then lowered the volume.

"Hey, Stupid, I was listening to that."

"Loud...Thought you were asleep."

"No. I aint." She knifed the three words as if they had the
virtue of sending Roberta to perdition. From the corner of her
eye Roberta saw the girl slink off, retreat within herself to a
torpid, feral wariness. It takes years and years to become so
suspicious and hostile. More years than this girl had on her.
What caused such premature animus? No reply from the
hapless little crone crouched beside her.

"I'm getting off the freeway next exit."

"Yeah big deal. Leave me off there, then."

Aghast at the power of her angst, Roberta was beginning
to suspect she would not be able to ditch the girl to an
uncertain destiny. "What...you a runaway...or something?"

"Hey, don't get no funny ideas. Just leave me the hell off.

No, I aint no goddamn runaway."

"I'm just curious, that's all...You read about kids... runaways...these days. It's your own business—"

"Don't you forget it, Chick. Stick your big nose out of it."

Driving in a daze Roberta was almost mesmerized by the brash setdowns flung from the lips of this sneering brat.

Rosie whooped, "Hey...sonofabitch. Look out." At once the cruising parade of traffic screeched and recoiled, cars bucked out of line like dislocated bones. Roberta swerved avoiding a collision as two trucks rammed together, tortured steel screaming.

"My God," she cried.

"Shit," said the kid.

Her mouth a hideous grimace, Roberta wrenched, clutching the steering wheel, diving it left and right, bringing the car under control, and stuttering it to a crawl. Her heart boomed, but her vision cleared and breathing leveled. The girl screeched, jabbing at her right arm, "You all right, oh shit...you all right?"

"Oh God yes, yes I think so." She maneuvered the car along the freeway slow lane to escape the high wail of sirens. Most of the bunched traffic behind had somehow stopped short of a pile-up. In her rear-view mirror she watched two irate truckers spitting in each others contorted faces. The girl was kneeling on the seat peering out the back window.

"I aint never seen nothing like that smash-up, hell's bells."

"We were lucky...incredibly lucky." She pulled off the pavement and sat shivering at the corner of the exit ramp. Like a mechanical toy unwinding the girl slumped down and resumed her disaffected indifference. Roberta leaned her head against the steering wheel. "Okay, where do you live? I'll take you all the way there."

"I don't...I said I'm going to Chicago."

"Okay. I'll take you to Chicago. Where?"

"Where?"

"Where in Chicago...Understand?"

"Don't get hyper."

"I mean, you can't just say 'Chicago.' Chicago's a major city...a big place."

"To my uncle's. I got a uncle there. That's where I'm going."

"Oh. Where does he live?"

"I said," she huffed indignant at the questioning, a what's-the-use annoyed sound, "I know where I'm going. I got his lousy address in my pocket right now."

"Your uncle?"

"Yeah, you slow or what?"

"Okay, dig it out. Let's go there then."

The address was in Oak Park, actually, and they arrived about two in the morning, Rosie curled up asleep against the door. Roberta's eyes fumed with speckled, hot ash. Crawling along picking out darkened street numbers in the vaporous dawn, she finally spotted the address—having already stopped at a gas station to find the street—surprised that the house seemed attached to a church. She called to the girl and slid the car in front of what was clearly a parish house.

"Say, uh...wake up," she didn't know the girl's name, "Could this be the place?" Whispered mostly to herself.

Rosie complained in a drowsy stupor, "Leave me alone."

Roberta shook her shoulder, "Wake up, huh? This is the

address, I think," mist fogged the numbers hazy and indistinct, "But it's a priest's house."

"Should be. My uncle's a priest."

A fact Roberta had trouble comprehending. Every probable situation she had expected to find palled against this event. She was stymied.

"You can't just walk in there," but why not?

"I'm gone, Lady," Rosie opened the door, "I don't got nothing else to do with you."

A light came on over the small cement porch. From the arched doorway, a tall man inspissated in the gloom. He stooped slightly, had a large, hooked nose, and behind wire-rimmed glasses peered at the glow from the open car door. The lights or noise of the car must have disturbed him. Maybe he'd been up early praying or writing his sermon.

The girl had clamored out of the car, "Uncle Chuck, it's me, Rosie," and hustled up the short walk.

Leave, Roberta outlined the thought with her mouth for emphasis. The normal thing to do is get away, an impulse along the brain passageways beeped an unambiguous command to her hesitant self.

The priest met his niece, hugged her quickly, stared into the dark.

"Who's that with you? Is that your mother?"

Was she his sister, this mother of Rosie—the father's sister's child—or the daughter of his brother? Rigorous, familial words of great consequence belched over the dusky scene.

"No. Just some chicky who gave me a lift."

"You hitchhiked? Oh, no—"

"I didn't have no ten bones for the bus. Listen, hey, Uncle Chuck—"

"That was crazy, hitchhiking."

Still idling the car's engine, still vacillating in the void of what might happen and what will. Or caught among the other dimensions when myriads of events may and perhaps do randomly and simultaneously occur. Senseless to consider infinity because one thing does happen and that, after all, is what matters. Roberta shifted into first gear, slid her foot to the accelerator, was applying pressure in that node when the car sipped its first trickle of gas, when she heard the man calling to her. What matters is what is.

"Just a minute. I'd like to thank you." The priest's face filled the passenger-side window, fingers clipped over the half-closed glass. "For bringing her here. Crazy thing for the kid to do. She could've been—well you know the kinds of people lurking around these days." He was wreathed in amused kindliness, spouting genuine concern, desperate for Roberta to size him up and put him in the good-guy column.

"Yeah, something like that made me pick her up in the first place. She—"

"You have to come in, get some coffee before you go where ever you're headed."

Feeling her mind dishevelled Roberta allowed herself to traipse behind the priest toward the parish house. Rosie had been waiting on the wet grass, the dew slowly seeping through her high-tops. The sodden damp chilled her sockless feet. She faxed waves of belligerence as they approached.

"Does your mother know? Did you tell her you were coming here?"

"No."

"You've got to call her."

"No way."

Roberta slumped against a round table in the pink glary kitchen. An aftershock from the freeway accident, she felt a jarring dislocation as if she'd been deposited in the wrong frame sequence. Here she was in the early hours of the morning watching a priest, for chrissake, pitty-patting about waving coffee filters coaxing this ragdoll of defiance, whose burst of enthusiasm had been sucked away, to do something as outrageous as call her mother. The girl, hunched in the corner near an open window over the sink, seemed spellbound by the mourning doves coo-cooing in the nascent sunlight.

"It doesn't matter what kind of fight you two had. You've got to let her know you're safe." The girl stayed mute, plainly meant to ignore his gnawing commands, further impressing Roberta that at only fourteen she had also mastered stoic silence. The last words Roberta had heard from her as they entered the parish house framed a nasty sneer, "Why the hell she following us in?"

Roberta stirred a heap of sugar and cream into the coffee the priest set in front of her. Lack of sleep, being half-hallucinatory, floated her backwards into her miserable day. She'd been badgered by Jill at lunch, Jill who moaned and baited at her from beneath mounds of garden vegetables. In the morning she had entered into a weird tug-of-war, clutching opposite ends of an ape femur, with some idiot technician at the museum. Afternoon had found her drawn into a confused squabble with Cameron about Margot. The day climaxed when she had endured a horrific visit with her father at the convalescent home. All today, all absurd, all too much. Her

elbow slipped and pitying herself comfortably, she cradled her
head, hair a pleasant veil over her eyes, in her arms, on the
wood-veneer tabletop.

The priest's clammy breath tickled the back of her neck
where the hair had pulled apart, "Why don't you sleep for a few
hours before you leave? Use my sofa." She opened her eyes and
forced her head up. "It's the least...you've driven all this way
just to help my niece." They were alone in the kitchen.

"Thank you. Maybe I'd better do that."

Terrible ruckus above. Must be coming from a room
upstairs. She had seen a staircase in the front entrance hall as
she'd been taken to the living room sofa. Struggling to stay
conscious, fighting a compulsive thickening which pushed her
back into sleep, she concentrated on the ugly, strident voices—
banging metallic acrimony against her mushy wall of
senselessness. She tossed the blanket from her head, flinched
from a sudden bright light, alerted by the savagery of an
overheard quarrel. Its import jolted her fully awake.

"So you send me to hell, then. Shit on it."

"Young lady," a howl, "I'm at the end of my patience. You
will not continue to talk like a slut—"

"But you got no right to tell her."

"If you won't, I have to. Get that through your thick skull."

"I swear if you call her up no one will never see me
again..." a low, animal threat.

"You're being selfish and inconsiderate."

"I aint gonna call that fucking whore." The sound of a
collapsing star, an implosion of sense when even noise is

rendered meaningless happens when you eavesdrop. To Roberta there were no further words.

It was past time to leave. She slipped off the sofa and put on her shoes. At the door she heard the priest's footsteps on the stairway behind her.

"Miss Branwaithe," They had learned each others' names. His was Frankel, Father Charles Frankel. This was the first time he'd used hers.

"I have to go. My boss will be wondering why I'm so late." She forced an arid laugh.

"I'm sorry. I hope we didn't chase you off before breakfast." He opened wide his lidded eyes. "That girl's a handful. My sister has had serious problems with her." Worry beaded his face like perspiration. "She refuses to call her mother, and says if I call her, she'll run off." Shook his head, "Nasty. I hate to ask this, but would you phone my sister? You see, I could tell Rosie it wasn't me then. Here, tell her Rosie's safe, that's all. That you drove her here and left her with me. That she doesn't want to go back home right now. Here, I wrote her number for you. But she's okay, tell her that. Say not to fret and that I'll get in touch with her when Rosie's calmed down."

At home Roberta like a zombie under mind-control conveyed the priest's message to Rosie's mother. No response, a dead vacuity on the other end of the line. Had the woman set the phone down and gone off and got a cigarette? At least the voice who answered had admitted being the mother. When the long silence became uncomfortable even for Roberta, she broke it.

"Mrs. Marone?"

"Yeah, well, what'd you want? What am I supposed to do about it?"

"I was just checking that you heard me." Resentment coursed through her being. Bloody waste of time.

"So, what'da you want with me? That little bitch lies to me all the time. Maybe good riddance to her. Maybe why should I give a flying fuck. Useless, stinking little bitch."

"Listen," anger sped away. It had found no purchase in the other's purblind vindictiveness, "I called as a favor, to deliver your brother's —"

"Maybe you should stick to your own goddamn business. My brother the priest."

Even if she hurried now, Roberta would be at least four hours late for work, and what story could she concoct for Professor Dorcus? He would have a hard time swallowing the tale of the hitchhiker. To put it mildly.

While in the shower she heard the phone ringing. Cam. Astounding. He was babbling, albeit professorially, about Jill in a rampage bugging him to try to convince Roberta she was sorry for harassing her at lunch yesterday. Remorse hit Jill like the thud of a rhinoceros. He been trying to reach her all night. Roberta wrapped a big towel tighter around her dripping torso. Thought, so, I wasn't here last night, as she scooped up the cat, tucked the phone under her chin shivering. They all insisted she had to stay in a definite holding pattern. She wasn't allowed any kind of spontaneous action. Hell, to some people any freedom of movement meant trouble somewhere. When she was younger, people had half-expected a little divergence from the norm of her. It had been emancipating when she had picked up the reputation of being absentminded, a bit unreliable. Those old days, she could blink and say just about anything—in her slow, drawl, composed from her over-flowing lexicon, words couched in learned, shy terms formed by years of voracious reading—and get away with it. Her cool grey eyes would peer out from behind heavy dark bangs. Back then, she could damn well let the suffocating world jeer. It only insured her the room to breathe. But now, getting a bit older as she hated to contemplate, did she, in addition, have to give way under the bulldozing delusions of others.

Cam's voice droned on. Years after their divorce he continued to intrude. Yes, he might still care about her, in a creepy, co-dependent way. But then, Cam cared about everyone—each from the perspective of his or her own karma. He had a unique conception of karma and had built a reputation teaching and writing about it. His caring was sincere, as far as his vision of Atman and the condition of his or her spiritual essence went. And true he was grieved if he saw someone with a heavy karma continuing to damage the elastic fabric of the universal soul.

Cam was wiser now, though less brilliant, than he had been twenty-five years before when they had gone to India on his Fullbright. While he eschewed money, he revelled in academic honors and accolades. Within his discipline, he had accumulated an awed following. But to Roberta Cam's personality seemed to get more evanescent, unfocused, dimmer every year.

"I'm glad to hear you're okay, Roberta."

"Why wouldn't I be?" Sprawled on the sofa she unplugged

from her thoughts and visualized drinking a hot cup of tea.

"By the way, where were you last night?"

"I spent the night in a seedy motel with a lover."

"Sure. Well, that's...great. Jill wouldn't...well, it's just...well, okay. You know. Did you figure out why you ranted at me about Margot—"

"Cam, yesterday, I didn't mean to go ballistic. I was simply trying to find out where she is. She's at another school. My last two letters to her came back to me in a note about her not being enrolled at Tilbury anymore. Why would she be at another school without us knowing, Cam?"

"She's probably in Paris by now—"

"Paris, what do you mean? Nobody's told me anything."

"Quit shouting, Roberta. I'd have explained yesterday if you hadn't run off. So give me a chance to now. My parents talked about taking Margot out of Tilbury. I didn't catch why."

"And you didn't care?"

"And I didn't pursue it. It was something about wanting to be in London for her last term. The way I understood it, she was to have a holiday with them in Paris, and then return to finish school in London, I didn't catch the name of the place."

"Why didn't anybody tell me all this was going on?"

"I tried to yesterday. You were in such a big hurry."

"It was bad timing. I had that new skull."

He drew out the pause. "And that's why my parents are in charge of Margot. No good flying off the handle like you did—"

"I did not."

"What's the matter, Roberta? You always start on my parents when something's bothering you."

"I was...nonplused when those letters came back."

"You should have called Alice."

"Should...I have to hunt all over creation to find out where my own daughter is?"

"You're making something out of nothing. I'll call my mother and get the details."

"Margot's whereabouts is not exactly a detail. Why she left Tilbury is not a detail."

He heaved, "She's all right."

"Yes, yes, I know. You explained it sort of. Only something sounded wrong. Maybe there's a residue of psychology sticking. Cam, I gave a ride to this pathetic, foul-mouthed, dirtball girl last night. I don't want to believe Margot could ever feel like a castoff."

"Fat chance. Margot appreciates us. All that we've done and what her grandparents are able to give her, too."

"She could be dissembling. What she really feels. Don't they all? I think I did. I think I hid what I felt until I was forty."

"She's fine, Roberta. She's doing great. I don't want to jinx it by saying anything. But she seems to be handling those adjustments, you know, the traumas of adolescence, pretty well. All that folderol, existentially speaking." He smiled in unperturbed condescension.

"Good-bye, Cam. Sooner or later I have to get to work."

"Oh, Roberta, that's it huh? Last night, you took a runaway home, right?"

"Nobody does that anymore."

2

Even he, smug in his ego, well-satisfied by the results of his persistence and sure of acceptance, for a moment was struck dumb at the audacity of science.

Professor Donald Dorcus approached with a slight limp and surveyed a table of fossils, hominid bones and teeth, at center of his lab. The mandible of an erectus leaned against a heap of fragmented frontal remains all under a hanging tube shedding florescent light on the collection below. Pushing aside a few of the bones, he lay his galley proofs, newly arrived, on the corner of the table. Professor Dorcus allowed himself to reflect how amazing it was that he had studied these enigmatic two-million-year-old remains and gleaned enough to have written the thousands of words entombed in the manuscript he had just set down right next to them. For one brief moment how the slight clues—but he would never have called them that—from these fossils had been transfigured by his written word became a personal miracle. Mostly he didn't squander his vaunted thinking processes with such idle speculation. But he had been theorizing last evening over a glass of wine with some old friends, and he was hung over today with boozy, evocative conversation. He considered himself a sensitive man. They had tempted him, these simple desiccated bones obscured by millennium. He had anointed them in oily interpretation. But meaning? His manuscript levitated before him. Even he, smug in his ego, well-satisfied by the results of his persistence and sure of acceptance, for a moment was struck dumb at the audacity of science. So he stood a moment in foolish wonder before snapping back to himself. Best not to get too carried away over one's own accomplishments.

Looking up he saw Roberta, arms loaded, bobbling the lab door open with her hip. She looked slightly embarrassed, but then that was too often her expression. The woman didn't stand up straight. Not that she stooped, no, but even though she had good height, she would never be called regal. And there was something about the tilt of one shoulder. It all signaled 'vulnerable' to him, more so than women's stances generally did. A sport, a freak of nature with a forceful intelligence misapplied. But she was mostly inoffensive. Her awkwardness was one legitimate reason he could excuse her brain and keep her on here. He unconsciously suspected she was smarter than he. She had told him once when she was getting ready to emblazon some wrongheaded theory, that words were untrustworthy in attributing meaning to the fossils. She unnerved him with such babel.

Under one elbow she was lugging VARIOUS NEW INTERPRETATIONS OF APE AND HUMAN ANCESTRY which she must have lifted from his desk. He'd been missing it for days.

"I'm sorry I'm late, Donald, I had a devil of a time getting back home after visiting my father yesterday. Not because of the visit, but lordy what happened afterward...I was stuck like a butterfly pinned until an hour ago. Doing penance over and beyond what was necessary."

He had a hard time following her. Luckily it didn't matter that he should. "Yes, well, I'm sure your excuse is valid," whatever it was. Dorcus backed up tidily to the table's edge and reached behind him for the proofs.

"I want you to help correct these. 'Locomotor Adaptations' just arrived this afternoon. And thank you for returning that text." They both glanced at the volume clasped to her hip. He set out his palm in the universal gesture. The book had been a review copy. Something ignoble compelled him to ask, "Was there anything interesting in it?"

"One of the mitochondrial papers, Lohmiller's." She eased the tome off her hip onto the table knocking aside a femur shaft. "The way he puts it it's almost mystic: an evolutionary timepiece. Click on the file and bong, here's where we come in. Very neat, almost Deistic."

She knows nothing whatever about it, he blushed in relief, "Yes, Darwin would be horrified."

"On, no, fascinated, Blyth would have been horrified. I'll get to these proofs right now, Donald." Gone quietly, he thought, she sneaks off, Apache-like, and wished he could dock her for being late. But the department didn't pay by the hour for his research assistant.

Roberta Branwaithe had a tiny metal desk in a converted

broom closet office where all this particular afternoon she labored correcting Dorcus' proofs. Within the deeply obscured, alien Pliocene her mind sloughed in pleasure until, as it began to be dusk, Cameron phoned.

"There's no address for Margot yet, Roberta. She stayed on in Paris with my dad. Mother said they hadn't decided which school for her senior year, form, or whatever they call it. In England, I guess...Roberta? You're upset about this, I can tell."

"Perceptive of you I'd have said if I were sarcastically inclined."

"But you're not."

"No. I'm not. I...I'm, I want to see her, Cam, right away, as soon as she's back in New York. She say when?"

"My mother's back in London."

"My daughter...will get back with them to New York? Did your mother say when?"

"Our daughter. They're going to stay in London next. A week or so, I guess."

No more hiding in Pliocene peace. Inflated with worry, Roberta was squeezed tight into her hard chair. Worried about exactly what, she baited herself. Come on, dimwit, figure out what's making you feel like a pickled bladder. Free-floating anxiety? Or inchoate apprehension caused by Rosie Marone and Father Charles Frankel? Something set off by Rosie's mother, the sister of the priest? Maybe Dorcus' unctuous tricks, chock-full of aggression, were finally getting to her? Oh, sure. Or simply because of the new habilis controversy? Perhaps because Farzi had become suddenly distracted, and Terry no longer made her laugh, and Cam pitied the whole unbalanced human race? Of course not. No, none, none of that bothered her. Was it because Jill had taken it upon herself after all these years to lead her back to God? Surely no. Well then, could it be because of her daughter Margot, growing up cheerful and bright, thriving on the good things provided by her rich grandparents and loving absentee parents? Certainly not, Fool. The grief of her seventy-six year old father slipping into self-induced decrepitude after a stroke had weaken him, but not hurt his brain? No, no, no. She was forced to the conclusion that there was nothing to worry her, oh, Pangloss, in this best of all possible worlds.

At the Union parking ramp she met Jon Martin coming from one of his perpetual night classes. A bald, sleek head, and short, spherical two-piece suit, charged at her from around a cement pillar in the fumy underground. Pink cheeks and cupid lips mocked his serious, green-eyed gaze. They had been neglecting each other without knowing it, the way people fond of each other but not intimate do. Meticulous, deliberate, clownish and erudite, Professor Martin was finishing the last part of his book on Ezra Pound. It had been tedious, unwilling work. Often he patronized Roberta because he could whine to her about his morbid inability to write his own poetry.

He insisted they leave off going home and have dinner together. Sitting opposite him she ate nachos with hot peppers and let the balm of his litany on self-sacrifice cloak her anxiety. Their talk rambled diverse directions, from local interests, Ezra Pound, of course, sexual dimorphism and chimpanzee teeth, to the arcane—how Tutankhamen came to change his name. Even went roundabout to the political—the deal over minority recruitment; and finally over the frontier to the aesthetic—hybrid tea rose judging, his true passion.

Back to Ezra Pound, "A crappy piece of doggerel, I think." Piqued, she was gazing through him, snapped "Roberta?"

"It must be wretched to be a writer," More annoyed, was she talking about himself or Ezra Pound? But she was remembering at that moment, an old woman in India who had squatted crossed-ankled in a gentle, clipping rain which glittered the vegetation to lime as it plummeted through the yellow sunshine. And she sensed that writing out such thoughts steal bits of your soul away.

Shaking off what he thought was her sarcasm, he muttered, "I think so, too, and I'd kill myself to be one," and begrudged that she had gotten more than he from this chance meeting. Even so, they both parted in better humor than they had been in when they'd met.

Under the car's windshield wiper blade, she found a note from Farzi. It had that brief, Farzi Bahroozi quality— searched all over the damn campus for you, call immediately. Farzi had been distant lately, self-contained. Roberta stared at the note removing the import, pondering the rich exotic handwriting. Something was not right, like a pimple coming to a head.

"Farzi?"

"Oh, Christ, Berta, thank heavens. Just listen. I can't—

where the hell were you?"

"At La Villita—"

"Never mind that. Listen, I'm in kind of a jam—"

"Oh, Farzi.."

"You will help me without being filled in on the big picture?"

"What do you mean? The big picture...Farzi, what are you talking about?"

"You can do that, Berta, when other people can't. Well, I couldn't either, but you can."

"What's going on?" Dread plunked into her stomach at Farzi's colorless monotone.

"Suffice it to say without getting into anything, that I'm in...this jam. And I need your help. First off, don't tell anyone, anyone at all, I called you."

"What is it, Farzi?" It had to be a hoax. "This isn't funny."

"No, most assuredly it is not. Now Roberta pay attention. Go to my house, pack a bag for me. The suitcases are in the basement. Pack up my clothes, make-up, anything you think I'll want. Use your head, Roberta, not what you'd need but what you think I'll need. And listen, don't tell anyone—not only that I called, but that you even know me. If anybody asks say, 'Farzi who?' Keep the bags at your place. When I can call again, I'll let you know where to take them. Thanks, Berta, I—"

"Wait, Jesus, don't hang up. You're scaring me. What in the world is going on?"

"You'll have to do without the big picture, Berta. I know you can."

"But I haven't got any pic—"

"Benedicite, Roberta, be blessed." She heard the dial

tone, dropped perplexed to the floor and put her hands over her aching face. The cat jumped on her belly and rubbed his head under her breasts. What in the hell was going on?

She rocked her head a little letting the puzzle of Farzi become absorbed and focused, take its place among the other apprehensions. Misgivings drained through her brain like water in a colander, runnels trickling away. Still solace crept forward coalescing—it was Farzi just now on the phone, not any of the others. She lifted her head, puppy-like panted a smile, pushed heavy asymmetrical bangs off her forehead. Farzi, it was Farzi causing this uproar. Farzi the melodramatic, the excitable, temperamental sculptor of clay and moods and phantasmagoria. Of course it would be absurd, as absurd and offbeat, as annoying and amusing as Farzi could be. So let it rest, thought Roberta, try to go to bed.

But it wasn't to be dismissed so easily. In bed she lay awake, her helmet of resolve sitting protectively on her mind, but the many worries sticky underneath it like a turtle's calipee. Farzi's words sank to her stomach's bottom and burbled there overripe and noisome. All the formless, evanescent accidents of existence over which she had no power capered by, mocking her. Let it all be, let it all go, she turned to the placebo of television, and immediately switched it off. Better to bundle up in her own head than hide in that ultimate distraction.

Years ago, her father had run for the state senate. It had begun in his office during a slow engineering period when he'd one day been moved to write a hard-hitting letter to the editor about global warming, and soon after began weekly letter-writing. The local politicos had tagged him as an ideal candidate. But he was really too intelligent to be effective at political rallies. He came across in the campaign, with his long, esoteric diatribes, as almost incoherent. All his charm, talent, his probity and understanding were distorted by his inability to keep things simple. His consequent defeat had humiliated him.

Lulled by thoughts of her father's fit of politicking, other tiny memories came to comfort, disappearing or diffusing, and a narcotic balm eased her troubled psyche. She felt a pulse of release.

Telephone ring shattered her doze. The cat who'd hopped next to her head on the pillow gave off tiny meows of annoyance. New York. A call from there. Roberta ordered her drowsy thoughts; someone in the dark, vague images of a city not totally alien to her, a city remote and huge, repetitive. A sluggish moment more to connect with an austere voice.

"This is Alice, Roberta. Did I wake you?"

"No." Why was she always compelled to lie when asked that?

"Good."

"Is Margot all right?"

"Oh, yes. I didn't mean to upset you calling so late. She's fine, just fine."

"You don't call..."

"Yes, well Roberta..." Why was the woman so obtusely outspoken. "You know how busy life gets. Margot and Harold are finishing our little vacation. I had to get home. I hope Cameron's spoken to you by now about her change of plans. She's been accepted to Eastbourne for next term. Cameron seemed to think...he thought you were...that a new school didn't settle well with you. I understand your attitude, but you don't have to be concerned. This is a wonderful opportunity for her. It's almost impossible to get—"

"Alice, I haven't any attitude. I've been wanting to reach Margot. Can you give me her phone number."

"Wait, I have our itinerary in here someplace. Brighton. You see Harold will call as soon as they're settled in Brighton...I don't normally...well, I haven't got a number for tonight, Roberta. Harold will call from Brighton when they get there tomorrow. If it's an emergency..." But it wasn't, and she knew it.

"Call me with the number, tomorrow then, please."

"Certainly, Roberta."

Hot tea might be good, or better yet, something really strong after Alice. But for years Roberta had refused to drink. Not since she'd rejected, regretfully, numbing chemical mindlessness. She wasn't sure why. But she'd determined that for some inarticulate reason, she would take it all—until she couldn't take it any longer—she would take it all straight.

Action, activity, movement, whenever her mind drifted off her work, Roberta took solace in concocting her evening. At dusk she collected Farzi's belongings. To her surprise the key was where Farzi had said it would be. Throwing everything she could lay hands on in fifteen minutes into three suitcases, she hauled them away in her car.

Before going home she made a return visit to her father's nursing home in a village about twenty-five miles west of town. She used the time driving to work up a defensive stand against her father. No matter what he said tonight, she would be pleasant. No matter what.

He was hiding in a dark corner of his room, perhaps sleeping. She turned to leave, she wouldn't want to wake him, when he lifted his head.

"What are you doing here? It hasn't been a week already, has it? Boy if it has, I've lost what's left of my mind for sure. Roberta?"

"I thought I'd drop back and check on you. I'm sorry. I didn't mean to get angry yesterday."

"I don't think you're sorry about anything."

Roberta sat on the edge of his bed, the window behind her throwing her face in shadow, so the old man had to jerk around in his chair and squint at her.

"Do you like the book I left?"

"Didn't have time to look at it yet. Can't read much anymore. Tires my eyes, you know."

"Yes."

"I don't want to forget. When you leave, tell the nurse, the one with the bad varicose veins, behind the desk in the entrance hall, that I take my dinner in my room. She's new, and I didn't get a lunch."

"Don't you think you'd be better off eating with the others? It must get dull in here. And, after all, you'll be leaving this place soon. You have to get used to being around people again. I think you'd want to...talk to—" He was looking at her as if she were sneering or taunting him.

"I prefer my own company—"

"Come on, Dad..."

"No. You come on. It's disgusting seeing all that suffering...old, deluded humanity...miserable people."

"I know. I mean, I think...I see what you mean, but you'll be out of here soon—"

"They drool. They're so old they drool, or they're too sick to care." Roberta cupped her hand over her mouth. "You don't remember your grandfather, Roberta. He died young. My mother, too. She had eleven children but several of them never made it past the age of three. Infants, they died. I was just thinking, sitting here, as a matter of fact right before you came in, recalling my father. He was not a man to respect learning. But that's an old story you've heard before. Once, at the funeral of one of my...I think it was a little brother, I myself couldn't have been more than five years old. I was so afraid in that long pew that I hunched over, scared of it all, you know. My older sister, Edna, was sitting between our father and me. And he whispered to her, 'Tell him to sit up.'" He began a low chortle. 'Tell him to sit up.'"

"Long time ago, Dad."

"'Tell him to sit up.'"

"Dad? Margot's coming soon. Maybe when you're well enough again, in a month, it sounds like by what the doctor said, you'll be going home. Could be sooner. The three of us could go someplace together. Maybe we could rent a cottage on the beach."

He drew in his eyes. "I haven't seen Margot in almost a year, Roberta." For a moment his face had cleared, then he dipped his head, searching, mumbling, "I've lost my alarm clock, damn it. See if you can find it in this mess somewhere."

"It's here, right here on the floor next to you."

He refused to believe he was getting better. Never in his life had he been afraid to confront evidence that smacked him in the face. She rose too angry to speak. Was this some loathsome game he was playing? Again somebody else's goddamn game?

He gripped the alarm clock on his lap, "I was all hunkered over because I was afraid, and the old man whispered to Edna..."

Peace, peace...Thou talk'st of nothing. Nothing. She slipped down the hall and out the back way fighting hot tears making her more angry still.

Arriving home Roberta left Farzi's baggage locked in the trunk of the car and was scrambling eggs for dinner when the mysterious men came. They were heralded by a peremptory pounding, a sputter of staccato on the door. This racket had to be about Farzi; no one she knew would announce that way. Sliding the cover on the pan so the cat wouldn't get the eggs, she whisked open the door defiantly frightened. Two tough guys, squat, dark, glowering, spoke at her with heavily accented, menacing phrases.

"We look for Farzaneh Bahroozi. It will be true you know her."

"Yes, of course, yes, I know her. Who are you?" She didn't invite them in.

"She now our cousin. Tell us we can find her."

"I can give you her address." Her tone leaked the knowledge that she knew very well that Farzi wouldn't be there, and that they knew it, too. Not too swift a bluff. She scraped her front teeth over her bottom lip. The men shifted their bodies, raising their bellies.

"Address we have. She is not there. You, her friend, can tell us where she is. This her landlady tells."

"If Farzi isn't home, I don't know where she is. There are lots of places she could be. The gallery to start with. She could be on a business trip if you can't find her there." Stupid thing to admit she might be gone. Roberta's insides started trembling.

"We have looked these places. Landlady says you know where Farzaneh is." The two men had alternated speaking in staccato deadpan. Now one of them began to cough, hacking away, spitting phlegm into a clean hanky.

"I really don't know where else she could be."

"You know."

"No, I don't. Farzi doesn't tell me where she goes. Why should she? I didn't even know she had a landlady." She shoved the door at them, but they held it pushed open against her. It was their first threatening move, and Roberta bitterly regretted having been so daft as to have answered the door in the first place. Not knowing Farzi's whereabouts didn't automatically make her safe, as long as these brutes thought she did know.

"You, woman. We search for two days. No one has seen her. No one say where she is. This not strange?"

"Yes, it is. Maybe I ought to call the police. It isn't like Farzi, you're quite right. I'll do that this minute." She pulled one foot back and planted it behind her appearing to the men as if she might stand there denying Farzi until they melted into a pool at her feet. They eyed each other tacitly agreeing that under limited pressure Roberta wasn't about to admit where their fugitive was, and decided that they were not in a good position to argue further. Opting for discretion, they wheeled and left.

Roberta closed, locked, bolted the door, tripped to the sofa and collapsed. Farzi had gotten herself into some very heavy stuff. She evaluated her part in the nasty little scene and confessed that, faced with the powers of ruthlessness, she had been more worried about herself than about protecting Farzi. Perhaps Farzi hadn't told her where she was, or what this was all about, because she thought Roberta was weak and would spill everything as soon as she was threatened. No, she retracted that indictment. Farzi wouldn't think she was a coward, only...circumspect. None more practical than Farzi. You can't tell what you don't know and thus ignorance should protect you. Well, telling what you do know doesn't make you safe either. The men's coming had spelled an evil portent.

3

*Feeling eyes watching her as if she had no right
to be carrying them, Roberta lugged
the incriminating bags nowhere.*

The actual transfer of the suitcases went off without a hitch. But the night before their delivery Roberta was left immobile by the relentless squeeze of doing Farzi's bidding. So much mumbo jumbo. First of all Farzi had not said, in the brief, elliptical phone call she'd made to Roberta's office, what the passing procedure would be.

Roberta had been finishing up Dorcus' proofs when Farzi called. As if reading a telegraph, Farzi had intoned her instructions for the next day. Bring her bags to the airport main concourse at five-thirty. That was all. She hadn't even waited for Roberta to breathe out and agree before she clicked off.

Then there was the problem of why these wild goings-on were happening in the first place which bedevilled Roberta all night. Had Farzi somehow gotten into deep trouble in the import business side of her gallery? Maybe because of her Middle Eastern connections? Farzi's father, Heshemi Behroozi, had maintained close ties with family members in the export trade filtering circuitously from Iran. Through him, Farzi and her partners, Denis Goldfarb and Anthony Cracroft, had acquired a thriving sideline in Middle Eastern artifacts. These fine art objects fetched excellent prices and subsidized their talented cadre of contemporary artists without financial discomfort to the gallery. Had Farzi gotten into a jam because she tried to cheat—not likely with Farzi, not at all. Or make too good a deal with some foreign sharper, something that got out of hand? Unlikely. Maybe, then, she'd fallen afoul some shady character? More unlikely still since her family was so respected as to be revered in Iran, and shady types were not to be found among them. But perhaps Farzi had unwittingly got hold of a piece of art that was stolen, or that wasn't to be taken out of the country, for national prestige reasons, and...god, a war could start over something like that. No, not possible. A blackmarket item? Not out of the question since Farzi dealt solely through Teheran. However, unlikely...Better yet, perhaps the business dealings had gotten messed up in the religious conflicts endemic over there: fanatics, Shiites, Summi, whichever was Farzi's family anyway? On the correct side, one could be sure, whatever that was...Could Farzi's side not be as inviolate as she had imagined? Farzi in the middle of a religious uproar? Not only doubtful, inconceivable. Worldly, secular, uninhibited Farzi? But the trouble must have to do with the business somehow for Farzi to run away like this, to hide. Probably something to do with art commerce, something mainly negligible, Roberta had temporized and was able to sleep at last.

An airport is a damn suspicious place to meet a fugitive. Feeling eyes watching her as if she had no right to be carrying them, Roberta lugged the incriminating bags nowhere. Relax, lots of other suitcases around. But what if the two foreign thugs had tailed her? Didn't it make sense that they would? So here she was leading them straight to Farzi. The sheer, utter nonsense of this farce was making her panicky.

Next to the women's rest room at the place where three main hallways met, as Roberta zipped her head about looking for Farzi, she spotted a very tiny woman in high heels approach and beckon her to follow. Feeling criminal and dirty she trailed her to the bathroom. If this wasn't some silly game, the world was making less and less sense. Nevertheless she traipsed after the tiny lady. Damn, damn it, Farzi. At times Roberta did question the sanity of situations. Reality, after all, is difficult to check. However, those other hiatuses in normality seemed nothing compared to this, this whatever—boundless vacancy of sense. Be calm, it's like looking between the stars.

At the row of toilet stalls the tiny woman stood nodding. When Roberta moved closer to her, she grabbed the bags and whispered, "Farzi says thanks, and she'll call you as soon as she can."

"Where is she—"

"Be quiet. It's not safe. Give me ten minutes before you leave here."

Nothing, therefore, left for Roberta to do but to go to the sink and run hot water over her suddenly freezing hands.

The last of the sun was glowing golden on the cat's white chest, when Roberta's telephone began ringing. Farzi's voice.

Roberta shouted, "Dammit, give me a chance to speak. Two scuzzy-looking men came after you here."

"I expected there'd be somebody."

"They weren't pleasant—"

"I'm sorry, Berta. The suitcases got delivered all right?"

"Yes. Okay. Now, tell me what trouble you're in."

"No. I can't. I am...as you say, in a bit of trouble. But I'm not going to drag you into it."

"What? You already have—"

"No. No, I haven't. People are vicious, Berta, and...you never understand that."

"I damn well do to."

"I've a hard time understanding this myself." Her voice dropped a notch; she was pooped. "Whatever can account for people, huh?"

"Adaptive radiation." That wasn't appreciated. "Farzi, what do I do now? Should we call the police? I think we better call them."

"No, no, don't do that. That wouldn't help at all. I should have lied to you, too. Maybe it would have been best. But I needed my things, and...I'm going to need some more help. No police and don't ask me anything. I'll let you know where I am, when I can."

"Farzi—"

"Benedicite."

Time passed under an almost constant hot drizzle.

It was turning into an unusual, wet, late August. For these long dog days Roberta's respite from a series of persistent worries was work. Professor Dorcus had become embroiled in the newest fossil uproar, and they had, as a result, been measuring teeth. They ran data through computers, condensed and analyzed results, reformed favorite theories to match unlooked for outcomes, pondered. For long hours Roberta and Dorcus haunted the lab. The deeper into the fossil story they fell, the more intricate and mysterious the questions became. Exhausted from numbers dancing, meanings aiding contradictions, bickering, Roberta was protected from an overdose of anxiety.

So exhausted by work was she that she was able to visit her father without much dread. Approaching his room her brain began to pinch a little, but mental fatigue refused to give it enough stimulus to annoy her. Nevertheless being cautious she stopped outside his open door. Her father was singing very low. Attending, she caught the words.

"I went to the animal fair. The birds and the beasts were there. The old baboon by the light of the moon was combing his auburn hair."

She smiled like an idiot alone in the hall. At the zoo when she was a child, her father had stood transfixed at the ape cage. She'd be impatient to go on; she had liked the lions better. In front of the lowland gorilla he'd bounce and make faces. On a whim the huge creature would toss his seven hundred pounds at the clear partition scaring the hell out of the staring people—momentarily. Then they'd see at once that they were out, and he was still in. And the big, calm gorilla would bare his teeth, then turn his backside up and swing-strut onto his rubber tire. Her father alone had never flinched at the gorilla's rush and impact. He would smirk back at the animal in victory. Now he sang about the baboon sotto voce in his tiny dark room.

The noise of her entering made him look up. The drapes were open letting in sunlight, an empty glass of milk was on his bedside table. His eyes betrayed some pleasure at seeing her. Fleetingly she wanted to tell him about Farzi's running away. But he spoke first and changed her mind.

"You know, Roberta, as I get older, people get uglier and animals more beautiful."

"What do you mean, Dad?"

"Are you going to sit down and stay?"

"Yes," she said not sitting. "How've you been?"

"Pretty bad, I suppose. No one tells me anything anymore."

She sat, then, on the edge of the bed where he lay poised, out of place.

"I couldn't get here any earlier this week. We've been working late in the lab. We're involved in a new species controversy. I guess we're taking sides this time."

He'd have run with that one if he'd been himself. He'd have asked questions, demanded details. Gone out and gotten a book. Whatever had happened during the stroke had not just stopped him, but made him a hellishly different man. No, she told herself, that wasn't true. Irrational backlash. Stop it. Yet strokes affect the brain, illness does. But he was the same man. Personality was infused...a part of the mind. What changes? Nothing, he was himself and that was clear. Or was she biased, a scientist telling stories, seeing what she expected to see? I see my father, I hear my father.

"Can you reach my clock, Roberta? What time is it?"

She ignored him, "In a month, tops, you'll be walking out of here—"

"You think so?"

"The doctor says so. I'm telling you the truth, Dad."

"Yes, yes, you always do that, Roberta. You're so damned honest. Really honest, not phony honest. Too honest. We noticed when you were just a little kid. Hey, kids lie, sometimes. But not you."

"I lied, Dad, just didn't get caught."

"I wished you hadn't been so goddamned honest." He raised his head propelling his voice insistently against her. Roberta was appalled not so much by his accusation, if it was one, and it sounded like one, but by his gleeful, withering, spitefully cheerful tone. She wanted to stand, if she could manage to, and bolt out.

"I have to cut this visit short. I've got a lunch date with Jill and Terry—"

"And I know that's the truth, too. You wouldn't just be saying that to get yourself out of. here, a miserable sickroom. No, not you. Someone else might. I might...and all that honesty was damn unhealthy in a kid. I remember telling your mother when you'd admitted...what was it? I'd been trying to find out who broke my saw blade. I think it was the saw blade. Anyway, I went around asking people, and when I asked you, you didn't deny it. Fact is you didn't even try to squirm out of it. Not pride, nothing like, I cannot tell a lie, I chopped down the cherry tree. That I would've understood. Little precocious arrogance like that. But you just didn't see a thing wrong, or right, with telling me that you'd done it. You should because you should, not because you should or you shouldn't. Know what I mean? I said to your mother right then what all that honesty would lead to—"

"All right," she shouted and that shut him up. "Whatever this is, I'd like you to stop."

"I'll say what I damn well please."

"And I don't have to stay to listen to it. Talk about something sensible, interesting."

"This topic interests me. Your incorrigible honesty... your intransigence, that's what he said finally got to Cam, too. Ruined your marriage."

"Nothing gets to Cam. He's in another world," and thought, Cam would never have said anything like that. She couldn't vocalize the thought because that would enrage him. It was too much like her telling the truth which had riled him up in the first place.

"Okay, then, just take off, Roberta...with your goddamned honesty. You're not going to harp on me about my health, or when I'll get out of here. Do you understand me?"

"I'll see you early next week." She wouldn't explain, wouldn't apologize, wouldn't capitulate; she would make it through the doorway.

"You could do me a favor and bring me some fruit next time."

Pushing out the room she heard him resume singing. She moved fast down the deodorized hall, reached into her pocket for her keys. Her fingers touched enamel. She pulled her hand out and opened her grip. A tooth. A prehistoric, hominid tooth. Christ, when she'd left the lab, she'd pocketed a two million-year-old molar. Clever jab from the cosmic joker.

Roberta didn't feel zippy enough for Terry and Jill—of their friends they asked inordinate enthusiasm and collaboration—but she had agreed to have lunch in case Jill had news about Farzi. She would give herself a little time, to ask people subtly and hunt around, then go to the police. Her father's tirade meant to bait and mock her, was a sharp-etched caricature of what she had challenged in herself at Farzi's enigma. Honesty for Roberta wasn't a clever ploy. She had dangled over that pit a few times and knew what it meant. However she had to trust in clear-headed reliability, or she would never be able to find Farzi, or help her.

Terry brought over drinks, and settled himself into an amorphous purple chair opposite Roberta. In the gaps between his loud guffaws, she heard Jill's voice carrying to them non-stop from the kitchen. Roberta shifted around, sipped the lemonade mechanically, and bid herself relax. These, after all, were her good friends since before Cam and she had split. She should unwind with them. Instead colors shimmered abnormally bright, their diamond-edged auras glaring. She felt too warm. Taking a deep breath, she shuddered at Terry's gutsy, bugle laugh.

When she sensed Jill's presence coming up behind her, the awful clarity receded. Terry had his beefy fists in the potato chips.

"So, how's your old man?"

"Oh. The same."

Jill sat on the ottoman between them. "Hey, Terry, quit now. We're having lunch in fifteen minutes—"

"Gotta fuel up. We're doing a big tree removal this afternoon on Highway V. County's clearing up road marginals."

They had never married, and Roberta thought, it wasn't likely they would ever need to. Years ago, he had come with the wood chips Jill had ordered for her new shrubs, and he had never left. It was hard to believe he was the gone-to-fat son of a millionaire.

During the meal Roberta struggled to be lighthearted and companionable. "You're not going to believe it. This morning I accidentally filched one of Professor Dorcus' teeth. If he's noticed it's missing, he'll be hysterical, gone off in a screaming fit."

"His tooth?"

"How could—"

"Not his own tooth. I walked off with a prehistoric hominid fossil. I can't believe I did it."

"That's real hard for me to swallow."

"I know. It's right here." Reaching in her pocket impressed with herself, knowing how she'd feel if someone could, during dinner talk, whip out such a peerless relic.

" Here it is."

"I can't see anybody being gulled by that evolution stuff."

"What stuff, Terry?"

"Didn't you just say that tooth is supposed to be an ape-man's?"

"Something like that."

"I don't believe in all that crap. It's against God. And anyway, people already proved it wrong. You come here—

I don't want you to bring up that bullcrap. I know you gotta earn a living and everything, but that don't mean I gotta have that junk in my own home."

There is no way to combat friendly fire. She could see that Terry was controlling himself, holding back from saying what he'd like to say, could tell that by his monitored syntax. So maybe the polite response was silence. Silence, however, is acquiescence. Avoiding this skirmish would disempower her. But did that mean one had to argue with every fool? In a flash she felt guilt, was about to shut up as penance when Terry reared back in his cradling easy chair and proclaimed:

"Such a bunch of shit."

You can't always pick your battles. Roberta reacted temperately, "There's disagreement right now in the field, looking at the fossils, about what bones belong to what species, and even how many species there really are. But there isn't any doubt that this particular tooth belonged to someone who wasn't quite us, but was almost human— over two million years ago. If you really want to be picky you could call him or her a proto-human. Maybe that's less of an insult," elevating the tooth in front of his face, "to whoever wore this."

Terry jerked away from the tooth exactly as the people at the zoo had done when the gorilla's chest hit the clear reinforced barrier.

"That isn't a human tooth, it's too big."

"Good for you. That's exactly right. For the kind of human we are."

"Nothing's going to make me believe all that shit,

Roberta. Where the hell do you think we all came from two million years ago? It don't make any sense."

"Closer to six million years ago—"

"Six million years ago in time? You're full of it. I'm not going to listen to this shit." Jill, who'd sat in silence through the affray, jittered uneasily making little conciliatory noises.

Roberta strategically retreated, lower lip slid down sideways, "Well, it's intriguing to speculate." Her ears burned.

Terry began shoveling in chicken parts at a terrific pace. Shy of where her last quarrel with Roberta had gone, Jill switched to a safer topic.

"What do you think about Farzi getting married?"

"Where is she?"

"In New York of course, having her wedding dress made. Roberta, don't tell me you didn't know?"

"I haven't talked with her in...awhile."

"We were on the East Side last weekend and dropped into the gallery. Denis said they had an O'Keefe print for my office. Something special—"

"Marrying who?"

"Tony, of course. Roberta, have you and Farzi had a fight?"

"No. Did she tell you herself she was going to New York?"

"She told me the very next day. They were asking too much for that O'Keefe. Farzi called to say they'd go down a little on the price. Then she told me she was going to shop for her wedding stuff in New York, but I should come in anyway and pick up the print from Denis or Tony. She made off that she was sacrificing on the price, but that's a laugh. What does Farzi know about sacrifice? Going to New York for her trousseau. Roberta, really I can't believe she didn't tell you she was getting married. What's going on?"

"I've been working late. I've been hard to find This all...marriage...sounds rather sudden anyway."

"It's hardly sudden. They've been going together for years."

"Well the...settling on a date sounds sudden."

"Then again maybe she didn't tell you because she thinks you don't approve of marriage. Because you're divorced. So she didn't let on to you about it. I'm not surprised. She can get so secretive. To tell you the truth, I think she really didn't want to tell me either. She acted a little put off. Maybe, well, you know, Terry and I, we've never gotten married."

Her man heaved his solidity out of the easy chair, "Hey, you two, I gotta get to work."

After Terry was sent off to his job with little, pecking kisses and many admonishments not fill up on candy bars, Jill took Roberta to her garden to show her a struggling clematis. They squatted beside it, Jill, round face reddened, pudgy form crouched on her heels, head cocked, lifted her eyes from the climber.

"It should have done so much better than this. There's enough sun. I took care of it. It should've been magnificent this year." Pathetic, yellowish tendrils clung to the wire fencing. "Look here."

Roberta tipped her body toward the plant not sure what she should be seeing.

"It seems...delicate. Still wispy from it's long climb out of the earth."

Jill wrinkled her short nose, pushed the neat page-boy roll off her broad forehead, peered at the wilted foliage.

"Maybe it needs water."

"Roberta, I always give the plants enough water." She straighten up, turned away from the dismal perennial. "This is it's second season. It should be spectacular this year."

"Give it time. It's early yet—"

"Roberta, it's August."

"I don't have any answer." Admitted more to bolster her feeble smile of support.

"Wish I knew what to do. I used to help my grandmother with her tomato vines." Unalterably tangled memory and impulse compelled Jill to chose this moment to attack Roberta. Too much food, too little beauty. She threw out a belligerent chin, "I believe in God, Roberta. He makes all that's in this garden grow. I trust Him to send the sunshine. Lately, I've been angry about what you've turned into. You laugh at things that are important to me. You make fun of them." Her trembling voice thickened, "Listen, you've got to stop coming over here and shoving that evolution down our throats. Maybe you didn't realize it, but you upset Terry. He went out to work on an acid stomach. I don't know what I can do. It's like you always put me in the middle, Roberta, and I resent it."

"How do I—"

"I never told you this before, but when you and Cam gave Margot to your in-laws, there was only one reason I was glad. At least she'd get some religion from them. Otherwise, it was just not right giving up your own flesh and blood like that. But I knew how you felt about religion, and Cam's no better than a Hindu. I can't be comfortable around you anymore, Roberta, and it's driven a wedge between us."

"I wouldn't ask you to believe or not believe anything. You and Terry are my friends."

"It doesn't work that way. And you don't respect us."

"How can you say that? What have I done to make you think such a thing?"

"You don't respect our religion, you can't respect us. And it makes it hard to talk to you. It's as if you like saying the outrageous things you do. Listen to you with Terry at lunch. I didn't know what to say to stop you."

"But that has nothing to do with our friendship."

"Yes, it does."

"I don't know how to make you see it doesn't."

"You could try going to church sometimes."

Sterile hope and vague regret flushed an admission as Roberta walked with her plump friend back through the lush flowered yard to her car, "I just met a priest."

"Yeah, well he could help. Science and God don't have to be separate. I know it's your job."

Leaving Jill at her doorway, Roberta set off across the front lawn. A damp wind, almost fall-like, blew through her thin shirt. She shivered. Didn't feel like August.

In shifting, moody preoccupation Roberta drove to the University after lunch. Seemed strange enough but investigating Farzi's semi-mysterious disappearance, if it was that, had given her some respite. Oddly comforting, the way mysteries are.

Farzi's predicament took up her mind. Better than mulling over her father's state and his bitterness, or all the implications of Jill's diatribe. Jill and Terry were charging her with treachery. Disturbing and sad, all that. And for months now she had tried not to think about Margot except in a forced-positive way. Since she wasn't able to ease the tension by pondering the intricacies of paleoanthropology today, she was thankful for the enigma of Farzi Behroozi's vanishing act.

If Jill's explanation was correct, Farzi was in New York shopping, and pulling some crazy stunt. Maybe a frenetic trick on Tony. Maybe she only needed Roberta to fetch her suitcases for her. Trouble was, however amusing or exciting Farzi's adventure might be to herself, Farzi's cryptic telephone calls had frightened her. Would Farzi do that to her? And what about the threatening visit by the strange men? They weren't in on any gag. Had they been a hallucination? That was a calming thought. Maybe the whole episode was a hallucination? Wait...what had Farzi said? "I should have lied to you, too."

Thus doubt and discontent pecked holes in her psyche as she curled the spiral turnoff to the lab on the fuzzy-treed hilltop. She couldn't make herself believe the sane answer— Farzi was shopping for her wedding things in New York. That was the lie. Even though she might question the reality of Farzi being in trouble, make it a dubious game, she couldn't shake her gut feeling. It was not clear what Farzi was doing. But she had not invented the fear in Farzi's voice. And Farzi abhorred practical jokes. One word from Jill and she had dismissed her own assessment of Farzi's situation. It was like the time someone had told her about seeing a ghost in a haunted castle in England. She knew that if she had seen even a flimsy, indistinct apparition, she would not have trusted her own eyes. She'd have called it imagination, the result of overwork, a break-down. It had frightened her to think that she would never have believed any ghost she saw alone was a legitimate visitation. She shook her head; her self-doubt could doom Farzi.

Roberta had considered every aspect of Farzi's mysterious disappearance except the obvious one: Farzi was running away to save her life. Damn it, she had heard Farzi's voice on the phone. She had been questioned by two intimidating men. There was no proof that Farzi was in danger, true. No one would have to believe her. But she was coming to believe herself.

Landing in her parking spot at the lab's graveled back entrance, she pushed her heavy hair off her forehead and whispered, "You've got to think." Slowly her pulse rate returned to normal.

She replaced the fossil tooth and went back to work.

She crept softly to the door and listened; then asked, "who's there?"

Roberta was sound asleep when the knocks jarred her sticky pre-conscience. Eliding the insistent vibrations she sucked in and gurgled out the pulling waters of reverie. But her dream state argued her into resolving a pesky intrusion when it couldn't be assimilated into the dream content, sensibly perhaps after all.

Because Dorcus wasn't going to be at the lab until three, she had given herself leave to sleep late. But whoever was out there wouldn't stop banging—stand, and unfold yourself. How had it gotten past the outer door without being buzzed? Second time in the last few weeks. Lord, what if it was the foreign men come after Farzi again? She crept softly to the door and listened; then asked, "who's there?"

"Father Charles Frankel, Miss Branwaithe. Do you remember me?"

Roberta let the man in, "Yes, sure I do. Nice to see you, Father. I'm sorry I didn't answer right away. I've been bushed from overwork and was catching up on my sleep."

She tucked her flapping, salmon robe panels together, pushed her hair off her face, and smiled at the priest. Gave him a healthy grin because Father Frankel was not hunting Farzi Behroozi. She wasn't much surprised at his unexpected visit having for years been Cam's wife when everyone who knew him loved him; and being a guru to everyone who knew and loved him, he let anyone show up at his house without warning anytime for all the usual, implausible reasons. Father Frankel's appearance didn't throw her at all.

"Forgive me for disturbing you..." His voice was like a fidget.

"Oh no, really, it's fine. Sit down, I'll get us some coffee."

Watching him move to the sofa, with one thought she saw him in memory as handsome, like an eagle, beaky but commanding; and now as a shop-worn, stuffed penguin. While he sat back in the fat cushions of her corduroy sofa, he abraded his snaggled edges with holy water.

"How's Rosie?"

"Well, I've still got her with me. But not being her legal guardian, I couldn't enroll her in the high school. They don't want to educate her for some other town, at their expense, you know."

"Yes, and you don't even pay taxes."

He laughed forming inward words like blunt and plain about this woman he'd taken it into his mind to visit.

"I've been trying to call you for several days."

"You have to call late. I've been at the lab—"

"So I risked this trip." He leaned back further into the cushions and stretched out his legs. Perhaps he'd finally made up his mind what he should say, not wanting to appear trapped into making a confession, "I don't know what to do with Rosie. I've decided I can't keep her, but I certainly can't kick her out. She's so strong-willed...she stays up all night. Sits around all day and mopes and watches cartoons on the television. I've even caught her making long distance phone calls. Then Wednesday she just took off, and was gone until four in the morning when she comes tearing up the drive sitting on the back of this big motorcycle, you know the kind, behind this huge guy twice her age with a beard and tattoos. She doesn't talk, doesn't answer me—"

"Fah—"

"It's...more than I can handle." The priest drew up and crossed his legs, clasped his folded hands over one knee. "I'm not shocked by this, any of this. Or surprised. I have a good idea how things are. I'm not cloistered for..." she thought he was going to invoke the Lord's name, "goodness sake," but he didn't. "What do you do? I've talked and counseled, prayed about this until I was blue in the face..."

"It's tough—"

"You did...speak to my sister, didn't you? You left a message?"

"Yes. I told her Rosie was safe with you."

"What did she say? You see, every time I call, she hangs up on me. We haven't been on...very good terms for years now. She remarried, and then divorced again. Now, she won't talk to me at all. She must have been relieved to hear the kid was all right?"

"She...I don't remember what she said exactly. She... doesn't want the girl either. I gave her your message. I don't know what she thought."

"It's not that I don't want—"

"I know, I know."

"I'm not set up to take in a girl. They won't even let her register for school."

"Send her to a Catholic school."

"Do you have any idea the kind of a problem that would be?"

"Then send her home. Although I'm not sure that's a wise move."

"She won't go home. She says she'll run away again. I think, however, if her mother actually came to get her..."

"Fat chance."

"Yes, as you say, fat chance...on her own. But I've an idea. Miss Branwaithe, will you call Sandy, her mother, again?"

"Me? Why me? Have one of the nuns do it...one of your friends. Anybody'd be better than I would."

"I tried Sister Cletus, she hung up on her, too. But you got through to her once. Maybe you're the charm. I've just run out of options."

"Father Frankel, what on earth can I say to your sister?"

Rosie's mother had ameliorated her bullet stance, come around a little bit, weakened her hard-line position. "What does he want me to do about it?"

"Come get your daughter." How to say what should be said without saying it, "Father Frankel can't handle her, the situation isn't a good one for the girl—".

"Listen. You don't sound like a stupid woman. See if you can tell Charlie just like I say it. It aint hard to remember...No. No, I don't want her back. I stuck with Rosie long enough to get the wickedest sinner he's found outta purgatory. She's a kid who pushes and pushes...I've had enough. She even made a play for my...this guy I'm gonna marry soon. So the kid wants to stay with him, he can keep her. Or you can. Whichever one of you's stuck with her now. With my sympathy."

Roberta filled in for the priest the half of the conversation he hadn't heard adding, "That's probably part of the reason Rosie ran away. The boy friend wouldn't leave her alone."

Father Frankel plucked off his wire-rims and rubbed his eyes histrionically, but not entirely for effect.

"Now what'll I do?"

"You could give her to the juvenile authorities as a runaway. But I don't recommend it."

"What will they do?"

"Send her home to her mother."

"And she'll run away again—"

"Better that she does—"

"How can you say that? The next time she runs she won't come to me. She'll go off with that pervert on the motorcycle."

"Maybe."

"I can't let that happen. I suppose I'll have to go to the authorities, see if I can get custody of her as my ward if Sandy won't have her."

"Or just tell the school that the girl is permanently with you. You can say that her mother deserted her."

"That's pretty much what I told them last time. They don't look at it like we do, though. They said no matter how the parents neglect, or abuse, or otherwise mistreat their children, they always end up wanting them back. Then it goes to court, and then they get them back. So, the school won't let Rosie go there unless I've got papers on her."

"Good lord."

The priest peered into his empty cup trying to will liquid in it so that he could hold it to his mouth like the holy chalice. "I shouldn't take up any more of your time." She wasn't offering any more coffee. Instead, she sat staring at him in deep silence, not waiting out a pause, more as if falling into a chasm. She had run out of patience. While they walked to the door, he thought in a panic that he had better keep contact with this woman who did seem to reach his sister, on one level, at least. She might find a way for Sandy to take the girl back. Awkwardly, he coaxed Roberta into having Sunday dinner with him at the rectory. He told her his housekeeper could cook decently. Thus Roberta promised to taste the decent cooking if only to satisfy some critical faculty, a misplaced curiosity about Rosie, rather than because the good father had swooped his way into her heart.

Before going to the lab Roberta stopped at the philosophy department and found that Cam wasn't in his office. He must be finishing a lecture. She lunged across the long swath of dandelion-pocked grass spotting Cameron coming from under the imposing porte cochere beside the Montgomery Building, greenery creeping over its massive granite walls. His collar up on his ivory linen jacket its elbows gray-leather patched, his puffy dark hair seducing the mellow winds, he hailed her as an accident, not thinking

Roberta could be meeting him on purpose.

She accosted her ex-husband, "I haven't heard from your mother yet, Cam, and its been days. She said she'd call with Margot's number when they got back to Brighton. What in the hell are they doing in Brighton?"

"Wait a minute. Margot went straight to London. She's starting at Eastborne in a week, about. My father's getting her set up. They went shopping I think—"

"Shopping?"

"Roberta, Don't get excited. I've got her new address and a phone number. If you come to my office, I'll give them to you right now." She wanted to snarl at his condescension, acting as if he was talking to an idiot. Although Cameron affected an unruffled exterior, he felt pique gambol up the rungs of his spine. "Eastbourne, what a great opportunity—"

"Why hasn't anyone told me any of this?"

"Roberta, I'm sure my mother tried to call you."

"Christ. I want to talk to Margot tonight. I want that number." They walked together to the back entrance of Carpenter Hall.

Cameron's office was a dark, book-lined burrow lit by a desk lamp and whatever sun filtered through one narrow, dirty window. Books were piled on the floor and in chairs as well as on high shelves and a sprawling desk. Roberta blushed at the aura of old university, wisdom and solace. A fleet image, she recalled Cam the way she had once believed he was, but used-up illusions quickly vanish, to be replaced by active, new ones. Cam was neither the first vision nor the later others. There were symbols with which she described him: intense, eccentric, intellectual, or self-absorbed, phlegmatic, greedy. She could not approach, no, nor completely reject. So close only can one come. She watched him sifting through the papers that clothed his desk. Did she still care if he were miserable or happy, or wasn't getting what he wanted? In searching for the information he looked uncomfortable and rigid.

"Here, here, Roberta, here it is." She snatched the extended sheet. "I wrote her yesterday."

"Thank you. Sorry I made a fuss."

"Yeah, it's all right."

"I didn't mean—"

"You never do."

"Do you think I generally make fusses, Cam? Huh? Get...frenetic or something?"

He leaned back against the curling leather ridge of the desk top, fingers gripping the rim. "What is it now?"

"I'm trying to piece something together...to figure out...oh, hell. What's the use?"

"What is bothering you? Margot's all right. For years she's been primarily my parents' responsibility, and you've never showed any doubt about their ability to take care of her."

"Well, you're right. Cam, when...over the years...when we were married, I mean, was I ever unfair to you?"

"You always let me know what you were thinking."

"Maybe I thought, or said, too much."

"Oh, come on. Neither of us wants to go through all that shit again." His snort-laugh ended in a pat smile. Bringing his palms off the edge of his desk, he crossed his arms, rubbing and caressing one elbow. Without wanting to include him she was following a line of thought wholly alone.

"I was probably too romantic..." a not bold line, only a series of thin dots, not colored nor textured nor true-sounding, only mixed up memories, and silky poetics, and trash."

"Oh, I don't know. When we were kissing, I always felt as if you were checking for a rounded dental arcade."

"Goddamn you, Cameron—"

"Leave it, Roberta. Quit worrying about Margot. Unless you know something I don't?"

"I miss her. It's seems longer and longer between her visits."

"Little late to be missing her, huh?"

"What do you mean by that crack, Cam? What're you saying? That I somehow gave up my right to miss her when we sent her to your parents?"

He crossed his arms, hardened his stance, "Back when we were married, Roberta, you were nothing if not melodramatic, emphatically melodramatic. And right now I'm not going to allow so much as a touch of emotional masturbation. Tell me what the fuck's bothering you or quit wasting my time."

Turning she stalked off, saving him his time, not being able to tell anything at all.

Finally Roberta had Margot's new phone number, and yet, although the need was smoldering in her mind, she did not call her daughter. Rosie intruded, what Cam had taunted interfered; she couldn't deny them, nor neutralize what they had spilled. Action stymied by the acid of society's collective guilt and by remorse at her lapses in maternal duty. While weighing bones, measuring bones, photographing bones, making casts, delicately removing matrices, she assured herself that she would today call Margot. The phone call went unmade. She asked for a moment's inner peace to talk with her daughter, but the request went unanswered. Might as well ask for death. Peace, peace, thou speakest of nothing...

At home, after dinner, she read physical anthropology journals and stroked the cat.

At nine-thirty Farzi called.

"Roberta, thank god it's you."

"Why, who were you expecting?"

Farzi flinched at the brush of anger in her voice. "Berta?"

"What's going on, Farzi?"

"I'm going to need some more help."

"Are you in trouble? Answer me plainly."

"Yes, of course. I'm not doing this for laughs."

"And you're not just shopping for your trousseau—"

"Who've you been talking to?"

"Jill."

"Roberta don't guess."

"I have to find out. I'm not making this whole thing up, am I? You really are calling me with an asinine mystery—"

"Not now, Roberta, for chrissake, not now. Don't have a nervous breakdown on me right now. I badly need your help."

"Jill says you're in New York buying wedding things. Why didn't you tell me you're marrying Tony—"

"Jill told you this. Who else have you been talking to?"

"No one. Perhaps I'm crazy, maybe I am. This is you,

Farzi, isn't it?" Farzi was expert at using American slang, and her accent was so slight that only a careful ear could detect it.

"Roberta. What do you want me to do? Tell you a stupid secret that only we share, something only you and I know, but no one else does? Want me to do that to prove I am who I am? Wait a minute, I have to think of one. Oh, lord. Shit, Roberta, why wouldn't it be me?" The ghostly accent was there, the beleaguered tenderness. It was she.

"Yes, of course, you're you. This whole week's been hellish."

"Sweety, I wouldn't...I swear, I would not do this to you if I didn't desperately need some one, one constant person, to help me."

"Jesus, Farzi, what's going on?"

"Listen. You've only talked to Jill—"

"Terry was there—"

"And Terry. No one else. Right?"

"No one else. But who were those men looking for you—"

"Yeah, yeah, I know about them."

"Does everybody think you're shopping in New York?"

"No, not everyone. I haven't fooled those whom I must. Be quiet, will you please? I can't talk much longer right now. I need money badly. I had no idea how much hiding costs. In the mail tomorrow you should get a check of mine to cash made out to you. Be very discrete about all this, Berta."

"My God, Farzi what if they've tapped my phone?"

"Don't be silly. They're not going to get to me through a phone tap. Will you stop pestering?"

"Can't Tony help?"

"I have only got a few minutes, and you're asking me these stupid questions. This is what you do. Cash the check at your own bank as soon as you get it. Immediately. What time does your mail come?"

"At noon."

"Okay."

"How will I get the money to you?"

"You find that out later."

"...So, I'm not nuts, Farzi?"

"No, Darling. That's precisely why I've come to you."

"Come to me?"

"You're the sanest person I know...Benedicite."

Roberta heard the empty, moaning line and wept.

After sleeping deeply through the night Roberta awoke feeling optimistic, encouraged by the thought that she was doing something for Farzi, and by a fanciful extension, for Rosie, for Margot, and even for herself. It's fine to be doing something, taking action against a sea of troubles, or some such thing. After eleven, plenty early enough so that she could get to the mail as soon as it arrived, Roberta stationed herself across the lobby from the rows of letter boxes and waited for the mail carrier to arrive. Ten before noon the mailman came, deftly opened the facade of receptacles, swinging them down from a single hinge after unlocking the whole band of them with one key selected from a ring of keys hanging heavily from his hip. Rapid fire he clipped the envelopes and magazines into the boxes. Roberta spotted Farzi's letter as he sorted it from a bunch pulled out of his bag, the large splash and curlicues of handwriting, and her eyes stalked the blue envelope until the carrier slid the letter into her slot. Finished, he clanked the facade back into place and relocked it.

Roberta reached forth knowledgeably and powerfully as she opened her mailbox and took out Farzi's envelope. Everything was going to be all right. Let it be. Yes. In the envelope sat Farzi's check with a note clipped on: "Give the money to the woman who took my suitcases from you. F." That was it. Roberta's head began to throb with anger and betrayal. How in the hell was she going to find this unknown tiny woman? She had to wait for more goddamn directions. Sickening the way she felt shoved around. Get the money, wait until Farzi calls to explain the next move. Just like with the suitcases. But a few moments ago she'd felt strong, undoubting, sure of herself. Power and strength, chimeras, like gas vapor, dissipated. Go to the bank, said the word, cash the check, wait, wait, he also serves who only...hell, she'd been waiting all her life. Where came the part when she would do? In the middle of the soiled lobby, clenching the check, her eyes set into inchoate orbs of disillusion, emotion welling from some atavistic cradle of remote, undefined, focusless briny time. Roberta mumbled to herself into the thin air, "And then, and then...and then we come to the part where I finally get it." She let the elemental anger creep off her in trickles like sweat off the epidermis, primordial, postcoital drenching, noisome. No time. She must go directly to the bank.

Roberta cashed Farzi's check in the vaulted, cool and brassy odor of The First National Bank. Here everything was efficiency and decorum. However, in these energetic days banks must be serious, but no longer solemn and unapproachable: a teddy bear or piggy bank for starting long-term accounts, and flocks of colorful female loan officers behind vast desks once reserved for men. When Roberta turned, having finished her transaction (in the vernacular), she tripped, and almost doubled over, catching her fall before she squashed a very small woman pressed up too close behind her. Jerking her torso straight, Roberta felt a shock of recognition the moment before her mind registered the tiny person's compelling stare. Barely moving an arm muscle, gazing above the woman's shiny, black head, Roberta slipped the tiny lady Farzi's money and rushed past. When she looked back at the door, she caught a brief glimpse of the woman undisturbed, doing her business at the teller's window. How damnably clever, how sweetly clever of Farzi. Anyone watching Roberta, planning to tail Farzi's money perhaps, would be hoodwinked. The money was delivered safely. No waiting. Stirrings within Roberta, surges of forlorn, ineffable desire amid incalculable disappointments; tendril-like phantasms prefiguring strength, and power, and action.

Before destroying it, Roberta reread Farzi's note: deliver to the woman who took the suitcases. Done. Roberta smiled.

On Saturday morning alone in the lab Roberta was finishing what Professor Dorcus had assigned her before he flew off to the ASI conference. She needed to complete the removal of a fossil skull's casing. The hominid cranium had been shipped from a colleague whose dig was uncovering more than he wanted to restore on his own. Some days beforehand Roberta had soaked the fossil, stuck in its calcareous shell, in a weak acid solution. She plucked the encrusted skull out of the liquid and patted it dry. Wielding the airscribe on the matrix in which it was embedded, she began to extract the cranium fossil. In the stillness of tremulous strokes like time beating—thousands of years since the bone had moved as she did now—in the whisper of the morning, she concentrated, engrossed without thought.

The door to the lab banged open, and Roberta fell backward a step startled. In broke Hashemi Behroozi plodding across the floor followed by the same two swarthy goons who had harassed her at her apartment. The three stout men, soaked in an emulsion of suppressed violence, bumped the work table setting the fossil skull trembling.

Roberta knew Farzi's father, but her innate, and lately descried, honesty kept her from greeting him. She first would discover why he had sent threatening envoys to ask about Farzi before she treated him civilly. Maybe he didn't deserve to be treated civilly. Behroozi glared in wordless, intimidating hostility. The thugs curled their lips expecting her to crumble into dust in fear. Roberta flashed back to the time she'd held off a rapist with her feet braced against a phone booth door while she'd dialed the police. The cops hadn't come, but the rapist had bolted when she had screamed into the phone. That had been frozen horror. Now she warily assessed the situation, her eyes revealing that she recognized Hashemi Behroozi and his henchmen, that she knew something of why they were here.

"Where is Farzaneh? Tell me where my daughter is."

"Mr. Behroozi, I don't know." She glanced at each of the

two thugs in turn. "I told them that."

"Yes, but you did not say what the other people say, that Farzaneh is in New York." Nodding knowingly he pulled his thin lips back uncovering fuliginous gums. The man on the right shifted his weight from one foot to the other. Roberta's fingers fiddled with the chisel on the table.

"Oh. Because I know where she really is?" Of course he remained impassive, voiceless. "I don't know. I said I don't know and I don't. But I'll tell you what, Mr. Behroozi. If I don't hear from Farzi soon, if I don't find out what's going on, I'm going to the police—"

The thug on the left crashed against the edge of the table wrenching her arm, twisting the muscles until Roberta contorted, slid to one knee in fiery pain. Instinctively she lifted the chisel about to jab it into his hand. But she held back, gripping the chisel in the long conscious throbbing struggle for control. She could stab him if she had to, it was allowed. That wasn't it.

Hashemi Behroozi commanded, "Let her go."

Roberta got up, compelling her twitching injured arm to be still. Behroozi's eyes shimmered rouge-touched golden and fierce.

"My daughter would be fool to tell one such as you anything. She is not fool. You, woman, do not be stupid. There is nothing to say to police except...that Farzaneh is not here...and that her father is looking for her." She saw he despised her but without passion as he would a fat moth or wretched dung beetle.

After the three men stalked out, Roberta iced her swollen arm sitting, shaken, in Dorcus' big, private, cushioned professor's chair. Under all the pain, and fear, and anger, something was stirring. Whatever it was, it made her close up hard, approach a strength buried within her and breathe deeply again.

Roberta lifted the fossil skull out of the acid solution about to begin once again the tedious cleaning. She stopped her uplifting hands in astonishment. There gaped in front of her like a mocking obscenity, a crenelated hole. An exposed part of the hominid fossil had been eaten away. Stupefied she shrank from the desecration. How could it be? Had Dorcus forgotten to coat the cranium in shellac before she'd dropped it in the acid bath? Why hadn't she noticed if he had or not? The damaged portion, pocked and distorted, gawked hideously at her. Feeling sick, she wanted to ask its pardon. For it had survived a quarter of a million years to come to her, to tell its story such as it could in big bold cryptic letters, to let us fathom what we might of its relinquished chronicle. All to be ruined by a senseless blunder. She lay the skull down on the cloth. It could not have been what we are. At once appalled by the deformed reflection, she meagerly, in stunned fascination, began scraping away the calcareous material, intent on saving what she could. She might yet uncover what, in the part still concealed, would make brave descant. Carefully she chipped the hard mute stone away from that which speaks.

Salvaging what she could, Roberta let ever so slowly the constructive activity stroke her mind. She heard the cardinal's tinny shrill whips from the big elms outside the lab's windows.

Effortlessly she worked late into the night.

"I'm interested," said the priest over coffee, "In Biblical

archaeology. So we do have something in common." He had wondered what on earth he was going to say to Roberta when she came for Sunday dinner.

"Well, that's not...actually not my field."

"Oh?"

"I have a friend in archaeology. Precolumbian North American cultures. She's part of the group that's left the site-specific focus and maintains a regional view. Not that I know much about it...Certainly not...anything about...the Biblical discipline...I'm interested in much farther back in time." Was it rude if she left soon? Dinner was over.

"I'd be fascinated to learn more about their religions." He sucked on his coffee cup.

"The Amer...uh, yes. They...pantheism, I guess, they must have had religions before they crossed over. Preconscious religious sensibility. This isn't my field, Father, and I don't know much about it." She felt clumsy not knowing this man, speaking so much nonsense. Nonsense often dribbled out when combating a pregnant conversational lull.

"Yes," he reached over the table and poured her more coffee.

"Religion is the key. It is, after all, what makes us human. From it we've received ethics and morals. Even on a secular level, I mean."

Roberta hated to speculate about tangential prehistorical matters about which she knew little. All afternoon she had restrained herself, but this bait and switch of his was at last more than she could bear. "Yeah, really? We've had a lot of religions for thousands of years, and aren't we in terrific shape. Made us better? You could just as well say that religions have made us worse." What an asinine thing to say. But once a person says something asinine, she has to say more along that asinine line or give up some personal ideal. Why else would people continue when they know they're saying the wrong things? And this ragging must be just what Jill meant. Why do it? Who cares?

Father Frankel smiled. He'd been trained, Jesuit style, how to respond to atheists of all ilk. "Now how can that be so? Of course mankind is sinful. It's people's sinful natures. Religion saves us from that nature. Directly through Christ, and indirectly through all the laws of the Church."

"By putting the fear of hell into people?"

"Yes, well..." He shrugged and widened his smile eloquently.

"I've got to give it to you. It's worked. Just look around it's really worked." That was she snorting. She was mortified.

"Man's sinful nature is strong, the devil is strong. Evil might look like it's too strong for us, but it isn't. Give Christ His due." Father Frankel, unconcerned, knew that he would prevail. His faith could handle the hapless flayings of a misguided soul. The Church, after all, had survived this kind of specious philosophizing for two thousand years. "Given human nature—"

"No. Not a given. Consider in the abstract for a minute. Keep so-called human nature out of it."

The priest shrugged, warm accepting laughter, "Are you going to be a nominalist now?"

"Okay. These discussions never do get very far...let me give you human nature and sinfulness and all the rest and let you consider them in the light of religion. I say religion helps them to grow. They are the conditions of religion..." she tried to stop. "People need to develop a moral-ethical sense without strictures or scriptures. Then we'll change. Then we'll be better, Father. When there are no more cop-outs."

The priest looking guiltily smug, leaned forward, "So now you'll bring Freud into it. Or are you a Deist?"

Roberta stopped trying, "Blame someone, huh? Blame the devil, or human nature, blame your subconscious, or blame it on the meaninglessness of it all."

Their eyes met. "Christ took responsibility."

"Father, he took the blame."

"Isn't it the same thing?"

"No." Skip it. The burden might crush us all. Or set us free.

"Perhaps...I'm more horrified at—"

"Human sinfulness?" He felt released, victorious, and expansive, "As a priest, I'm used to it all."

"My point exactly." She moved her chair back, had to get out of there.

"But there is, well, there is one thing I have difficulty with."

"It's getting late."

"No, no. Wait Roberta. You know, I am human. I've always had some trouble counseling in the area of sex."

"Understandably, Father Frankel."

"Come on now, Roberta, you said you'd call me Father Chuck."

"Yeah..."

"Sex bothers me, except as it relates to sin. That I can see. Uh, counsel, you know."

Thinking, I've got to leave this charade, Roberta considered being rude. "Nobody knows anything about sex from what I can tell. So I wouldn't worry. We've made the same mystery out of sex as we have of religion. Exactly. And if it makes you feel better, I think that's Freud."

"I know what you mean, Roberta. Sex is like breathing."

"What?" She couldn't handle this, not right now. Not ever.

"Or shitting," he used the word tenuously as if it were in quotes. "An instinct. I can't go beyond seeing the...sex act as a function. I think it's a sin of mine to feel that way." When would he stop? "You're supposed to give up a part of yourself when you have sex. But, I can't imagine what it would feel like to give up part of...What kind of monster would be left?"

Roberta rocked back into her chair and sighed. She was being after all only a passive receptor, no more than a computer. Not programmed yet.

"Once, when I was eighteen, Roberta, an older woman...would it be polite to say seduced me? But, I was already thinking of entering the priesthood. I let myself be convinced that I was testing my chastity, letting myself be tempted." Roberta sat very still glad that he kept looking away from her. "After it was over, I raced home really terrified. I went into my sister Sandy's room where she was sleeping. I woke her up and told her the whole sordid story. We were both in tears, and she comforted me, stroked my hair, soothed me. Oh, God forgive me. If that evil woman hadn't...yes of course I shouldn't have gone with her in the first place. Sandy helped me through my sexual doubts." His anguished words for all their sincerity and brokenness, were rehearsed. He'd confessed this many times before. "Sandy and I were always close. If only I knew what happened to us."

"Father Chuck?"

"For years we haven't really spoken."

"Why?"

"I don't know." Her interference had broken the charm. The father would confess no more that night.

Abraxis, the kitchen door banged open. Through the slot between hall and dining room, in came Rosie followed by a giant, hairy man.

"Hey, Uncle Chuck." Rosie was encased in her own uproar, laughter not of pleasure but as defensive and secretive as a sneer. She choked off the sound as if attempting to bridle all that mirth would be too much for her, as if no one else but she could see the joke. In fact, the joke was on you.

"Rosie, you remember Roberta Branwaithe who dropped you off here—"

"Got something me and Ronnie can eat?"

"There's another hen in the kitchen."

"Come on, Ronnie."

"I aint so hungry."

He had tattoos of naked women crawling up both hirsute arms, chains around his neck. Over his tee-shirt he wore a sleeveless leather jacket with a burst zipper. Embarrassed, belligerent, a little arrogant, he thought of himself as bad and tough...with a capital b and t. In his own world, Roberta would bet, he had power, raw enough to be sure and usable. His fear would always be of losing that power; his fear would never be of the dispossessed. "Just get your stuff and let's get outta here."

Rosie slid into another room while the biker and the priest surveyed each other in silence. Roberta continued to muse on power as if she'd suddenly been given second sight. Rosie returned lugging a backpack.

"Where do you think you're going?"

"On a trip. With Ronnie and some of his friends. It's gonna be a big party." She stuck out her little chin. "We're sleeping in tents."

"Oh no you're not. You're not going anywhere," the priest never raised his voice, but he almost levitated out of his chair in anger.

"Who's gonna stop me, dude?"

"Yeah, you gonna stop her?" Ronnie talked as if he was wasting his breath doing it. He slouched toward the back door signaling Rosie with a twitch of his bushy head.

The priest threatened, then tried desperately to reason with Rosie trailing them out of the room.

He returned, gagging, blackfaced, and contrite, "God will deal with the likes of that creep."

Roberta hoped God hadn't forgotten to soak Rosie's exposed surfaces in shellac. "You'd better call the police, Father Frankel, she's a minor."

"What good would that do?"

"Well, they'd arrest him maybe. Bring her back anyway."

"Sure, if they can find them."

"But...you just can't let her go."

"She went of her own free will."

Just like I sat through this dinner of mine. Roberta took her leave at last. She drove home hoping that maybe, underneath, that it'd be all right, that he was a nice guy, not sure if she meant Ronnie, or the priest.

Things had changed. And Rosie knew from her uncle's voice that she'd pushed him to the point that her mother had been at before Rosie had taken off. It was all right with her that he'd reached that point since he'd been on her too much, nagged and nagged and shat on her. Just like her mother had. So she'd blow that place. But they all wouldn't leave her be, gotta do this, can't do that, as if she was a squalling baby. Tried to make her stay a kid all her life. Motherfuckin' kid. Hadn't been a kid for a long time now. What did they want from her anyway? They lived their lives the way they wanted to, so why shouldn't she? Nobody interfered with them, no matter what. Shit, she had the same right as them. So what if she wasn't eighteen, what was the big deal about eighteen anyway? So when she's older what's gonna change about her that she can't live her own life right now? I'll do what I want, screamed Rosie.

Well, she'd run off now and she'd be free. He'd kicked her out anyway, the fuckhead. Priests aren't supposed to do that, so he'd burn in hell for it. She fully expected that he would, treating her like a piece of shit. And he deserved it, too. Kicking her out for going to a party. Free now, though.

Stay with Ronnie. The roar beneath her, the rumble moving up her legs, wind crushing, heating her ears, insulating her. For minutes she stopped herself from thinking.

So that weirdo lady had been there with him. Gave her a lift that day, then come around for some reason. Maybe had the hots for her uncle, maybe got it on just for priests. That's what turned her on seducing priests...she'd fry in hell for that. Disgusting. What a pervert.

Every time the machine went wailing around a corner, Ronnie bracing himself against the tilt, Rosie would frantically tighten her grip around his middle. She'd squeeze her eyes shut against the wind's sting and hold on.

There'd be sex, booze and stuff that'd really mess you up good at this party. Cocaine, too probably, but nobody ever offered her that. And later, when Ronnie was sleeping it off...He didn't want her hanging around anyway. Last night he'd called her jail bait. A joke, she thought. Ronnie wasn't scared of nothing. He was better screwing than...lots of them. But there wasn't many—I aint no goddamn slut, she informed the tearing wind. Damn them, damn them all to fucking hell.

The motorcycle revved climbing a hill, around and around grinding disorder, a percussing din that collapsed the senses mid-shatter. So everybody talked about loving and making love. Sex was making love that's what they said, so what was wrong doing it? She was supposed to be good, and loving was good, but making love was bad, so what was going on? All of their answers you could just put in a garbage can, they don't make any sense at all. Anyway, Ronnie said he loved her when they did it. She was no stupid bitch. She knew why he said it. So what? He said it. And he wanted her with him, not like a kid.

Into a groggy haze they roared coming out in coldness to rock on the cycle, bending with its turns, Ronnie caressing, cutting back then feeding the engine fuel line, the bike gurgling, spitting, ratcheting as he cased the park for the campsite.

Under the frigid stars and beside the rushing woods she let sex infuse her thoughts. Wanted her like a woman did these unfocused males, wanted her. She had accepted them like the women in the movies did. It had been exciting, yes, throbbing, pulsating, taking their needful pricks inside her, that's what it was all about. They couldn't hide it from her any longer. Sometimes the good feeling, sometimes not, but no more the pain of the early times. In fact it was a lot like anything else. She could think of lots of words, not just the nasty words, there were lots of words for doing it. But there was something she couldn't say. Something besides the sameness of all the words. There was the shame, sometimes, but that was nothing. There were words to explain that, too. Once in awhile she ended up hating the guy she'd had sex with. Not that though. Deaf and dumb Thomas hanging around the neighborhood. There was something...mute.

Ronnie stopped the motorcycle near the pine-enclosed campsite. A stillness pounded with tremulous strokes of time beating from way back when that skull Roberta had held breathed as Rosie did now, like a deep booming in the night. Rosie momentarily did not think but knew. Sex was not somewhere you could go; sex was running away. Yet there had to be someplace she could reach.

The words ran together,
and he wanted to fire her then and there,
force her to admit her fault.

———————

Roberta watched the wet green of the just-cut and watered nursing home lawn creep up the rims of her shoes as she walked in that early evening luminance—colored with poignancy—what had Emily Dickinson said...a certain slant of light...that oppresses like cathedral tunes. Something like that. Yes...there arose the transfusing clarity of deep vermilion, gold-edged. Yes, softened depression mellowed to that inward turning which heaven to gaudy day denies. Roberta laughed at herself. People like Jon Martin always remember the exact words. Didn't mix things up like she did, mess and mismatch. The vermilion splendor stretched to suffusing pinkness lifting her spirits. It was an alien time.

Her father, again, was sitting in the dark. She split her toes on the chair she groped at when she stumbled in.

"Dad, why don't you put more light on?"

"What for?"

"To see."

"Did I invite you here?"

"What?"

"Did I say, 'Roberta, come visit me Sunday night and complain?'"

"Oh. Well, I just about broke...never mind. What have you been reading?"

"Nothing."

"Yes, you have. Here's," she picked up a volume from the table and squinted at it under his little bedside lamp, "Descarte, good lord."

"Someone left that here."

"You had a visitor?"

"Yes. Sometimes, Roberta, people do come see me. Jerome Ludington came by today." He ran his hand across his broad forehead clearing it. He was well-supplied with pure white, soft hair.

"I remember him. He was a...political supporter years ago."

"Yes. Of sorts."

She felt he was putting her off. Was he sorry she'd come, or did it take too much energy to talk with her? Doane Branwaithe could have told her there was a pressure in the room which would build to squeeze them, flatten them both against the wall, splat, reduce them then to a sheet of single atoms, if he said too much more than he had. The hurt crossing her face was a tiny pressure valve.

He was talking about Cam, "Came to see me a few days ago."

"Bully for him."

"You don't have to be so bitter, Roberta. You don't have to keep on badgering him—"

"Badgering him?" She'd let herself be cornered. It was her fault insults alighted on her like bird droppings.

"It was nice of him to come and tell me about some new paradigm he's been studying about—"

"And the two of you had a convivial talk."

His glare could have sheared the flesh from the bones of her face like the fossil from Bodo. They'd discovered marks of just that kind of mutilation. A face savagely defleshed five hundred thousand years ago.

"You've held it against Cam too long. Neither one of you wanted the marriage, then neither one of you wanted the divorce. Let it alone, for chrissake."

"I can't forgive everything." She didn't mean Cam, but Cam, too.

"Roberta, you can't forgive anything."

It wasn't hard getting out of his room this time. She stopped listening. Later, jumped up, and in one swift motion removed herself from his sight.

"Oh, Jesus Christ," Dorcus lifted the decimated fossil skull, cradled it, cupped it in his blue-white hands. Whispered, "Jesus Christ" over and over. Then, setting it down, shaking his arms as he did so, tried to focus on Roberta through his red haze of anger. He ended up glaring out the window.

"It was never prepared. It wasn't soaked—"

"Obviously."

"I thought you prepared it."

"How could...why didn't you notice that..."

"It's...always been prepared before I get to it, any fossil

I've worked with." Everyone sees what they expect to see, everyone hears what they expect to hear, she was singing in her mind.

"Williams, or Conklin? Who was it that was supposed to..." What one expects...

Finally he switched his eyes to Roberta available to be blamed because she wasn't on the staff, she was an employee. She hadn't spotted an unprepared fossil. Or one of his graduate assistants had blundered. It must have been they or she. The words ran together, and he wanted to fire her then and there, force her to admit her fault. But he couldn't kick her out; ultimately he'd be satisfied with railroading one of his graduate students for this desecration. As for Roberta, he'd have to settle for pushing her nose through the dung for awhile. She was not so smart, no, not so smart as she thought she was.

"An inexcusable, unspeakable error. I can't fathom what's been destroyed here," more mumbling over the skull.

Roberta, as the afternoon dragged by, tired of his posturing self-pity. His tirade was at bottom, infantile, his wish to demean her, vicious. She let him carry on ignoring him as much as possible. Yet her part in ruining the fossil would stay vivid in her mind forever. Unforgiving. But Dorcus, ah, Dorcus, was everlasting innocent.

So she waited for his tantrum to end, and for his verdict in her favor which must come because she was too valuable and competent for him to lose.

"Let's see what we can save of what we've got left here, Roberta. We can do some reconstruction. But by God what am I going to tell White?"

At lunch during her second cup of coffee while she was throwing salad around with her fork, Jon Martin pulled out a chair and sat without ceremony across the table from her.

"The great Cameron lectures tonight I'm told."

"That's all I need to hear."

"He knows his Wittgenstein."

"Who, after he claimed he'd figured out everything, had the decency to shut up."

"For a while."

"You can help me, Jon. You're so lucidly ambiguous; clarify this problem of mine into obscurity."

"You're making fun." He pretended to pout looking like a well-fed monk.

Roberta rubbed up her cheek bone, "No, my life's gotten so damned confused..." She laughed, "In the last twenty years."

"Hey, you all right?"

"I would be, if I were a poet. But, I long for clarity. I'm embarrassed to say it, but I do." She told him about the fossil accident.

He thought that he followed her now and was relieved.

"Oh, that's no tragedy. I keep telling you to forget about your miserable old bones and write a novel or something."

"Too simple."

"Well, excuse me," he feigned being insulted broadly. A poor actor who anyway enjoys playing roles, his saddest that of the bad poet. "All right, I'll bite. What do you mean by simple?"

"Words have patterns like strings of numbers—"

"Oh, don't tell me: look for patterns and find the

meaning. Trite tripe, woman."

"No." She smiled. "Look for patterns and change what comes next."

"You're full of malarky."

"So everyone seems to believe."

"Aren't I misunderstood doesn't sit very well on you. What's bugging you, Roberta?"

"Yeah, well, Dorcus is pissed, but after all, I screwed his tale for him."

Jon hacked a coarse laugh and felt pleased with her again, "I see, you ruined whatever that old skull had to tell."

"The Pleistocene fossil doesn't speak. It lets me be...to think. To think beyond what all you...all your...I'd write a novel like everyone else is, if I could do it without saying anything."

On her way back to the lab Roberta regretted the lunch conversation with Jon. She replayed in horror her picky, contentious voice. And had she been offending Jon lately, turning harmless chatter into personal crusades, comebacks into strident renunciations? All that blather over the years. She stood in a kind of resentful awe in front of Science Hall, looking past its solid facade: people used to stone one another for doing something they didn't like. Fossilized... everything that survives turns to stone.

Why couldn't she call her daughter? And where in the hell was Farzi Behroozi?

She climbed the flight of stairs to the lab. Pinching her eyes against the new fluorescent lighting, she hunted for chips and flakes to fill in the holes the acid had gnawed away. Why with such a feeling of desecration?.

Roberta curled tighter in fetal position on the soft impress of her bed as from far away in REM sleep, she sensed the phone ringing. Coming back, she thought Farzi and jerked immediately awake. It must be Farzi.

Farzi's distracted, garbled discourse frightened her.

"Roberta, are you there? Did I get you up?"

"Yes...Farzi, will you come home. Why can't you come home?"

"Not right now, Berta."

"What's going on—"

"I put you in danger if I tell you. Why are we going through this again? Just stop and listen, something new has come up. Tony's getting restless—"

"Can't Tony help—"

"So I told him I'm going to the Adirondacks for a week. He's beginning to think I'm trying to put him off...I can't talk to him anymore."

"If you tell Tony what's actually going on, he can—"

"Berta, Christ, listen. Roberta?"

"I'm calling the police, Farzi."

"Will you listen to me? Good God, I'm shouting. Listen, will you please, Berta? I've only got so much time to call, and you can't say these things and ask ridiculous questions. Roberta, you've got to handle Tony for me. He'll...get hurt, unless he stays out of this. Tell him I phoned you—"

"But, Farzi—"

"For Christ's sake, Berta, shut up. If you don't shut up right now, the next time I see you I'm going to give you such a sock in the head." Roberta squeezed the tears back to the bottom of her throat. "Tell Tony that I'm asking for some time, to go away and think, and that he must let me have it. Tell him I'll call him in a week or so, and everything...will be all right. But he shouldn't say anything to anybody. Tell him—damn it, what else should I tell him? If he tries to come after me, Berta, or if my father thinks Tony knows where I am...but Hashemi doesn't think that. He knows me better than that."

"I'm going to the police, Farzi."

"No, Berta. Good-bye. Tell Tony."

She fell back against the pillow, panting. The dream had been about Father Charles. She, naked, and the naked priest playing out a kind of anointing ritual, touching each other intimately with holy oils. The priest chanted, head between her uplifted knees, unrecoverable litanies. She wouldn't remember the words. Shivering Roberta banished the memory of the dream already fading from her consciousness. Only a titillating murmur of it remained.

Tell Tony. If he'd been unsatisfied with what Farzi herself had told him, why should he acquiesce to her? But she would tell him what Farzi said to, and nothing else. Anyway, if she told what she knew, it would all sound crazy to him. What did she know, that Farzi wasn't in New York? Or was she? Tony probably thought Farzi had second thoughts about marrying him. Could that be all there was to it? No, that answer didn't make any sense. Farzi would never run off. She'd simply tell Tony she'd changed her mind. And this business about Tony possibly being in danger? Why the hints? Why the partial warnings?

"Am I in danger?" She spoke aloud listening to the sound the words made. Dawn sponged the darkness from the contents of her bedroom. The cat jammed his head against her jaw signaling for his breakfast.

The general idea of asking Tracer Hawksley for advice poked around Roberta's mind as she was eating breakfast at Arty's Diner having decided after all that she should not go to the police. Tracer might be helpful. However, Roberta wasn't sure she was back from her field work in New Mexico yet. They didn't write or e-mail. As far as Roberta could tell, Tracer had never in her life written a letter to anyone. And she abhorred computers.

Stumbling over the quadrangle Roberta headed to Archaeology before she went to the lab. It might be a waste of time. One of Tracer Hawksley's people had been an Indian. There was a certain risk in confiding in Tracer; one never knew what outlandish things she might say. No matter the modernity of the situation she seemed to view whatever from the perspective of a sixteenth century Toltec.

In fact Tracer had that day returned to the university and was unloading crates in the basement. As Roberta came from the darkened foot of the stairs into the single, bare bulb's glow, she saw an Indian shadow hovering over the tall, sallow, muscular woman, square face obscured by dense, black hair. Tracer piled boxes from a dolly onto the floor.

"Ah, Bertie," her wide-set, green eyes trilled, "I've got enough shards now to keep me happy. What're you doing down here?"

"Looking for you. Welcome back. Wanna go get some coffee?"

"I've got too much work."

"Could I talk to you while you unpack? It's sort of important."

Tracer overturned two empty packing crates. "I'll take a break. Let's sit down."

Roberta wavered, disarmed, "I've got a...well, a little dilemma of sorts..." Tracer apparently wasn't paying attention to her friend. Her eyes kept wandering to the unopened crates. As she paused, Roberta was sure Tracer had forgotten she was there.

"What's this about, Bertie?" Her voice echoed off the damp walls.

"This particular problem...uh...it's really somebody else's trouble. So, I have to be a little cautious explaining it."

Reaching for an crowbar, Tracer pulled over a loaded box and began prying it open. Undaunted, Roberta kept on, "I'm in a mucky quagmire. One wrong move and someone might...get lost, uh, hurt."

Tracer got up and began rummaging through a dirt-filled bushel basket, "Oh, a hypothetical situation is it?"

"Not exactly."

"One of those 'do good to one person, and hurt someone else' things," she brushed dirt off an e'cru figurine."

"No, it's—"

"Saving one person almost ruins another, such things happen, Bertie." Her blunt fingers grazed over the artifact's contours lovingly.

"Only one person besides myself is involved here,

Tracer—"

"Double approach avoidance conflict, like in the case studies..." she cranked her head up and blinked.

"Wait a fricking minute, Tracer."

"Bertie, you can't generalize with me," walking away.

"I can see that..."

She returned cracking off chunks of dried mud from a potsherd, "I haven't the mind for it." Grinning fatly at Roberta from behind a round, striped storage jar. "I don't believe in generalizations or case studies, Bertie."

"Okay, okay. Well, then, how would you help someone when you might be hurting her badly if you make the wrong move?"

"I don't know what the hell you're talking about."

"Farzi Behroozi could be in a lot of trouble."

Tracer stopped diddling with the storage jar and stared at Roberta.

"Farzi? You gotta have it wrong. Farzi couldn't be in trouble. The world is Farzi's playground. She knows the rules to all the games and scores better than anyone. Come on, that fortunate woman can't be in a bind. Everybody loves Farzi, chooses her first. Hey, who doesn't want her on their team? And as for being teacher's pet—"

"She's in a jam...I think. I didn't realize you despised her—"

"How in a jam?"

"She's missing, and her father wrothy and sending goons after her. She told people she's shopping for her wedding things, but she isn't."

"Who's she going to marry? Tony ?"

"Yes. But I don't know. She isn't in New York shopping, I don't think. And when she's called me, she's almost incoherent. She told Tony—"

"Wait a minute, Bertie, how can she be missing? You've all been talking to her."

"Tracer, her father's searching for her, and he came with these Iranian mobsters to spook me into telling him where she is. They were threatening—"

"They were foreigners—all right, don't get riled. I suppose it does sound a little fishy. Farzi running away from her daddy's money."

"I had to sneak the things she'd need to her. This very tiny woman—"

"Hold on, I want this whole story from the top. How tiny was the woman?"

"Tracer, go fuck yourself."

In the musty, cold basement filled with the detritus of innumerable digs, cryptographs forgotten, abandoned here by scientists who left the university or simply lost interest in the plethora of relics stored below them, in the rank gloom, under the lone burning light, Roberta managed at last to inform Tracer Hawksley.

When she got up to the lab, Dorcus wasn't there, so Roberta resumed salvaging the abused fossil unmolested. Tracer's advice had assuaged her panic. Farzi, Tracer determined, it sounded as if she was safe enough, and Roberta should pass on her message to Tony. Part of her comfort came from the sound of Tracer's nepenthean voice.

While chiseling along the fossil's maxilla, Roberta felt a

strange heat spread inward torching the neurons in millions of her mind webs. Hot hands trembling, she set the fossil down. Farzi's disappearance and retreat terrified her at some ineffable substratum. Until this moment while believing Farzi was in danger, she had denied her own belief. No longer would she protest. Regaining control she put aside the fossil. Tony, too, was concerned. She would do more than deliver Farzi's message. Tonight, at Jill's party, she would find a way to talk to him.

A few minutes after eight Roberta left the lab, and not bothering to change her work clothes, showed up at Jill and Terry's dinner party clutching several bottles of wine. Take a message, bring the wine, she would do the chores of all the disembodied directors. Letting Terry rid her of the wine, she was drawn into the crowded living room, a lobster into boiling water.

Anthony Cracroft, elbow leaning on the fireplace mantle, stood and laughed, conspicuous amid a group of women, Jill among them. Go there, unload the message as she had the wine, whole, unbroken. Right away.

"Roberta," Jill saw her coming, "Did you bring the—"

"Terry took it. I hope it's the right stuff, Jill. Uh, Tony—"

"You look tired, Roberta."

It wasn't going to be easy telling Tony. She floated, oil on water, listening to their conversation, saying nothing, understanding little of this art talk, being ignored in the friendly, diffident way of party-goers. She wanted to get this goddamn message business finished. But she was stuck nodding, rehearsing drivel, sipping a flat soft drink, watching the whole flirting, twirling mass spin about her.

When she was about to accost Tony and drag him into the corner, Terry ballooned up against them hauling a tall, sloop-shouldered man with long, black hair slicked straight back off his forehead, an eccentric mustache slightly distorting his round, puckered mouth. He looked like a frontier undertaker. Terry pushed his bulk into the center of the group blocking out Tony and Roberta in his anxiety to introduce his wife. "Hey, Honey, you gotta meet this guy. Our papas grew up together the best of friends."

That lunge maneuver left Roberta an opening. "Can I speak to you for a minute, Tony? Over here."

"You know who that is? That's Bill MacBeth, I think," he was trying to reach around Roberta and shake Terry's sleeve.

"Just for a minute, Tony, over here please." A corner of wall jutting into the passage to the dining room gave them some privacy. Roberta looked around, "Over here."

"I'm sure that's who it is. Bill MacBeth. His father's a cabinet minister in Canada. He's got big bucks, real big bucks. Roberta, you're hanging on my arm."

"I've got a message for you from Farzi."

"What? When did you hear from her? I thought she was to be incommunicado in the Adirondacks."

"Last night. She called me early this morning, maybe it was, late last night. Or early. You know what I mean. I'd been asleep."

"Calm yourself, Roberta, what did she say?"

"She understands how worried you've been about her, Tony—"

"Not worried. She's got a set of cold feet about the wedding, and I'm fed the fuck up. It doesn't matter what she admitted to you. I'm flying to the Adirondacks tomorrow, and we'll see then what she has to say, face to face. Why on earth would she bolt? We've been practically living together for years. She hasn't ditched me for somebody else, Roberta, so stop looking like that—"

"No, no. Don't fly anywhere. You don't really know where she is—"

"Of course I do, what's the matter with you? So...give me the message?"

"That's it. Farzi said to tell you to stay where you're at. Take care of the gallery. Well, she didn't say that exactly—"

He reared back, "Roberta—"

"Leave Farzi alone right now. Of course she wants to marry you. She just needs a few days by herself to think. It's only natural. She said to tell you everything will be okay if you give her a little time, a little space. She said to—"

"Why the hell is she sending this message with you? Why couldn't she tell me this junk herself? Last time we talked, she seemed evasive, and now you say...Why send a message with you?"

"She doesn't want to be run after, and you won't believe her. She feels it might convince you if someone else tell you. A friend. You know, like you said, face to face. It's a better way to make a point."

"What else?"

"Give her a couple of days, no harm. She loves you."

"I suppose I'd look ridiculous charging after her, but I can't figure out what's got into her. You think this is like her?"

"I know what you mean. Have you talked with

Mr. Behroozi?"

"Not for weeks. The bastard, pushy bastard. When we do business, it's always got to be his way. Who the hell does he think I am?"

An imbecile, Roberta fancied.

"Last time I talked to her old man, he really lost it. We got into this shouting match. You know how they are. He kept screaming at me, inches away from my face like some maniac. I impinge on his honor of Allah, or some such thing."

"Whatever could he mean?"

"I told you, the man's a bastard, a bore, a bony prick."

"And filthy rich."

"Yeah, well. Anyway, I'll wait and give Farzi her space. Whatever she wants for now. But she'd better get her head on straight." He disappeared like Gabriel after the annunciation.

Roberta escaped the party as soon as dinner was over. She had gained Farzi a little more time...to do something.

Tony searched out Bill MacBeth, who stood at the buffet table talking to a small group. He was determined to meet this enigmatic man, so hyped by his friends. He was reacting, also, to Roberta, in his stomach an ominous, god-awful, tightening twist. What could she have been hinting at while giving him that goddamn message? Farzi and Roberta, for witless reasons, were somewhat friends. Roberta would waltz into the gallery at noon and, often as not, coax Farzi into going off with her to lunch and dumping the customers on Denis or himself. Roberta could make him palpably uncomfortable even at the thought of her, owl eyes wide apart, the way she gawked at pictures in the gallery with an obtuse lack of intelligence. Her hands fumbled toward the paintings as if she had to touch them.

Tony insinuated himself between Jill and Terry nudging Terry's round over-ripe flanks, working his bright smile on the group. MacBeth was speaking, "Angelique, come tell one of our New York stories. What hicks we Canucks are. Tell it, Angel...We'd only been in the City a few weeks and, you tell it."

Strikingly beautiful, dark as the source of the Nile, the tall, aloof Black woman withdrew a step, afraid of being driven to repeat some tripe her husband called amusing. Each time he forced her to recount the incident, she felt punished for ever having told him it. Mrs. MacBeth the younger, whose mother-in-law didn't acknowledge her though she was a Wellseley Phi Beta Kappa, tried to turn the story aside.

"It's a stupid story, Billy. Oh,well...I took...the first time I took the subway from the Bronx, I asked the man at the change booth if this train stopped at 42nd Street—"

William MacBeth roared, "And the guy snickered, looked at her like she was some kind of twit. Every train stops at Times Square—"

"It's a silly anecdote."

Tony found an opening for himself, coming to her defense, "I always take taxis. None of us here would have known any better."

"I would have," said Jill.

Bill MacBeth spun on Tony lowering his mustache tips,

"You are?"

"Anthony Cracroft, of Persia Gallery," nodded idiotically.

Angelique revived, "Oh, Farzi Behroozi's gallery."

"She's one of the partners, yes."

"She often comes to the Harley with Janine Chilburn. I'm sorry I missed her last week at the Wolshine showing. She can get lots of things that other's can't. By that I mean—"

"Of course. Imports. Are you in the art trade?"

"No. No, I'm afraid not. I didn't mean to imply...Farzi is a very charming person. Perhaps I'll catch her at Messinger's."

"You should've seen her at the Wolshine show. She was there."

"Everyone else was, it seemed."

Suddenly bored the Canadian businessman led his wife on to another verbal island.

Irritated and despondent Tony attacked Terry and Jill, "Do you think Farzi's pulling something on me?"

"Tony, for chrissake."

"I mean it. Something isn't right. Farzi should be back by now with the wedding only a couple of weeks away. She doesn't need any time to think any damn thing over."

Jill interjected, "Who says she does?"

"Roberta. She called Roberta of all people. When I talked to Farzi yesterday, she was vague as hell about this Adirondacks shit. And now...Why wasn't she at the Wolshine showing?"

"Angelique just didn't see her there."

"And then, Roberta sounded nervous and phoney with her stupid message. This is strange, I tell you."

"Hey," said Terry, "You think somebody's kidnapped Farzi? Why didn't they ask for ransom?"

Jill tried to laugh, "You two are talking crazy."

The fossil repair, tedious and meticulous work, absorbed Roberta on Sunday morning as she labored in the lab alone. As an act of atonement, she chipped away overtime on the ruined skull trying to revive it, urging it to recommence riddling its stark riddles.

Hearing a noise Roberta looked up expecting Heshemi Behroozi, disoriented momentarily by a familiar form.

"Cam?"

"I saw your car parked in front. You weren't home... I thought you might be here." He gestured to the fossil skull, "Handsome brute."

"He is, isn't he?"

"Roberta, a couple of things have come up."

"Margot? Is she all right?"

"Yes. You still haven't called her?"

"Not at the right times." She had been fighting an immense longing to have Margot with her, afraid she wouldn't be able to endure reaching her then losing her somewhere between their distances when she hung up the phone. No, she hadn't called her daughter.

"She's doing fine. Gets your letters twice a week like clockwork. How can she be so grown up..."

"Last spring I spent the week with her feeling like a lame pony. While Margot went along and humored me, her quaint half-idiot parent. An idiot savant. She's tolerant of her benighted mother after all. We have one sophisticated child, Cam."

"Granted, she seems self-sufficient, but she's only seventeen. There are things you ought to talk to her about, as her mother. My mother thinks so, too. We're all wondering why you've...pulled away a little."

"She's growing up...the best schools, tutors, holidays in Paris and Switzerland, warm and sunny in Spain. She revels in it all, Cam, don't shake your head. And she isn't a shadow either. We talked about what she's been reading...decent things, and, her thinking may not be polished, but...it's like yours when you were twenty. She loves Artaud, but that's okay. I'm a bumbler in her mind, I could tell." Roberta's throat constricted in a painful tickle, acid squeezed back down her esophagus. She moved toward the fossil, faced away from Cam.

Cameron tugged at his tie bottom feeling the knot bounce off his Adam's apple. Out the tall windows the sky became overcast. He felt tainted by the formaldehyde and mouse piss odors, and violated stones from ancient lake beds.

"I didn't come here to discuss Margot. She's okay, and if you don't want to talk to her, that's your business. Jill called me. She thought I might be able to find out what's bothering you lately."

"She set you off again? Nothing is bothering me, nothing at all. I don't know what gave Jill that idea. I was at their party last night, but I hardly spoke to her."

"You did speak to Tony."

"Oh, good lord."

"Tony thinks you may be cracking up."

"I'll bet he does."

"Jill said you were babbling to him about Farzi. You told him some strange tale which he doesn't think is true."

Roberta leveled a stare at him, leveled it like a club or a hunk of dirt, like a stroke of time when its end has come, met his wavering, hesitant, arrogant gaze, "Farzi's not coming home right now. She asked me to tell Tony. What does that suggest to you about whose mind might be upset?"

"I think your understanding has soured as you've gotten older, Roberta. I didn't come here because I was worried about your stability. I came as a favor to Jill and Terry. I promised them I'd check on you. I've done that. I don't know what kind of game you're playing with Tony Cracroft, but I'm happy I can report to Jill that you're as sane as you ever were."

Roberta had backed against the table and picked up the fossil rubbing its parietal bone as Cam spoke. She attended to each of his words. There was a cold and ancient timber reverberating, a cadence knocking on the inside of the walls of her own bony encasement at about the spot where she caressed the fossil. She stroked it as Cameron talked on. When she heard his voice stop, she pulled her fingers from the skull and searched for Cameron's eyes in the suddenly dusky room.

"Do you know you said 'I' ten times just now. Ten times in those few sentences."

"I pity you, Roberta." He tramped out of the lab.

Roberta flicked on the overhead work light. She placed the fossil on the drop cloth beneath it, and walked to the window.

Two weeks on the road and Rosie Marone had had enough. She'd slept in tents, under viaducts, on hay mounds, behind billboards, in sleazy motels, all beneath her giant boyfriend's smelly, drunken carcass. She'd fled, Jack Kerourac fashion, over the long, dry roads, through the ubiquitous small town that clogs the American countryside, chased by coke and booze, fists, knives, guns, uproars, lust, continual cacophony, and an occasional police car. She wanted a bath, baked chicken, and to be left alone. But she never once told herself that she did. To cling to this man was her salvation, she said. She must sear her fate to his cloth. Otherwise there would be nothing. He was not so totally a nightmare, this sluggish, moody biker, blindly selfish and marginally unkind, that she would give up and go back to the void. The blank before them all. Had there been something before, as a child, her mother's boyfriend Kyle had taught her sex?

Now the biker needed cash and was heading back to his rented room and some job, any job. Ten miles out of town he'd ditched Rosie so that he could return unencumbered.

Rosie misread the source of the relief overwhelming her as she trudged along the highway. She thought she wept because she'd lost her boyfriend. And she imagined some hero who might roar up next and rescue her, pluck her right off the edge of this road. No one came to get her. Not even the bitch who had given her a ride last time. She began to fear that this time she would have to walk all the way to her uncle's rectory.

Roberta could detect some background noise muffled perhaps by Farzi's hand.

Roberta slipped onto the sofa as the tabby cat lengthened himself over her lap and dropped down. Oblivious, she plucked at his soft, gray striping until he kneaded her belly, purring a subterranean, secretive rumble. Roberta began to relax. Dorcus had been pleased with how well she had begun to repair the fossil skull, and his uncertain praise rinsed away the residue of Cam's visit, dissolved into mind runnels. Roberta brought the cat up against her chest and put her face into his silty fur, nuzzling him.

When the phone blared, the cat lurched at the side table and zipped off. Roberta let it ring six times, then crooked the receiver between her jaw and collarbone, shutting her eyes tightly.

"Roberta?" little more than a whisper.

"Oh, Farzi..."

"Did you talk to Tony?"

Roberta could detect some background noise muffled perhaps by Farzi's hand. Sculptor's hands, long, thin fingers shaping. In the studio attic of Farzi's townhouse through the raised skylight poured the sun's freckled beams. Farzi stood one foot each on tall ladders, stretched between them like a slender colossus lit by the sunshine sparkling white as she molded with clearly articulated fingers the curved contour of the form beneath the drapery. When the gallery was getting started, Roberta had asked Farzi if she would be content just collecting and selling others' work. Let her only be surrounded by beauty and someday she would create it, she'd answered. It was a simple enough response.

"Roberta, are you there?" an alarmed note coarsened her whisper.

"Yes. I've talked to Tony. I'm afraid I didn't do an adequate job..."

"But is he quieted down now? Not coming after me?"

"I think so."

"Think so, Roberta, can't you say?" Each word either spiked or plummeted.

"Is somebody there with you?"

"No, no. I'm still safe." Relief escaped between her colored vowels. The last three words anyway were true. She was safe, but she wasn't alone.

Roberta composed her report, "Tony, I'm pretty certain, won't fly off to go find you right now."

"Good. One more thing, Berta. Not such a small thing either. I mean, I'm having to ask you to do a lot..." She waited, needing unquestioned acquiescence.

"No more. Not until you tell me what's going on."

Farzi spoke up. "What do you want to...I mean...what do you absolutely need to know? I can't tell you what's going on the way you ask. What do you have to understand in order to do what I'm about to request?" The foolish speciousness, the blinkered word choice, the calculation in her friend's voice warned her; Farzi was game-speaking for the benefit of whoever was there beside her eavesdropping.

"To start out with, can you tell me why you're hiding?" She knew she wouldn't get the answer; however, not-the-answer would serve, and Farzi knew that, too. Why it was so neither of them comprehended. But it was.

"There are deals cut in the import business, Sweetie, sometimes we have to remain circumspect about them."

"Like the Byzantine mosaics."

"Which?"

"I heard it on the radio. An art seller bought some Byzantine mosaics from a Turkish antiquities dealer in a fedora—"

"In a what?"

"Fedora. And she found out later they'd been stolen from a church in Northern Cypress."

Farzi whispered again,"They had..."

"Yes. Is it something like that you're involved with? This woman isn't in too much trouble. You could get a first-rate lawyer. You know. Well, the people she supplied are really pissed, okay, sure, but—"

"To say nothing of the Cypriots."

"But you can't stay away just for that kind of thing—"

"Berta, shady business deals can be very heavy. I will come back soon. I promise you. And face...whatever. But I need you to do something for me now. Something important."

·"All right. What is it?"

"You've got to get Tony out of the country. You've got to get Denis to take him to Europe. Yes, to Europe, that'd be best.

Roberta coughed a stunted laugh, "This is insane. Okay? I can't do that. How do you expect me to do that? I have absolutely no...control over Tony. I have a...negative effect on him."

"That's why you have to use Denis—"

"Farzi, for chrissake, call Denis then."

"I can't."

"Why the hell not?"

"I don't trust him."

"Don't trust Denis, how can you say that?"

"Roberta, I don't."

"This is in—how can I get them to go?"

"You have to. And then I'll come home."

"How, how?"

"Denis likes you. Denis thinks you're clever—"

"I'll tell them you'll come back if—"

"Certainly not, no. Roberta use your head. They can't know I want Tony out of the country, or they'll never leave. You'll have to trick them—"

"I can't. I can't trick anybody, Farzi. And I'm getting damn angry."

"I know you are, Sweetie, and I'm counting on that...Benedicite, Berta," voice barely audible, a click, then the infamous bellowing void.

Roberta clutched her hair by the thick forelock, jerked it upward, sighing and giggling like a purgatorial shade or a fey muezzin. Then she rocked backwards comforting herself, telling herself that this all might still make sense. Say there was an art transaction which, with the shifting of priorities, had become illegal. Could be in that case the gallery and all three owners were in a fix, perhaps even in danger. And maybe Frazi figured out the danger before the others had an inkling of it and had to...no. Without warning Tony and Denis, no. This tale which they'd concocted together spontaneously on the phone was a cover story. For the person next to Farzi listening in? Or if the phone was tapped, or maybe as protective coloration. "For me," Roberta spoke aloud to the peeking cat.

Tony was compelled, even driven, to learn more about Macbeth. He was frankly fascinated with the poise or brassy pretentiousness, the political power, the wealth of the young Canadian. Craftily working Terry, Tony finagled an invitation for himself, too, when Terry took Macbeth to the racetrack. While Terry was explaining trifectas and quinellas, bloodlines, and jockeys, talk which bored Tony although it caught the evanescent interest of Macbeth, Tony wormed himself into their dinner plans. He even tagged along with them to the hotel to pick up Angelique planning to charm the Canadian couple into a friendship with him.

Of the three men just arrived, Angelique seemed most pleased to see Tony.

"Perhaps you'll take me before we go to dinner to the famous Persia Art Gallery." She lifted every third word in an affected sing-song which grated suddenly on Tony.

"My Darling," said her husband, "We have dinner

reservations—"

"I want to see this famous, classy establishment," smiling at Tony who looked away not wanting to risk offending Bill by accepting this inconvenient praise. "We won't get another chance." This wasn't a town she expected to return to.

"But we'll be late," glancing at Tony, "Some other time?"

"Of course, anytime," Tony folded. Terry's large buttocks bumped him in his hurry to leave.

"Sure, Tony will show you tomorrow. I've got these reservations at Squire Malloy's—"

"And they can't be put off a half-hour? We can go fast through the gallery. I insist."

Denis Goldfarb met Tony at the art establishment's wide glass door, "I need your okay on something, Tony." His eyes shot past his partner, picked up Terry, floated over Macbeth, and lingered on Angelique.

"Fine, first I want to introduce you to some friends. This is my partner, Denis —"

Angelique looked baffled, "Where is Farzi Behroozi?"

Denis spoke up quickly, "In New York shopping for her wedding."

"We're getting married next month."

The allure of the gallery stole over the group splitting it apart as each person went off to ogle various art works. Denis jerking on Tony persisted, "Can I talk to you now?"

"Sure, fine. Excuse me, you folks. Feel free to look around at everything." Another tug, he snapped, "Just a second, Denis."

In the glass enclosed office with giant mahogany desk

and computers, the business center of the prosperous gallery, Tony glared at his partner. Through the glass wall he could keep track of his guests as they moved about the outer room. Angelique had obviously an educated palate. Macbeth, Tony sullenly approved, seemed interested; Terry looked grumpy.

"Oh, all right, Denis, what is it?"

"Farzi's old man is in the back. He's waiting for you. Two big guys with him."

"I can't talk to him right now."

Denis moved in front of him. "Honest to God, Tony, he looks crazy. Violent. He was yelling about where Farzi is hiding. Hiding? Christ, isn't she in New York? What's going on?"

"Yes, she is. I'll go talk to him in a minute. Denis, don't get excited. Just stay out here and show the Macbeths...show them the Shanoma pages in the private room. Oh, shit, here comes Roberta."

Entering the gallery's main room floor covered with bright geometric colors on rugs breathtakingly chic, Roberta felt the rich plush ply beneath her feet and was momentarily taken aback. She looked around in dazed distraction as if she'd never been here before. Her manner baffled Terry who almost didn't recognize her and was put off by it. The Macbeths did not turn from the picture they were contemplating. From the little office Tony raced out, Denis overwrought, pursuing him. Caught between Mr. Behroozi and Roberta, not a fortunate position. In a flash Tony spoke and shattered the wavering tableau. "Roberta." Almost shouted, then voice squawking he quieted down, "Denny, will you show the Macbeths the Shanomas."

Roberta, her rehearsed words for Denis forward in her mind, thinking this was Tony's day off, what was he doing here, knowing she wouldn't be able to accomplish Farzi's task, escaped from the awkward situation by watching the Macbeths.

Angelique seemed pressed up against a picture she'd been contemplating, a thoroughbred horse in colors being led to the gate. Roberta framed the one picture upon the other, long legs of the smooth black woman in a molded blue skirt which tugged gently outward beneath muscled strength, shaping silky cotton, an equilibrium of vision-motion halted. Leaning lightly against the back of a railing, the wonderful thighs stretched endlessly out as the horse's withers shivered upon the wall. One vision absorbed the other, lines converged, and the horse and Angelique conflated until the woman took on the equine mystery, and resonated with the horse. Roberta had to speak, "That's Regret."

"Pardon me?"

Terry pointed over her shoulder, "That picture...is of Regret, the only filly ever to win the Kentucky Derby."

Angelique gave Roberta that puzzled look which women sometimes give one another when there is between them a veil of misunderstanding shielding unspoken depths of common insight.

Scenes change occasionally without the lights dimming or the curtain falling, right before the playgoers' eyes, and, as in Japanese Bunraku puppet shows, the audience knows that the play is artificial, that there are three men manipulating the elaborately realistic dolls, that the true is somewhere else and that this is part of the transformations of illusion. It gives another dimension to the performance. So the change of scene now becomes part of the event at the Persia Art Gallery, or at least sits upon the event horizon. For a few moments Terry began to retell the story of Regret to the Macbeths while unobserved by them Denis frantically signaled Tony. Tony, meanwhile, was glaring horribly at Roberta. And Roberta bewailed the fact that she wouldn't be able to do right then what Farzi had asked.

Then, incredibly, to the uninitiated, out thundered Hashemi Behroozi from the back workroom, a toady-guard on either side of him, shouting, "Which one you bastards going to tell me where Farzerah is?" Roberta heard the words twisted and thick in his stunted speech and was shocked at the hostility whipping crazily out, particularly at her. One of the bodyguards pushed Denis aside in his lunge after his employer, sending him reeling. Denis gripped a wrought iron rail protecting a walk-up to another level of the gallery and slid with a thud to the ribbed rubber mat on the little ramp. He flushed less in embarrassment than at the pulsating anger he felt enveloping them all.

Tony tried to appear calm and unruffled, "Terry, you and the Macbeths go on to Malloy's. I'll meet you there as soon as I've finished up some business." Terry gladly ushered the Canadians out of the gallery. As soon as he saw the door shut behind the Macbeths, Tony faced his irate future father-in-law who had pounded up behind him. With a giant swipe, Behroozi punched his knuckles into Tony's mouth.

"My daughter. Tell me now where she is."

Tony stumbled back gagging, "Are you mad—" Behroozi lifted his hand again motioning the thugs to grab Tony's arms while he crushed another blow into Tony's face. He was about to slug once more when he spotted Roberta speaking into the phone behind the glass partition. Dropping his fist slightly he backed off.

"Miserable scum of a stinking dog. You don't know where she is. You find where, and you tell me. Or I will make you sorry." Boring at Roberta through the glass, he then called to his goons and retreated.

In the ensuing silent heaviness, Denis picked himself off the floor and crept over to his friend. "Tony? Are you okay?" Quivering in anger Tony couldn't reply. "Tony, there's blood all over your mouth. Tony?"

"What the hell does he mean?" Roberta walked slowly out of the office. Denis heard her approach and without taking his eyes from Tony, said, "Did you get the police?"

"No. I didn't dial them."

"But I thought..."

"Yes. Are you all right, Tony?" She put her hands over his and lead him to a bench.

"He's got blood all over his mouth, on his teeth, even."

Tony howled, not milking the incident, he'd been and was frightened. Psychic numbness in its beatitude be damned, he was going to remember this beating forever. So thought Tony as he shook himself, "I'm okay, really. I just need to sit a little."

Denis brought a wet towel, "Yeah, you're okay. That filthy bastard. We'll get that son of a bitch, Tony, we'll sue him, have him arrested for assault—"

"That bastard is going to be my father-in-law...Jesus Christ, leave me alone. I'll go clean myself up—"

Roberta leaned past Denis examining Tony's face, "You must have cut his knuckles with your teeth. That's not all your blood. His hand is going to be badly infected. The bacteria in the human mouth is the worst of any others. Human bites are dirtier than any other animal's."

Denis was piqued, "What god-awful things you know."

"I'm going to clean up," Tony stood, his posture showing pride he'd taken a blow, that he'd somehow protected Farzi from whatever devil her father was manufacturing. Yes, thought Roberta, abashed, go wash your mouth.

Denis collapsed on the bench, "I wonder what on earth that was all about?"

"I don't know."

"Does he think Tony's hiding Farzi? Whatever for?"

"I don't...Denis, is it something related to the business? Is everything at the gallery going well?"

"Fine, of course. What could Behroozi be angry about here? He's not that much in it with us."

"No. But maybe the export end. He helps—"

"Hell no, Roberta. He hasn't anything to do...well, maybe Farzi's money, I don't know about that. No, his going nuts isn't because of us. Where is Farzi, anyway? Why isn't she back? Tony's pissed at her, too. What's going on?"

It was an opening, "Denis, what would you say to you and Tony flying to Europe for a week or so—"

He looked at Roberta as if she'd lost her mind. "What?"

"Okay. Look. Farzi's father's irrationally enraged

because he can't find her. She doesn't want to come back yet. I don't know why not, I truly don't. Maybe, I thought, the business is involved in this mystery somehow—"

"It isn't. What do you mean doesn't want to come back? She's in New York shopping—"

"Anyway. Look what's happened. Behroozi could have really hurt Tony today. Until Farzi comes back and settles him down, maybe Tony should be taken out of his way. And Europe. Why not the two of you go to Europe? Don't you go on buying trips—"

"Not all of us at once. We don't close down. What is this?"

"It's an emergency. So close the gallery a week—"

"What emergency are you talking about?"

"Didn't you just see Behroozi pound Tony?"

"Then call the police. We don't go to Europe over it. Roberta, what are you loony? Why should we leave the country?"

Tony came back with an ice pack on his mouth. "I should call the police? No. Wait till I talk to Farzi. I'm beginning to think she's pulling something myself. I'll fix her. She doesn't come home in a couple of days, and I'll go get her and drag old man Behroozi with me. He must think I've got something to do with her being away. But I'm not going to take this treatment."

Trapped, appalled, Roberta tried once more, valiantly, "Aren't you afraid?"

"No."

"Of course not." They echoed one another.

Artistically, Tony stationed the ice pack on his mouth and stood. A customer had entered the gallery, a tall, tailored man, hair cut short, juggling his head this way and that as if to take in all the art works at once and have done with them. Denis jumped to greet him while Tony headed out to finish repairing himself.

As she left the gallery, Roberta brushed past Denis and whispered, "Get Tony to leave." He shook his shoulders impatiently pointedly ignoring her, but the motion was wasted for Roberta had already hurried out the door.

In the sunlight Roberta paused to clear her head. "Tracer," she heard herself say before she'd realized she'd been thinking it, then flicked her eyes to check if anyone passing was close enough to have heard her talking to herself. Tell Tracer, tell Tracer. Tell Tracer what? That Behroozi had assaulted Tony but no one knows why. That if Farzi was purposefully hiding either from her father or Tony or the law or on a goddamn whim, the situation had deteriorated so that Roberta needed to take some action. But to do what? Why would Farzi hide from a rich, indulgent father with whom she had always been on the best of terms? Why run away from Tony, a non-threat as far as that goes? There were other ways of breaking an engagement which were more Farzi's style. Then again, why want Tony to escape from what? And lastly, why involve Roberta herself? What motive could Farzi have for any of her behavior? Tell Tracer and if she could make no more sense out of it all after that, she'd have to ask Farzi to...what was the word Tracer liked? Manumit. Release her.

7

"You should forget the whole thing. Next time Farzi calls, tell her you're out of it. You quit. Or better yet, hang up on her."

Roberta searched all over the campus for Tracer. In a panic as she hurried from place to place where Tracer might be, she smacked into Jon Martin walking under the elms in his dignified bald-headed way. She had not seen Jon since before Farzi's disappearance. He seemed at this minute an irrelevant anachronism, her once dear friend, Jon. When he stopped her, disjointedly preoccupied, she tried to respond to his affectionate pestering, but the colors around them brightened about their edges, and she barely hung on to the base meaning of his words. Still, she must have spoken well enough to pass because he was treating her as if she were normal. She told him she was anxious to find Tracer Hawksley.

"The awesome Indian."

"I've got to locate Tracer. I'll see you..."

"Your good fortune, Roberta Branwaithe. It is really always a stroke of luck to be friended by me. I just happened to have passed her as I walked out of Myer's

Pharmacy. She was talking with ornery Professor Mauw. They were heading into Pacho's." Roberta exuded gratitude, and he felt rewarded. Giving a dramatic sigh, he smiled to himself. It was easy to see she believed in his charm.

At Pocho's Cafe Roberta found Tracer at a round table hunched under a coat rack in a dark corner, working on a mound of glistening French fries.

"I need to talk to you. Right now. Are you alone?"

"Yes. Do you want some French fries?"

"Lord, no. Why are you eating that junk?"

"Don't start, Roberta."

"Sorry." She dropped onto a hard, little chair dragging it up close to Tracer. "I need to—why do I begin so badly all the time? Why do I alienate you when I've got this desperate need for your help?"

"Hey, wait. For once let your emotions dampen before you start a thing. You'll fare better. D'you want to know why I'm eating this...garbage?"

"Tracer, I should not have said that. I need to talk to you about the trouble with Farzi Behroozi. It's driving me nuts." For a few seconds Tracer made no motion nor spoke. Then she picked up a greasy French fry.

"You simpleton, I told you what I think about Farzi Behroozi. I don't want to hear about her anymore. You never get upset about my angst. I've just had a revelation, a nasty revelation which has dispelled, I think, my last illusion—"

"Oh, Christ, Tracer. Don't tell me about your last illusion. I don't want to hear how you lost it. You're right about your dreaded anxieties. I can't talk about them now. And, yes, stop eating that crap in front of me. I need your help. For once." She began to cry, absurdly, softly just underneath at first, then so that it was noticeable, until tears dribbling she put her head in her crossed arms on the wooden table and let Tracer pat lightly the crest of her hair. "I think Farzi's in danger...somehow, and I can't do anything about it, and I'm supposed to...somehow." She told of the assault on Tony at the gallery and Farzi's demand that she get him to leave the country; they drank six cups of coffee, and Tracer finished off the mound of French fries.

"Tony's too stupid to be scared," pronounced Tracer.

"Well, I wouldn't put it that way—"

"That's the problem; he's the problem."

"None of it makes any sense. If only something made sense."

"Want to know what I think you should do?"

"Yes, what the hell you think I've been asking—"

"You should forget the whole thing. Next time Farzi calls, tell her you're out of it. You quit. Or better yet, hang up on her."

"This isn't helpful. You know I can't do any of that."

"Why not?"

Exasperation leaked out between clenched teeth, "Farzi is in danger..."

"Who says?"

"You haven't talked to her, Tracer. You haven't heard her voice."

"Upset, okay. But in danger?"

"Why else would she be hiding?"

"Lots of reasons."

"None that I can think of and you haven't given me any."

"That's because I'm too polite."

"I can't say what's happening. If I could, you would listen to me...take me seriously. There's a difference between what I sense and what's being said or done—"

"Wait up, Roberta—"

"I'm not going to get philosophical, like Cameron, but it isn't just a matter of semantics. Christ. All right now. Take a piece at a time. What does it mean...forget Farzi for a minute...that Mr. Behroozi hit Tony?"

"Tony."

"That Tony is somehow part of this disappearance—"

"She hasn't disappeared."

"She has."

"You speak to her."

"Christ. Am I going bonkers? I'm trying to say that the differences here, the slips are giving me a definition. Disappeared. Why am I the only one worried about Farzi?"

"If you ask me, Roberta, I think some mysteries should remain mysteries because when solved, they're big disappointments. This is probably one of those. I say leave it alone. Hang up on Farzi. She'll come back and get married when she wants to. Who cares why her old man hit Tony, or why she hasn't told him or anyone where's she's gone. I'm gone for three months and nobody gives a damn. You act as if something bad, something evil, is happening to her, or might. And there's no proof of that. You're a scientist, Bertie, think of evidence. Let it go."

Roberta was so dispirited she could barely see. "The difference is bothering me. The difference means something.

It tells me that Farzi...you know, Tracer, they say there's no difference between good and evil either. No differences at all."

"If that were so you wouldn't have to say it. Like saying there's no difference between red and red."

"But there is. There is a difference between red and red."

"Yes. There's a difference between everything. And some people would say that that's only your semantics, Roberta, only words."

"Illusions of separation."

"Illusions of unity. And my last illusion, lost now, and you don't want to hear about it." They both began to laugh.

"Yes, only words. Well, Tracer, I can't let it alone. Too many times I've been stopped because people said it...wasn't. Because if it wasn't what they thought it was, they thought it wasn't."

"Bertie, do you think what you just said makes any sense to me?"

"I don't think it's Toltec sense," voice clouded, insistent, "But I'm not going to quit. I'll wait till Farzi calls again. And...I'll get it out of her."

"All right do. I only told you what I think. And I think you should leave it, Bertie. Because you aren't being given a fair chance. The dice are loaded, the cards are stacked, need I go tritely on—"

"No. In all the years we've been friends, I've never wanted an honest answer so badly. Why, no joke, do you think I should give this up?"

Silence. Tracer lifted her chin, her drape of heavy black hair fell over her wide shoulders. From behind her blue-painted eyelids a primeval knowledge surged unstoppable.

"Because you're getting hurt. I don't like what it's doing to you."

"I see."

"Farzi can take care of herself."

"Not this time."

The fossil cranium's left side had been badly eaten by the acetic acid bath which had removed the breccia. Roberta pondered while with a magnifying glass and a dental pick and scalpel, she worked the parietal area scratching at it smooth in the gentle morning light. Over her shoulder Dorcus noted what repairs had been done.

"I thought you were finished."

"By the end of the week, maybe."

"I'll be in Boston until Sunday," he picked at a bit of flake." When it's completely clean, I want you to take it immediately to...the anatomist, a new man here, Johnson, somebody Johnson...wait, I'll get his name and office number for you."

Dorcus returned. She stuck the anatomist in her bag, continued scraping meticulously; Dorcus hovered sometimes clucking critically. When Cameron entered the lab, Dorcus seemed to speak from the top of his head, "Professor Hudson."

"Morning, Professor Dorcus. I'd like to talk with Roberta a minute, if I may."

"Of course. I'm going now, Roberta; drop the copies at the office before noon and make sure I have enough for the entire conference." He was still talking as his right leg led him out the door.

Cameron pursed his lips and popped, "Where have you been?"

Roberta covered the fossil skull with a rag, "Do you want to walk to the copy room with me?" Morosely he followed her out of the lab.

"You've been hard to catch. My mother called a few days ago. About Margot." Guilt surged and did Roberta in. She wilted. "Margot wants to come back to the States. She doesn't like Eastbourne. After six years abroad, she wants to come back here and my mother's astounded and feels...well, that it's ungrateful of her—"

"Really?"

"I can't understand—"

"Stop it, Cam. Do you remember a damn thing? Your Fulbright year in India?"

"What has that got to do with Margot?"

"We got off that nineteenth century train in that miserable little village. The hideous poverty and stench of disease and rot. Remember how the ragged old man carried our luggage to the wagon and refused to ride because he might harm the insects if we drove into them. Remember, Cam? And when we got to the monastery and were looking around for the Jain, the others pointed to the old guy who had carried our luggage and refused to ride. Margot's the daughter of those two people, Cam, whatever we are now. Let her come home."

He was staring at her as if he wished she were shut up in some lunatic bin or dead. "My parents have given her a chance of a lifetime."

"If she comes home, she can go to school here."

"Oh no. If she comes back, it's to them in New York."

"If that's what she wants—"

"What the hell is bothering you, Roberta? Flying at me about this. Terry told me something about Farzi and Tony. Some scuffle at the gallery the other day. Are you involved with that nonsense? Something going on? You've gotten real testy lately."

She turned toward the closed copyroom door, "I'll see you...later, Cam. I'd better call your mother—"

"Don't bother my mother."

Turning back again she swallowed it, "Good-bye, Cam."

"Hold on a minute. Terry says Farzi's pulling a fast one on Tony and Denis. He thinks—"

"Terry knows less than nothing about it."

"He's got eyes and ears—"

"I have work to do." Faced the closed door again.

"Roberta, can't we be decent?"

Back again as in a fun house maze, "I haven't—"

"I miss you, sometimes...well, I do remember India and other...times, too. I don't know what makes us nasty to each other."

As honestly as she might, "I'm reacting to you—"

"As I am to you—"

"Bullshit."

"There you go. I told you...one thing I do know about me is...I did love you. More than I'll ever love anyone else." He reached with his eyes, gathering in the light before her, clutching the colors and tying them together like pictures of rainbowed wheat sheaves. His eyes conveyed that he believed his declaration was true; but his assertion meant at once a great deal and very little to her, it's meaning inherently precarious. At the moment what his words conveyed to her loomed foremost. Their marriage had, put simply, broken up because she had decided she would search out what love denoted, live with the hope of defining love, or learn to live without it. If perhaps love was as Tracer implied, one of the big illusions then...She stood bracing her head with her hand as she spread fingers through her hair, aghast by Cameron's disclosure. Later she would reflect that although Cameron spoke what he felt, there was a corollary: he had never suffered to express it. While she, in her desperate attempts at inescapable definition, feared the ice, feared falling on ice, feared skating on ice, running on ice, walking on ice. Meaning shot with infinitesimal black holes.

"Maybe we can have dinner sometime?"

"I think not, Cam. We have to make some kind of decision...about Margot. After I talk to your mother." She heard him say something about obstinacy, his voice tailing off in his good byes, managed to shut the door against him and listened to his retreating footfalls. She knew that it was necessary in rejecting Cameron now, to have to reject the earlier Cameron again, too. And that seemed such a pity. An odious pity.

When Roberta got back to the lab, she noticed that the fossil skull had been unwrapped in her absence. Dorcus had left further instructions pinned under it, in addition, a message to return a call from her father. He had never called her here before. She didn't use the office phone. There was a pay station in the corridor.

"I don't feel very well, Roberta." His voice trembled, "It's this new medicine." He had been for months pretending to take medicine. Almost fully recovered he had none prescribed for him. Why he pretended, Roberta was afraid to think.

"I was coming to see you tonight...do you want me to check with Dr. Suharda?"

"No."

"I guess I can talk to the nurse out there," lousy at charades.

Her father's room was brightly lit this visit. Roberta heard an untoward burst of sound as she finished knocking and opened the door expecting people there. But the noise came from a radio located next to his bed. The old man sat alone scrunched in a chair, his melancholy features distorted into a welcoming half-smile.

"I'm feeling better. You didn't have to come after all."

She took the desk chair, sat pensively, unconscious of him for a few moments, staring at the distraction of the window's inward glare.

"All right. You're here. But I'm better now. This new medicine—"

She had never humored these self-delusions, "You don't have any medication. They've released you. You're paying extra to stay here. You don't need any medicine at all. The doctor is letting you get stronger before he kicks you out."

"Is it my money you're after, Roberta—"

"I've," she pulsated at him, "about had it with you."

He was unusually meek, "I thought I was dying. Maybe you might have wanted to see me before I go. I was feeling bad enough."

"You are not dying."

"I thought I might be—"

"Then you are. If you give it up, you are dying. Life's a struggle to survive. Your refusal to admit...but maybe that's what this is, not a separate thing. When we were primitives, we struggled simply and cleanly so we wouldn't die off. Every day was...an endurance test. When we got things, food and tools, it meant survival, the race goes on. Maybe it's no different now. It's just that it's more sophisticated, more subtle. We've abstracted everything but the meaning is the same."

She had caught his interest somehow by this rampage. He said, "What do you mean?"

"Like working to get rich, or spending the money."

"Power, things like that—"

"So we won't die."

"But we do die."

"Exactly. Or go on pretending to die. Which isn't going to stop you from dying someday, either, Dad. But you are going to survive right now."

"You paint a bleak picture of soulless humanity. Aren't you ashamed, girl? You're a mishmash of heartless, gutless ideas. Nothing in particular that I can make out. Now, let's see, Roberta, what comes next? Okay, let's play your game. Give me a great mystery, Roberta, and I'll think about it. Is anything a mystery anymore to you?" It echoed Tracer and made her stutter for composure.

"The Neanderthals."

"You know what I mean."

"Yes. The Neanderthals, where'd they go?."

He became alarmed, "Oh come on. What's so remarkable about your damned Neanderthals?"

"They were the first to bury their dead."

Roberta banged into her apartment, phone screeching at her, angry, morbid, obtuse. She picked up the receiver, noise still blasting inside her head. If it's Farzi, it's got to be Farzi, please—

"Roberta? Father Charles Frankel. I'd like to see you. Can you get—"

"I'm pretty busy right now, Father—" she clenched her teeth.

"About Rosie. She was picked up by the police last night, shoplifting, curfew violation, runaway. She's being held in the juvenile detention center."

"Yes, but I can't—"

"I'm at your police station now."

"Here? She's been picked up here?"

"You've got to come. My sister's making trouble, and I can't cope with this alone. Since you're right in town..."

She met the priest at the new precinct station filled with milling cops, bored cops, controlled tumult, and antiseptic violence. Everything had the appearance of modern and clean, but beneath beat the old hideous crime and punishment, the power of the compulsive need for order so that disorder can prevail. Never fear, if the building's insides had none of the seediness of old stations both in fiction and fact, it was a seething sinkhole of corruption just the same.

A hard-looking blonde officer left them in a conference room where they sat in soft, new, tweedy chairs and looked in dazed confusion at each other. A moment later she returned leading Rosie in. The stiff, boxy woman shrugged, her folded shoulders broke their stapled corners and bent slightly sideways. The disheveled girl approached Father Charles who struggled out of the cheap already-saggy chair. From her corner Roberta studied the priest and despised herself for her part in this spectacle. His mouth muscles lifted the skin around his teeth making it look as if he had a white, molded moustache invisible except for being whiter than the skin around it. Fascinated, Roberta watched the mouth take on a resigned detachment.

The mouth wailed, "Rosie, what did you do?"

"I don't know." Her eyes drilled Roberta, "What's she doing here?" echoing Roberta's reflection. What was she doing with them in this place of detention? The girl loathed her, so much so that the priest's insistence on her presence was unfathomable. Just because Rosie had been arrested in this particular town, and the girl for some reason had called her uncle who for some other irrationality, wanted support from Roberta who is so hated by Rosie, and the hopping in a circle gets more and more frantic until the circle collapses. Nothing more than that, please, she breathed, please nothing more. She had initially, delivered Rosie to Father Charles at the beginning of this coil to spring these shocks of consequence; so, of course, he must drag her back in with him. That's all, nothing more.

"She's here to help. I want to know what we're supposed to do now, Rosie. Your mother hangs up the phone. Do you want to come back and live with me? If you do, no more messing up. Do you know what I mean? Rosie?"

"What's that chickie got to do with it?"

"She's helping me. She lives here. You'll have to go back with me, I suppose, until I can get a hold of Sandy. They have to release you into someone's custody. A social worker will talk to you this afternoon, they said. You'll have to return for a court appearance. I don't know when they'll let you out yet."

The girl glared over her shoulder at the policewoman, "Hey, policebroad will you get me outta here?"

The priest bridled, "Will you stop and think for a minute. If you changed your attitude, your behavior, I know your mother would want you. She'd come and get you right away. Control your mouth, will you," he reached out and grabbed the girl's arm as she twisted stiffly like a frostbitten scarecrow knocked by a passing raccoon, "I'm relieved you called me when you found yourself in this jam, but there's your mother...I'll try to talk to your mother, Rosie, but you've got to give me your promise...you'll have to do better. You can't skip school, and no more of those men. Your mother—"

"She has her old man—"

He chomped, "But that's not the point. There's more to life than..." totally defeated.

"Sex," supplied Rosie. "More than having fun, partying... hey, man, what you talking about? You want me to spend my life praying?" She had condescended to come out of her stupor and react.

"There's the life of the spirit, the life of the soul. There are worldly joys, too, Rosie, that don't destroy the soul.

God wants you to be good here, on earth, so that the even greater joys of heaven..." suffer the little children.

"Yeah, yeah, yeah. I want outta here, cop lady—" sullenness rising.

Roberta butted in, "Okay, Rosie, I get it. Your uncle's heavenly kicks don't seem anywhere near as much fun as you're having now?"

"Whatta you know about it?"

"You're having a ball, right?"

"Sure. Uncle Chuck what's this fuckin' broad doin' busting in on my personal business. And your heaven, fine, when I'm too old to heat up, but there's nothin'...nothin' for me in your heaven now—"

Through a numbing aureole Roberta fashioned a Father Charles, wary, beaten, although self-righteous as ever; again, she spoke without intention, "You're an ignorant brat, Rosie. And I know what his heaven would be for you, nobody telling you what to do all the day long, no worrying or crying about being dumped by your boyfriend on the highway and being picked up by the cops and locked up. Maybe heaven to you is just a load of negatives. And that's the only way you see anything."

"You fuckin' bitch—"

"Yes, I can see you're having lots of fun, party on—"

Rosie stomped up to the deadpan policewoman at the door, "Let me outta here. I'm outta here until this bitch is gone."

The hot sunlight filtering in made the room unbearable. Roberta put her hands up to her face, "I'm sorry, Father Charles."

But the priest reproached her, wary and suspicious, "You don't do much good that way." He walked to his raincoat draped over the back of the cheap, new chair, "I'm not good with kids, but it seems to me, we do more harm attacking that way," and slowly picked up his coat, sticking each arm in it, straightening its cuffs. "Rather, we need to find some way to reach her, to bring her back."

"But what if innocence is truly a thing, Father, not a vacuum, but a force, a kind of anti-evil, like anti-matter, and what if it's destroyed early, too early before it accrues enough energy. What destroys it too early could never touch it later for then it has a field around it. But only later can it be transmuted into what people have who are...good...what we call good. What comes of innocence pummeled in the very young, perhaps destroyed? What are we doing," she began to search through watery eyes for her own jacket, "to our young?" When she looked up, the priest was staring at her, his eyes large and fathomless, dark, like the ocular cavities in the fossil skulls.

Leaving together they were whisked cleanly and efficiently down the elevator and in silence vacated the sterile safety building. Before he could leave her, the priest, despair and bitterness pushing up, insisted she understand although he did not trust her, "In the right way, we can still reach Rosie. It was only momentarily I didn't know what to answer her."

"There's nothing...'The children of the world are wiser than the children of the light.'"

"What?"

"Luke, isn't it? Good-bye, Father Charles. Let me know how she comes out, if you can find it in your heart to," moving down the street. She could be with him no longer.

*". . . Since Farzi doesn't want to be found, I should let
her be lost. . . Maybe she's hiding from this mad dog -
her old man - for reasons Iranian?"*

Through its broad showcase windows Persia Gallery
glowed serenely bereft of customers, odd enough for a cool
evening in August. People, Farzi had once observed, like to
buy art when the weather turns chilly. Art heats one up.
Roberta realigned her spine and poked herself through the
doorway. Denis stood behind the desk partially blocking
Tony who sat slouched over it. Turning toward the sound of
someone entering, Denis' expression changed from
controlled alarm to untapped anger when his eyes fixed
Roberta. He strode around the desk unveiling Tony.

"Jesus," gasped Roberta, "What happened to you?"

"The amiable Heshemi Behroozi came back. He
figured—I guess...he's tenacious, one tenacious guy—that
he could beat it out of me where to find Farzi."

"But the last time...but you said you'd take him...to
the Adirondacks."

"I'll be damned if I do." He pulled up a smile, which
was hard to watch without wincing. "Anyway, I don't think

she's there. She said—"

"If only she'd call again, we might—"

"You don't know squat either, Roberta. Why are we kidding ourselves? Since Farzi doesn't want to be found, I should let her be lost." His bitterness cooled, "Maybe she's hiding from this mad dog—her old man—for reasons Iranian?"

"I've been thinking that, too."

"But why? It doesn't make sense." He tried to get off his chair, caught his breath, and tucked his arm round his ribs. Denis loped over to steady him.

"Did you call the police?"

"On my father-in-law to be? Yes, I did. They just left here. I squealed, told them Farzi's missing and probably in some kind of trouble."

"Oh, no, you didn't—"

"Shit, it's all right, Roberta. The man said if she called me, she's not missing, so there's nothing the cops can do about it. Not about Farzi and precious little about Herr Behroozi."

"You've got pay attention, Tony, Denis make him listen to me. Where are you going?"

"I'm going to get him a doctor's appointment."

"Yes, of course. But isn't it clear now? You're in danger. Leave the country, Tony. I truly don't know what's going on, but you should get away for awhile, that's obvious. Why not, huh...go to Europe like you do on buying trips? Let Behroozi simmer down, or whatever, get over it."

He looked at her, contempt flitting about his lips painting his words, "He's blaming me for Farzi's disappearance, screw him, and I'm not running away. I'm not a goddamned coward."

Roberta prepared a spicy vegetarian chili for dinner adding each ingredient with precision as if to mix up a magical brew, "Ah, a little thyme, doesn't that heal everything?" With the airs of Beethoven, or somebody— she wasn't sure who'd got on at that spot—lilting about her, she felt soothed. It was good to be back in her grotto alone, licking a hot chili spoon, cooking. But the phone must ring, mustn't it? It did.

"This is Alice Hudson."

"Yes, I was expecting—"

"Cameron's talked to you, I suppose, about Margot?"

"Yes, he has. I'm not surprised about any of it, her last letters have been...indicated some dissatisfaction."

"So she's flying here next week. Cameron agrees—"

"And so do I, Alice—"

"We'll get her into school here at once, perhaps Lawrence."

"If that's what she wants—"

"Have you spoken to her, Roberta? You haven't called her since her birthday, have you? As I said, next Friday she'll be home. We'll see her settled at a new school right away."

When she went back to the pottage, Roberta figured she'd better shake out more garlic. Garlic, that cures a hell of a lot faster than thyme.

Three a.m. the second call, the one Roberta had been waiting for, didn't awaken her because she was up reading unable to sleep. Farzi's voice seemed smoothly tangible, "How did you do, Berta? Did Tony agree to leave?"

Roberta snapped off an immediate and perilous response going simply on fear, "Yes, he'll be flying out Friday to Rome, flight 492 from O'Hare, take-off, I think, is at five forty-three, United. So you come home now, stop this absurdity."

"You're fibbing, Berta."

"What? You've got the nerve to accuse me of lying?" Fatigue made her voice indignant, solid. "After all I've gone through getting Tony to agree. It wasn't easy convincing him, you know, so dammit, Farzi—"

"Can it, Roberta."

"He's leaving on the twentieth, what else do you want... you said you'd come home then—"

"The trouble is that you are such a crappy liar. I don't know if that's a pity, but it's lucky for me."

"I'm telling you he's agreed to go."

"Enough already. Do you remember when you missed the Moore showing which would have been a focal experience of your whole life? You told me it was an important crisis that kept you from it? You knew I'd be mad as hell so you made up some stupid story about a possible reconciliation with Cam when really you were shacked up in Colorado with that dimwit geologist you were temporarily insane about—"

"You knew?"

"Of course. You lie like shit. Just like shit. Here's what you can do to try to make it up to me. I'm...this is important, Berta...I'm going to get an airline ticket placed where...uh, where you threw your wedding ring the first time you and Cam split. Tell Tony he is to use the ticket, and I'll be at the ticket's destination. That'll get him out of the way. I didn't want to, but I will have to do it sneaky like this, Berta. I honestly thought you could find some way to get him to leave, but—"

"He wouldn't even consider it. I've never seen him so furious. He insists that he will not run away; his manhood's at stake. You don't know how wild it's been around here. Your father and his goons beat Tony up—"

"Oh my God, already. Then I really have no choice."

"But you won't be meeting him—"

"No. Of course not. But he'll go if he thinks I'm going to be there...I know it."

"Farzi, why is your father—"

"Roberta, hush. Tony will be out of the States, and I'll come home. I promise."

"Roberta caught her up, "When will I get the ticket?"

"Soon."

"Damn this all to the deepest depths of hell. Why can't you just come home now?"

"When Tony's safe."

"Why, Farzi, why?"

"Berta, quit. I've got to go. I promise."

After Farzi's call, Roberta sat up sketching angles. Her commission to do book illustrations of fossils had first got her interested in paleoanthropology and ultimately had lead to her research assistantship. Flipping through the pages she did some figuring. Her perspectives shifted with dead-eye accuracy. Easily and without numbers she could draw estimated ratios, come up with drawings which uncannily recalled the speculated pictures. With quick confidence she sent the pencil strokes through contortions rearranging the drawn pieces, giving the fossil cranium three congruent volumes. Amused, at peace, she let her shoulders drop, then her head slumped with little twitches. She dozed at last having toyed with the sketches enough to have sent herself into a relaxed torpor.

Tracer Hawksley pounded on the door.

"What are you doing out so early?"

"I have a long drive ahead. I'm giving a nine-forty lecture at Loyola. And, uh, Jill made me promise that I'd talk to you before I left. She begged me; I hate people who beg, Bertie. And I only have a minute. We've got a load of burnt potsherd we're running some thermoluminescence dating on...Uh, it's this, Jill was at Farzi's gallery yesterday and heard about the beating. For some reason she thinks—hell, I don't know why—she thinks you, or you and Farzi, are hiding something drastic, or else Farzi is—she nagged me to check on you—don't get irritated, Bertie—"

"It's too early to. Want some coffee?" Tracer did, and they ate the remains of the chili cold for breakfast, Tracer downing the last of it without seeming to sense its magic. She was in a large, expansive mood, her face active under a floppy, felt hat sprouting illegal hawk feathers filched while on some dig. Such things became Tracer.

"Farzi's not on any shopping trip, god knows. But I don't have anything to do with where she is or what she's up to. I'm not involved at all."

"So tell this to Jill, and she'll feel better about you."

"Better?"

"Yeah, that it's not your fault Tony got beat up."

"My fault?"

"Well, you know...of course it's not your fault, and Jill

shouldn't be carrying tales. But with your scruples...Hell, Bertie, you always feel responsible—"

"For Farzi. I don't feel any overwhelming sense of responsibility for Tony. That's ludicrous. Jill's not going to make me feel guilty no matter what piffle she's spouting. She raises her self-esteem by elevating her blood pressure. And Tony's being obstinate. If he does get hurt —"

"There you are, if. So what, that's what you've got to say, not if."

"I am not blaming myself for his beatings. For any of this. Why the hell should I?"

"But you do feel guilty, Bertie, because you believe in original sin—"

"I do not. I've recently had a similar disputation with this fanatical priest—"

"But you do believe in it. Not the religious kind."

"What other kind is there?" Exasperated, she sighed.

Tracer rubbed the side of her head, "Well, whatever ...you always feel responsible..." She brightened, "Like your feelings about animals. How you think about animals, original sin." She nodded at her staring friend.

"Tracer, I don't want to think about anything right now. I'm getting a stomach ache."

"You know what I mean? You want animals to be treated like humans because you believe humans are just like animals, only smarter." Roberta shook her head. "No. Maybe not that, maybe just have...more cunning instincts."

"Okay, that's a worthy perception. Okay, right. So let me ask you something, then. How do we know that what we do is...thought provoked? Maybe what we do isn't think, maybe it is like a higher order of instinct. But we don't see it that way because we're too proud, or maybe because we're not wise enough to recognize it as that. We're inside the pattern—"

"So see, so you're ashamed of yourself because you think people don't behave as well as animals. We have malfunctioning instincts. We're not quite as good as the other creatures. Isn't that right?" Roberta averted her face, "Bertie, isn't that right?" She moved her eyes over the sticky dishes, over the mauve table cloth, "Bertie, don't be obtuse. This Homo sapiens' guilt is just another kind of original sin."

Roberta's tacit agreement softened the creases of her friend's large eyes, "Leave me alone. I don't believe in original sin."

"But you feel guilty because you belong to the human race, the arrogant human race, master of all the earth. We look so nasty to you sometimes...deep down inside...you feel guilty being a part of us. I have a vision: Roberta Branwaithe speaking with a Hindu Brahman. She says, 'You're all off base, Holy One, the human species is—'"

"They don't call them 'Holy Ones.'"

"'—Not the highest level of being, not nearest achieving Nirvana. Transmigrating souls, if they have good karma—'"

"You don't know a thing about this—"

"'Ought to culminate not in humankind but in the holiest of creatures...the lovely, evanescent, shimmering blue and green dragonflies...which eat mosquitoes and thus have a pure and good purpose for existing. How foolish to believe that humans are the apex of creation. Oh, no, Mr. Hindu Brahman, the lovely, little, blue dragonfly—'"

"Oh, shut up, Tracer. What would you believe? Huh? What do you believe in?"

She stopped short on the tip of Roberta's glare, then slipping a grin like mercury across her deep brown face, chanted softly again, "In the spirit of everything. Like the Toltec that I am."

"You cunning bully. End of conversation. Oh, you're right about the instinct thing, Tracer. It's an old idea. Some guy named MacDougall thought of it long time ago. Turgenev said it better than anyone. And that's what's so depressing. There aren't any new ideas, and that's an old, old idea, too. It disturbs me; it's like there's nothing, nothing to know or discover, except what's been said before."

"Wait up, Bertie, there's tons more to learn, or we wouldn't be here on earth."

"Oh yeah, what? I want to know something unthought of, not discover the unified field theory, or how to clone a person—those things are gestations of old ideas. Give me one radical concept that, as soon as it's thought of, isn't wrong. Is there no end...and then beginning, Tracer? Can we wipe out...No, not resurrection. I won't have it."

"Stop, take a breathe, Bertie, you're getting too upset."

"It can't be that we see to the end of all knowledge. To say that is inconceivable arrogance. Yet it's what I hear. If there is not anything which would appear to our sparks of being as infinitely more, then what there is—whatever there is—what it is we do not comprehend—must lie crushed forever within our limitations. And I would, if I knew how, cry to...somewhere, will this little consciousness be snuffed out for eternity and never know? That's the real horror of it.

And when I ask, whatever, for a glimmer, I fear that what I might spy, immense and cataclysmic, would be illusion. You want a prayer, Tracer, to evoke your Great Spirit: grant to this little consciousness one moment of knowing before the stars...reabsorb it all."

"Roberta,you've gotta settle down. You're going off half-cocked—"

"I dreamed, before she disappeared, I dreamed I saw Farzi's eyes shimmering at me behind a yashmak. And the dream stays with me. Even as Farzi hides—" Roberta dove for the bathroom Tracer behind her and retched into the toilet. Feeling awkward and clumsy, Tracer knelt putting one hand on her back steadying her.

"It's all right, Bertie, breathe deep, it's okay... all right?" Sitting back on her heels, wiping her mouth with the towel Tracer held out, Roberta, coughed up acid, began to shiver, "We...humans, we share almost...ninety-nine percent of our genetic material with the chimps. What are we, Tracer, what...are we?"

"Oh, Bertie..."

"Word has it," said Jill Schommer to Cameron, "that Roberta's close to a nervous breakdown."

"I'm not interested in what my—with what she's doing. She's chosen to fight the material world instead of be guided by her perceptions. And I could light the path for her; however, she mistrusts me. I won't have anything more to do with Roberta's folly."

"I've just left Tracer who did a quick favor for me this morning and talked to her. Tracer said Roberta's very upset...about something to do with Farzi. So I thought I would come to the university and try to reason with her. Get her to tell me what's going on. Maybe I should intercept her at her lab—gad, she's hard to get hold of—and see if I can help? But you don't know what's happening with her, Cam?"

"No. Roberta's a private person, when she wants to be."

"Well, I don't want to invade anyone's privacy. It's just, I've got a couple of points. Go ahead, eat. I can't have anything myself. Just this coffee. See I finally got Terry on a diet, and I feel guilty as sin anytime I eat anything."

"So, what do you think is bothering Roberta?"

"Well, it's hard to put in words...First point. Farzi has not come back from New York. That's strange, Cam, she was supposed to be back last week. And Tony now thinks she might not have got to the Andirondacks. Something about what came out while Mr. Behroozi's men were beating him up. And that leads to my second point. Terry says that Tony claims it's because Farzi won't come back that Bahroozi thinks, crazy you know, that it's all Tony's fault. That she's hiding. But Tony can't think why that would be. Point three. I finally got a chance to leave the office before seven, we've been shorthanded—the woman who runs payroll quit so I've had to do all the computer work. Anyway, Denis told me that Roberta pleaded with Tony to leave the country. That's weird, isn't it? Next point, see if this all adds up, Cam to you, huh? Roberta's a kind of go-between, Tony thinks, because she talks on the phone to Farzi. So did Tony, but not anymore. What could it all mean?"

"I don't know what you're getting at. Can you...connect your points or something?"

"Well, I think there's a fishy smell in how they're running that gallery. Probably in the import side, because of Farzi's father's anger. Somehow Roberta's been talked into taking a part in a compromising business deal." She smugly tipped her coffee cup against her upper lip and drained the last tepid drops. Then she sat back folding her arms as if she'd just stated her case with lucid brevity.

Cameron finished the last forkful of his fettucini and lit his pipe. He was thinking, for he, too, had discussed this puzzle with Tony and Denis. Both the partners had been adamant that Persia Art Gallery had nothing to do with Farzi's enigmatic retreat. Nor did, Tony furiously insisted, their impending marriage. Cameron was sure that the hodgepodge hypothesis served up to him by Jill explained not a thing, but it would be useless, as well as unkind, to say so. Why was it that women—he took back 'women', that wasn't the right way to look at it anymore, nor kind, again. So, some women, perhaps better say people, but he knew what he meant, could not see the illogic as they spoke, come peeling and curling and twisting out of their mouths like grapefruit rind. But he was curious about the inconsistencies that he noticed in all the differing stories.

"Jill, don't you think it's strange that she's so worried about Farzi if Roberta knows what's going on?"

"An act—"

"No. Not Roberta."

"Yeah, Cammy, I tell you, you might not know her as well as you think."

"Something doesn't fit—"

"Anyway, I guess I'll go home now, make sure Terry

doesn't get into the left-over pot roast, get him a lunch, and then waylay Roberta later at the lab. I'll get her there when she's not expecting me, and I tell you, I'll find out what's going on or know the reason why. Tony called the police, you know."

"Sorry, I can't help you."

"You don't see it, Cammy."

Disdainful, he shook his head after she left.

Terry bumped the car up the curb and shouted out the window. On the front walk Jill spun around wrinkling her brow at him.

"We're taking the Macbeth's. Did you forget?"

"Oh, gad, I did. Let me go use the bathroom and put on some make-up."

"You can do that at the restaurant. Come on, get in." She hustled into the car next to her panting boyfriend.

"I went to talk to Cam about Roberta—"

"Forget that stuff for awhile, will you..."

But on the way to the airport, Angelique MacBeth's brief reference to Farzi so upset Jill that after the Canadian couple were delivered to their plane, she insisted on dropping Terry at his business and taking his Mercedes—which he never let her drive, even with him in it—to the campus. Must not lose a minute, Jill asserted in a dim demanding way, must certainly talk immediately about this revelation to Roberta. But at the lab Dorcus informed her that, quite out of character, Roberta had left early. When she tried the apartment, Roberta wasn't home. Perplexed and seriously disquieted, Jill mulled over Angelique's startling bulletin and fretted.

Monday when Roberta got to the lab two messages sat cheek to jowl on her tinny, little work space, one in Jill Schommer's expansive hand, "It's important please call me;" the other, a telephone message, cryptic and enticing, tainted only by having been scribbled by Dorcus himself. It was a beautiful message, really, and she looked at it in admiration for several moments before she absorbed it's meaning: "Woman called. Left no name. Said to tell you to look, that it's there."

Roberta went to the wooden rack of slender, long drawers each labeled meticulously and always kept locked. In the compartments were stored fossils too small to be left in the larger, deeper bins with the rest of the hominid miscellany not connected with any group or individuals in special collections. These were teeth mostly and small, fractured bits of skull, picked up in isolation, too worn or tiny to give a name to. Just single, mute pieces lying on strips of felt or thin foam. On top of a row of enameled molars in the bank of drawers nearest her work table, sat an airline ticket. How in creation did Farzi remember where she had once stored that damn ring? It frightened her, but only for an instant as she gripped the paper folder between her fingers, relocked the cabinet, and caught the ticket's destination: Montreaux, Switzerland. Laughter howled through the empty lab, Farzi's rare, brash, totally uninhibited, gulping laughter, embarrassing all other expressions of joy. Before anything else this was a stroke of genius, hell, a thunderbolt. Of all the cities where Heshemi Bahroozi would be most baffled, where he could not easily win, of course...Wicked Farzi, thought Roberta repenting her earlier self-doubt, come home soon.

"Well, isn't it strange?
How did this come from Farzi?
Why meet her in Switzerland?"

Tony slipped the clipboard over a hook, shut the closet door behind him, and rejoined Denis in the office. He hissed, "We can't come down on that figure." Denis held up three fingers meeting the expectant eyes of the customer across the black lacquer desk, "Price is firm."

The customer gave a tense smile, "I've seen something like that vase before."

"Very likely," Denis contended, "it's not unique." The haggling went on in silence a few moments more.

"All right." At the acquiescence Tony left them, filing across the Kashan carpet, through the oval showing room. He found Cam waiting at the side entrance.

"Sorry I was rude. Touchy deal in there."

"Yeah, Tony, whatever this is, I'd like you to hurry it up. I'm meeting someone at the theater."

"I heard you were seeing Susan Alvarez."

"I will be if I can catch her before rehearsal breaks."

Tony lead him through nearby double, glass-doors to the back of the main gallery. Cameron felt hushed and over-warm; Farzi's gallery profoundly disturbed him. They sat at right angles to each other along a narrow, maroon, Florentine table which struck Cameron's niggardly mind as pretentious. From a concealed drawer, Tony retrieved an airline ticket and set it on the table's hand-tooled leather top.

"Roberta brought this to me earlier today." Cameron shrugged. "She said it came from Farzi. Farzi wants me to meet her in Switzerland." Cameron said nothing. "Well, isn't it strange? How did this come from Farzi? Why meet her in Switzerland—"

"So, the old man doesn't want you to marry her, huh? Is that what all this is about? A kind of elopement? To avoid getting him mad?"

"Getting him mad. Getting him—"

"Well, he's a...you don't know. I've heard it happening. A few years ago some Moslem had his daughter killed... in Miami or someplace."

"Believe me Behroozi's always been rational...and civilized. Anyway, Roberta didn't say Farzi wanted us to elope. She simply said she wants me to meet her in Switzerland for Chrissake. But if all this running away and hiding and beating me up is because Farzi's old man doesn't like me, then why the hell doesn't Farzi tell me? She knows I'll go where ever she wants to marry her. So why doesn't she call me, huh?"

"I don't know. Maybe she can't, maybe she's afraid to...to protect you—"

"Behroozi's here—"

"Or herself, somehow."

"I can't believe the guy's that big a jerk. And why set it up through Roberta? All she had to do was ask me."

"So, what are you thinking?"

"Roberta's lying. The ticket didn't come from Farzi."

"Ah, Jesus."

"Lying like Beelzebub to get me away. She's been trying for days to force me to go to Europe."

"Just for the sake of argument, I'll go along with this implausible scenario, but then, why? Say you're right, does that give us any hint what Farzi is up to?"

"Fuck it, Cam, I don't know. But I told Roberta, I won't use the ticket. And I won't budge."

You're a fool, thought Cameron, and why was I elected to be the devil's advocate? "Thing is, Tony, Roberta wouldn't concoct a lie to get you to—"

"Hell she wouldn't—"

"Why would Roberta do that? Listen, Tony, what if Farzi's involved with another man?"

Tony's eyes popped, he jerked his head up a notch, "Then she'd tell me. There's nothing, nothing that would make Farzi just disappear."

Denis came over and dropped a price book on the table as he slid into the chair next to Cam. Appalled by Tony's scruples, his covert fear, Cam regarded Denis with relief.

"What'd you think about the plane ticket, Denny?"

"I think, you know what I think? I've said it all along, Roberta knows where Farzi is." Both men stared at him. "I do. Face it. Whatever's bothering Farzi, Roberta knows what it is, and she knows where she is."

"I don't think so, Denis. If I had to hide, Roberta's the last person I'd trust."

Cam gargled, "Got a point there."

"Farzi's no pushover. She's played tough in a hard world. She'd depend on—"

"Strength."

"I still," pumped Denis, "think Roberta knows more than she's telling."

"Phone's ringing, Denis."

It had failed. Tony had asseverated: he would not use the ticket. Of course, he did keep it right there with him, so maybe later he'd change his mind...no, and Farzi wouldn't come home, or couldn't...or wouldn't. Roberta's lunch time was used up delivering unwelcome tickets, and now she had to go back to the lab hungry. Then at three-fifteen Dr. Suharda's office called to summon her to her father's nursing home to consult with the doctor. So she left work early assuring herself that whatever, all had failed. Failure was a relief. She stopped for a sandwich and eavesdropped on a near conversation running it a safe distance through her mind, and concluded rather comfortably that whatever, it was, indeed, good to be finished. Time comes when the decent thing to do is stop. So what, ah, Tracer's blessed, blessed so what. Failure, bountiful failure. Ended, done for. No, failure was finished, not done for.

Doctor Suharda in her father's room conversed with rapturous ease while the old man gazed up at him, mute, but framing his response. Suharda took the daughter into his patter when he spotted her under the transom, "All normal.

I recommend some mild daily exercise until you build yourself up. Then, I'd say, you might as well go home."

"I'm feeling awful these days."

She walked the doctor to the lobby, "If you think he should leave here, you'll have to get this place to kick him out."

"What are you implying?"

"He'll stay until he's ready to leave, and that might be never."

The doctor conceded, "He's a strong-willed old man. When did Doctor Jordan last speak to him? I thought by now with some therapeutic counseling—"

"My father's well-versed in psychoanalytic theory."

"Well, I'll get Jordan to talk to him again. Maybe you need to be more convincing. Have you—"

Some small pique crawled beneath her epidermis; an urge to insult this doctor, to finish up, at last, a day ripe with dialogue fugues, and maybe, somehow dent his smug, cordial, tepid act so generous and complete.

"You probably haven't encountered in your safe world, Dr. Suharda, a wholly sane, delusional, principled man, so you have no clue how to deal with my father. And neither do I."

The sun was combing its translucent yellow strands in through his filmy window panes when Roberta returned to her father's room. From the center of the softening light he spoke out in harsh, reactive suspicion, "I've been reading some of that junk you brought me."

She looked at volumes piled next to his chair, "You mean the journals?"

He waved his hand dismissively, "Your Neanderthals are getting the worst of it. They aren't coming out of this very well."

"What?"

"Those people buried their dead, huh?"

"Yes."

"They're not even sure of that anymore. The evidence for that is moot, shaky at best. What do you say about it?"

"It's interpretation, Dad. Or call it selection. What you decide to leave out or in. This...explication... probably won't change many people's minds. Just sets up a discourse. You'll get the replies in the next few issues."

"Keeps you on your toes. In your field. But you never finished your degree, so you don't do your own research—"

"Something happened between the middle and upper Paleolithic—"

He motioned toward the journals, "What they're saying is that those Neanderthals died out when our people came. Am I wrong?"

"Adherents...of a kind of theory about...population replacement...well, yes, put baldly, something like that is one reading of the evidence. It's all speculative—"

"Pretty bad off, your Neanderthals. Couldn't make it."

"We don't know what happened to them."

"Easy to see. Others came, the new men, stronger, smarter. Wiped them out, our ancestors did." He gave a vast nod.

"Wonderful, Dad, just wonderful." And humankind suddenly woke up and found itself very cold.

Clutching the slippery journals against her rib cage

(He didn't want them around anymore. They were rubbish once they had indicted her), Roberta vacated the Tower Home linking failed and finished in alliterative duet. A snap storm out of the lowering dark sky flash-flooded the street with gushes of brown water so that she was soaked up to her knees by the time she reached her apartment. Two people hidden by the ferocity of the rain had clambered into the lobby behind her. She heard the voice of Father Charles, turned, saw his clerical collar popping out of a rain splattered trench coat, sensed his aura of troubled ambiance. The girl, Rosie, hair a soaking black mat against her small face, quivered, a mini-tempest roiled within the natural storm outdoors.

In Roberta's living room Father Charles, slipping out of his coat, sprawled unpriestlike on the sofa. Rosie refused to take off her sopping jacket and battered espadrilles. She sulked, as usual, closed, miserable, unrepentant. Roberta ruefully regarded the gloomy apparition: didn't even have the good will to pretend gratitude for being taken out of the rain. She'll never fool a living soul, not for an instant.

"We're going back to Oak Park." He sent his fleshy mound of mouth around the coffee cup. "The judge gave me temporary custody when her mother didn't appear." He raised his nose to drink again, "How's that hit you?"

"A good...arrangement, I suppose." What to say? Back against the window pane there dripped the adolescent in question showering spite.

"I've had a horrible day," intoned the priest. "I had to wait three long hours in a smelly, noisy hall amongst the riffraff, God bless them, before her case came up."

"Rosie...are you sure you don't want some hot chocolate, or a sweet roll?"

"Jerk-off. Leave me alone." She edged closer to the window putting her face deeper into the evening shadows.

"As if that wasn't enough, afterwards, they sent me to the wrong holding tank, or whatever they call them, to pick her up. Males instead of females. Some man-sized boy, very big boy, ran smack into me, and before they got him under control, he'd half-ripped the shirt off my back. He was bellowing nonsense speech, cripes such babble," shaking his head. Beak slid along the coffee cup rim, "Why don't you sit down, Rosie? Warm up, huh? We'll be off in half an hour." Eyes sidled over to Roberta, "We don't mean to barge in and take advantage of your kindness, Roberta. But when I got through that court appearance, and we finally got out of there, all I could think of was a refuge, getting a breather somewhere. Sit down, please, Rosie."

The girl dropped on the floor where she'd stood. "I seen that guy. Them cops said he's autistic. What's that mean?"

"That he has a mental disease," her uncle responded.

"He's crazy. Them cops said he pounds his head into the wall till it bleeds all over the place. And he screeches."

"I'll...get you some hot chocolate, Rosie."

The girl snatched the steamy cup, pushed her shoulders against the chair leg to look up at Roberta, "You think I'm just like that crazy dude, huh, Chickie? Looney bin bait."

Slurp of the priest draining his coffee cup, "All very instructive today, really. Well, Thy will be done."

"Done well by you anyway."

"Ah, Roberta, you want another round? We sinners do

the best we can with the devil and our own human natures to contend with."

"This whole world stinks." Rosie crawled to her feet and delivered the empty cup to Roberta, "Hey, can I use your toilet?"

"Over on the left. Yes, right in there. Sometimes, I agree with her."

"Because you haven't considered His whole plan. The struggle, the striving, is God-given. The goal of course is unattainable, but there's salvation at the end."

Roberta reminded herself he was guest in her house. "Would you like more coffee?"

"Uh, not right now, thanks. We've got to run along." Straightened himself, shook out his long fingers. "That autistic boy is a good case in point. He teaches us a number of valuable lessons."

"Remember one of our earlier conversations, when we were talking about balancing evil?"

"Oh, yes, evil. You were wishing for a cosmic censor. Rather naive, but sincere. Anyway, the world isn't made like that. And a good thing it isn't. Think of the loss of free will. Think how much we learn, even the weak, from what's bad, wretched, sordid."

"Not...what I mean. You believe in what you're saying. That it makes sense. That it's the final expression of truth."

"Striving, laboring for perfection is part of His plan. But attaining it is a chimera, you know. Heaven is for after, not for now. That's why we must fight our sinful natures. Ah, but we can imagine heaven, even if we have to live amongst evil."

"There, right there. I don't want a cosmic censor, Father.

I want a world the other way around. Not evil is unthinkable, although that's a fascinating idea if you let it come. Instead, how about: we could imagine evil, but not create it, instead of we can imagine perfection, but can't attain it. Wouldn't that have served your God just as well? Think of the pain he might have spared us—"

"Free will—"

"Is about as real as your perfection."

"Your heresies aren't original."

"I know."

"And we're in this world as it is. God made the universe for our instruction. Not just to tempt us. Take this huge boy who came at me spouting grotesque drivel. He's been created to teach us, to help all of us to salvation as well as gain salvation through his suffering for himself. You've fallen under the most tempting spell devised for humanity. It's the greatest sin to think we can do better than God can at creation. You're dead wrong."

"Yes, I am. I'm wrong. There's no need for what's unthinkable or unattainable. When the autistic's words begin to make sense we'll find that out. Father Charles, the human race's idea of it's own nature is autistic." His words festered, and a bright chill seeped out of her skin as if she and not Rosie, returning now from the bathroom, was rain-sodden, and shivering. Rosie, intrigued, drawn to Roberta in compulsive tremors came as close up to the woman as she dared.

"I tried to talk to that nutty dude."

The priest was put out, "Go sit down awhile, Rosie. We'll be leaving soon." She retreated to the window half-facing the downpour, like a guilty thing surprised, thought Roberta.

"I'm sure you're very clever, Roberta," he continued, "but without a glimmer of faith, what does clever get you?" He muttered ambiguously, "A scapegrace who will be taken in, too, in the Lord's good time."

Roberta trembled on the fringe of blackness. What surfaced at this moment had been a long time coming, a hard delivery; she didn't give a damn from where it finally sprang. She was almost thankful. "So simple, and I'm a dolt." With a relief compounded of all failures, she elongated smoothly into a dawning, willowy, uncertain pink opaque essence. "What would you have done, Father, if you'd lived when Clement was pope in Avignon and Urban was pope in Rome?"

"You haven't got much of an argument there whatever you're getting at."

"What would you have done when Clement and Urban were both pope?"

The priest was offended that he must answer, "I'd have prayed, then followed the pope I had faith in, the rightful one. Not that honest men can't be misled, but I'd have chosen—"

"Taken sides. There you are."

"Yes. God spits the lukewarm people out of his mouth. You're either for Him or against Him." Misdirected lives, he shook his head, announced it was time to leave.

At the door the priest nodded at Rosie, "Well, Roberta, you've been good to us through all this mess." The girl's round eyes, chestnuts set too far apart, could not reward, could not invoke. Roberta shut the door behind them.

Whipping around she stalked to the bathroom, tore open the door, entered in a frenzy and flung it closed behind her. With a smash. As if in the face of the priest...into vacancy. "That priest and Freud, they can go suck each other...go suck...each other," leaning over the basin, palms pressing cold porcelain, hanging over the empty sink, "And you know what, they already do."

While she was bathing her face, the phone rang.

"Mother?"

"Margot."

"Roberta? It's me, Farzi, are you all right?"

"Yes."

"You sound out of breath. How did it go?"

"This isn't...it isn't working. It's all falling apart." Her voice alarmed Farzi. "I tried to...but Tony won't leave. He won't use that plane ticket."

"What exactly did Tony say?"

"He said he's not going to run after you. I think he suspects me of making the whole thing up."

"Maybe it doesn't matter if Tony won't leave. Maybe it wouldn't have worked anyway. Maybe there's a better way. It's just that I wanted to come home..." The wordage baffled Roberta. When Farzi was frustrated, she chose a convenient phrase rather than an authentic one. "Berta, I've been warned since I sent the ticket. Things have changed. Never mind. I don't think it would do any good if Tony went away and I came back. It wouldn't solve the problem. How childish of me to have thought so."

"You promised me you'd come back."

"When I can. Can't you see? I want to. I jeopardize... they'll get me. Nothing will help me then."

"Get you? Who? Tell me what the danger is, why can't you?"

"Not if I love you."

"The police?"

"Aagh."

"It can not be that bad...there have got to be ways we can get you out of this. If I knew what the hell you're in. Sweet Jesus, we'll find a way. Tell me."

"I promise, Berta. One day."

"This doesn't make any sense," she wailed.

"Stop it. Stop that noise." Farzi's barely perceptible accent thickened. "It pains me not to tell you. But I can't risk people...bothering you. You'll only be safe knowing almost nothing. People who once come to question you will afterwards leave you alone."

"That isn't necessarily true. Your...they beat up Tony, and he doesn't know a thing."

"Different, Roberta."

"How?"

"The difference is you don't tell the outright lie, not even, Darling, to yourself. Benedicite. Benedicite, pouvre Berta."

The telephone droned its lonely, demented dial tone. Dropping the phone into her lap, Roberta let it bellow. "Dearly, my delicate Ariel." Dearly. And the next line, too, what was it? "Do not approach till thou dost hear me call." Had Farzi managed to disclose anything in that messy, truncated, inefficient conversation just ended? What, that would help, that she hadn't known before?

Roberta took a damp, chill walk at daybreak, an orange blaze, in measures, pursued to phantoms the linear forms of the crenelated town. An impressive sunset lit up in glory the violet sky for one long, absorbing lapse. Then the shade purpled, and Roberta still skulking in her afternoon melees—her battle with the priest, her frightening skirmish with Farzi's inchoate fear—saw an apparition rise up and stand resolute before her in the fading light. Father Charles. She spoke aloud: what if I am wrong? My wrong is better than any of your rights. He sank his brows together into the hollow between his eyes. So I'm wrong, but I'll hold to that wrongheadedness. That way I'll inch down an angled path, because—The shadowy priest intoned: say what you will, you haven't the Truth. She choked on her reply...Because. The specter approached nearer on the ellipse. Because...if I don't hold, there will exist what I can never see. The priest-form expanded: You will get nothing. He wavered, blown to corporeal distinctness. Her voice quickened. And, if I only sense why it should be, that little will be enough. Dark descended brushing dusk away to empty corners, and the priest dissipated. She walked on. Plaiting the sunrise, weaving the new words, if only to figure out where wrongheadedness goes.

On the steps to her apartment building another figure hovered. "Roberta, what's happening with Farzi? Can I come in?" She was staring at him to establish identity or maybe substance. "It's pouring out here. I need to talk to you."

"Yes. I think I still have some coffee left, Tony. It's starting to rain again?"

Roberta filled two cups with the last of the coffee as they

huddled around the kitchen table, a suggestive, new pot brewing.

"She called you, wonderful." He brooded. "What'd she say? Where is she?" He seemed convinced Roberta would know. How could he have become so sure?

"She's afraid of someone."

"Or something."

"And she's in danger, but she won't tell me how... or why."

"In danger. And you've known all along? In danger. Why the fuck didn't you tell me? We've got to drag the cops into this now. If anything happens to Farzi, Roberta, I'll hold you responsible—she's stopped calling me."

"She doesn't...didn't want you to know anything. You can't conceive how little she tells me when she calls. And she...insists that the police are useless. Anyway, you tried with them—"

"Yes, but if she admits she's in danger, that's different. In danger. And she doesn't want me to know?" His voice became stronger, rather than flimsier in the confusion. Was it beginning to make sense?

"Didn't want you to know to protect you. I can't figure out what her motive is now."

"That's saying I don't need protection anymore, or--"

"She didn't, doesn't, think so. I guess."

"Roberta, what the fuck are you saying?" He spit out deeply flavored bitterness like the dregs in her cup.

"Don't go off on me. You came here thinking I know something. Well, I have talked to Farzi– last night. But I don't know any more than you do where she is or what this is about. I think it has something to do with her father..."

"Oh sure," he sulked, "But how? Or why? Has he gone nuts? Oh," deep acrid pause, "he used to be charming...yeah aggressive, demanding, in the deals he helped us with, but cosmopolitan, how can I say--a charmer. No, not lunatic. He wasn't angry with me as such, even when he was hitting me. Just kept asking where Farzi is. Calm, beating the shit out of me calm. Doesn't make sense. Christ, I've been sleeping with Farzi for years, he's never made a fuss."

"I don't think it's you personally, Tony."

"Other women."

"What?"

"I've had occasional affairs, Roberta."

"Not...news to anybody."

"Oh...Oh, hell, what sense does it make? Do you think Farzi's old man might have decided, you know, because of an occasional other women, that I won't make a good husband?"

"Then he'd be glad Farzi left."

"She hiding from both of us?"

"She's hiding. I don't know if it's from anybody." They sat, quiet, drinking coffee for a moment.

"Angelique was my last fling. And she is going to be the last." Roberta scrunched her shoulders despising this penitent assault. "You might not believe this, but I think our marriage will be a lot different from what we had going before. The way I feel about the state of marriage. When I do marry Farzi, that's it with other women. Farzi should understand this. Don't you see?"

"Does it matter what I think?"

"No. I'm pissed at everybody. I've been jilted here,

ignored, beaten fucking up. So you inform Farzi, next time, next time she condescends to call you, that I'm fed up. Anything she's afraid of we can handle together when she comes home. So she comes back within a week or the whole marriage is off. Or, or tell her, if she calls me and can explain all this silly running away shit, I'm patient. She knows that." He bounced to a close.

"I don't know, Tony, but if I were you, I wouldn't issue any ultimatums." He had gotten smolderingly sensitive and preoccupied watching himself take on a studied bad humor, as if he were writing a lurid chapter of his autobiography. Now with that unsolicited advice, at last, genuinely, he ignited.

"Inform her when she calls you. And make her believe it, Roberta. Because I mean it. She can come home and get over this thing, or she can go to hell."

Someone began banging on the door.

10

She hadn't developed the knack of restrained assertiveness so valued by the modern world.

———

Tony announced, "That's probably Terry. I told him to pick me up here."

And if I hadn't come home to see you standing like the frog-prince in a drizzle at my doorway, thought Roberta as she answered the knock...but getting stuck, or even inconvenienced wasn't what Tony ever expected. Things worked out the way he planned them to. Up until now.

Cam and Terry stood leaking raindrops on her carpet. And now these callus orangutans showing up like respectable callers. Why hadn't they come earlier leaving cards? Although it wouldn't have mattered because ladies no longer could instruct the parlor maid to tell the gentlemen they were indisposed.

"You going with us, Cam?" Tony asked from a distance. The two men entered freely.

"No. I met Terry coming up the elevator. Where you guys off to?"

"The track," Terry's plump voice faded as Roberta,

who'd been given brief greeting, left to make more coffee. For herself; to stop herself from losing control and kicking them all the hell out. She hadn't developed the knack of restrained assertiveness so valued by the modern world. She would have to either be polite to them, or insult them all so horrendously she'd never see any of them again. So she brought coffee out to the table where the men sat huddled. The place smelled like damp wool and aftershave. Cam appeared anxious to talk with Roberta alone; but big news hung heavy in the air, and only Roberta sensed his suave discomfiture.

Macbeth had uncovered Tony's romp with his wife after Angelique and he had arrived in New York.

The news fascinated Cam, "Well, you did it again, big boy."

Tony bunched his fists and squeezed them into the tabletop, "But how did he find out—Fuck it, lord, no."

"Bill is shitting mad."

"Sure, cuckold's cold soup." Cam seemed pleased as well as intrigued.

"What happened, Terry, for chrissake?" Tony's composure reasserted itself.

"It was crazy. MacBeth's horse, the chestnut, Salem's Marquise of Night, was running at Saratoga. That did it."

"Jesus, Terry, make sense for once."

"MacBeth's got another horse running this weekend at Arlington—"

"Would you forget the fucking ponies, Terry—"

"So he decided he'd fly back here for that race. He had told me he wanted to when they left. We took them to the airport, and he said it then. Angelique, I kinda remember now, there was something strange in the way she looked when he said about Arlington. Jill says Angelique had told her she didn't want to ever come back to this part of the country again. She got this funny look on her face." Tony snorted, forcing the sound up against his pallet. "At Saratoga they got into an argument about coming back here to watch Saber Blade run. And, I guess, Angelique had got Blade and Marquise mixed up and hadn't understood—"

"Make sense, Fat Man." Tony's thumps of anger became palpable; wary, Roberta drew away.

"Cut the crap, Tony, it was your hot prick got you into this, not Terry," Cam spoke beatifically. Roberta peeked at her ex-husband. He could say almost anything, and make it sound consecrated.

Tony's head swirled, "But he's not making any sense, Cam. Horses—right now I don't want to hear about race horses..."

"Don't go off on him, Tony."

"For chrissake—"

"Well, anyway," continued Terry, unruffled, "Angelique threw a fit when Bill insisted on them coming back here. So they had a screaming match and in the middle of it, your afternoon of romance got blurted out. MacBeth was mad enough to—" Spit nails, thought Roberta, or split rails, a plastic cliché unmade. Yet spit nails had a fine, furious edge to it. The three men had fallen silent, and in the sucking oral void, Roberta took a deep breath. Stars burn in the vacuum of space; but space is not, not really, a vacuum. Yet there is such a thing. Roberta tried to pacify her raucous thoughts.

Sitting still, slumped sideways, Tony steadied his head with his hand—peccavi. I have sinned. Terry glanced about the kitchen fancying something to eat. Cam leaned his rounded shoulders into the wooden ladder-back, eased himself by lacing his fingers, pulling them against one another, breaking their tension. And Roberta thought, leave it to Cam to perfect silent knuckle cracking. Spotting her looking at him, he made a spout of his mouth, a private signal which she obtusely refused to recognize.

"It wasn't a panting lechery, a screw of the moment, it meant something. I'm not making any excuses, Cam, I don't have to."

Cam half-hid a smile, " Don't misunderstand me when I say this, Tony, but didn't you describe to me how you and the dark lady did it standing up in the hall at the hotel —"

"Shut the fuck up, Cam. I wouldn't talk. Susan Alvarez isn't an unknown item—"

"Both of you shut up." Terry wanted no details of Tony's exploit, nor of anyone else's. Idle sex talk didn't titillate his solidity. If food was to be taken let it be the legitimate thing. So he was relieved when Roberta asked if anyone would like her to cook him an omelet. But Tony wanted a strategic retreat, and Terry acquiesced anxious to get to the track. After their exit, she had only Cam to deal with.

Roberta took up a little sigh and focused on Cameron's blank blue eyes as he waited for her to make an opening for him.

"Want an omelet, Cam?"

"You look tired."

"I am."

"Margot's in New York."

"I spoke to your mother."

"She's...Roberta, you haven't talked to Margot in two months. I don't get it?"

"It's not a mystery, don't make it a mystery, Cam. They flew all over Europe in the summer, and I was always a day behind their itinerary. My letters were forwarded, but phone calls can't be, so I quit trying. Then, this decision to go to Eastbourne...and dropping that...I called twice at Eastbourne and talked to head mothers, mistresses, whatever—once it was too late, they wouldn't wake her...Your mother's insisting on some school in the city now, and Cam, I'm not sure..." she interrupted her own pause resolutely, "but, I need to discuss this with her before she makes another change."

"She's at their apartment now. Not flitting all over Europe."

"You seem a little off yourself."

"Do you trust me, Roberta, do you trust me at all?"

"How do you mean?"

"Don't turn this around on me. It's you who seems bothered. Noticeably so. We've all noticed. You're always distracted lately. Then Farzi disappears. Jill even saw you leaving the police station with a priest. Will you tell me what kind of trouble you're in?"

"Father Charles."

"Is this the priest you spent the night with? You can trust me, Roberta."

"That...was a...joke, I was baiting you. Why wouldn't I trust you? There's no reason...The priest, Father Charles, I think he's out to save me." She seemed to be holding back laughter angering Cameron who felt blisteringly fed up.

"Will you stop it? Will you quit, Roberta?"

Not Cameron but the thought of the priest was

uppermost in her mind, "If he can convince me to renounce my shady intellect and embrace faith. But I do embrace it, Cam. I have faith the sun will come up in the morning."

He shook his heavy, streaked blond head giving up on her. "Everybody thinks you know what Farzi is up to."

"I don't know." She was beginning to be frightened of that answer. She didn't know—she was beginning to like saying it.

He wanted to pin her down to something, "Okay, the priest's a friend, and Farzi calls you, but she won't tell you where she is?"

"Partly true."

"What? You just said you don't know where Farzi is—"

"That part's true. I wouldn't say the priest is a friend."

"All right, have it your way. Play games. But what it boils down to is you don't trust me. It would be easier to tell me to mind my own damn business then. Why go through all this rigmarole?"

"Why do you come to me when I make you so angry? Why did you come here?"

"You won't believe me—"

"Margot?" She smiled and shrugged.

Cam put his fingertips against the table edge and jiggled them, "India...you think I've lost it all. When I was young, there seemed to be more then, not to me, to the world. Why do I come here? Why do I waste time searching for anything?" Looking up from staring at his fingertips' soft movements, "Seems like ideas, the idea of ideas maybe, are vanished. So much political bullshitting now. Why do I come here?"

"There's nowhere the ideas have gone to. You would hit it off well with Father Charles."

"Don't be a goddamn idiot, Roberta. I'm trying to talk to you."

"Get out of here. Take your ideas and existential transcendence or whatever...and..."

He jerked his chin at her in amazement, "Roberta, I came to help you." Hair fell into his eyes in a peculiar, old-fashioned way.

"I know. You hate the inexcusable parts of life. That's probably why I married you."

His confidence returned, "You see, Berta, you're from the part of my life that sustains me."

"Because I'm past? Leave now, Cam, before your angst drips like the rain did all over my carpet."

"And why the hell won't you call Margot?" An exit line.

Science halls of great universities are best approached obliquely. Passing between the avenue of trees beginning to take on fall colors and the dwarf shrubs clustering the front of smooth granite, Roberta resonated in the muted bronze light. Inside the building she climbed swayback stairs of marble to the tiny cell Tracer worked in when she wasn't in the field nor in the musty subterranean lab recently bequeathed to paleo-Indian archeology. Tracer's square bulk eclipsed the rheumy blue school desk at which she sat tapping on an old computer.

"Bertie, what a relief. I was just starting to be appalled at my own ignorance." A grin split her stoically tanned face.

"What were you doing?"

"Writing up some analyses of cut marks on these bones."

She gestured, hand over her broad shoulder to a littered table behind her. "I don't know really." Roberta sat next to the mound of computer sheets on one corner of the desk. In truth she was disrupting her friend who had greeted her in reflexive friendship.

Roberta glanced somewhat bewildered about the small, dark room, "That's new."

"The sand painting?"

"Effecting. Like something from the collective unconscious." She shook her head. "But it doesn't matter."

Tracer had spent a lot of time locating just the right painting, a significant one. Also, her painful last visit with Roberta still caused her some discomfort. She snapped, "Hey, you don't like the painting?" Being disrupted brings intense people to unkind backbiting. However, Tracer wasn't self-centered, particularly, nor disloyal. Roberta had been jumpy wrestling with Farzi's disappearance, she supposed, or her father's illness, either or both pinching her overly thoughtful nerves maybe causing spasms in the psyche.

"I'm touchy today. So, what are you up to?"

"On my way to the lab. Dorcus called earlier in an excited state—"

"What a picture."

"He's got something phenomenal to show me. I should rush right up."

"And with such enticement you stopped here first?" Bit of a jab, but there was so much work to do.

"Well, I, I was wondering if you could remember this place Farzi used to talk about. I can't..." She rubbed her forehead, "this place in New York she used to go to."

"A gallery?"

"Oh, no. Just this little place she used to say she liked to visit...it doesn't matter."

"Nope, I don't know of any little hideaway Farzi might have mentioned. Anyway, why are you staring at the sand painting? Forget Farzi, she's a lot harder nosed than you, she can take care of herself—"

"No. I've had a lot...on my mind, and...Really, I didn't mean to barge in," she stood saying this and backed toward the door.

Tracer relented, "Wait, huh? That was ragging you, Bertie. And I'm not going to do that anymore."

"I thought I'd do a little detecting on my own. I don't want to interfere when you're busy—"

"Don't go away mad—"

"I thought you might have remembered—"

"You'll upset your stomach—" her white, even teeth dented pink buccal mounds.

"It was the cold chili. We shouldn't have eaten it cold."

"Will you sit back down, Bertie? So you started something. You got an idea where Farzi might be? So finish."

"You don't give a damn. Finish your work."

"Okay, sit for a minute, huh. I wasn't getting anywhere with this stuff. What were you going to say?"

"I figure...if I put together clues from her telephone calls, I should have an inkling where Farzi is. I could challenge her with that. At least I might find out where she is. It'd be a start."

"Strange. Someone like Farzi, who's got everything.

Screwed if I know." Again Roberta was staring at the sand painting.

"You know, Tracer, what the hell good is an unconscious collective memory?"

"What? You mean to a species?"

"Yes. How would it increase a species' chances for survival?"

"I suppose that's an interesting question—"

"This collective memory comes from how we made our fears abstractions...and, lodged them, yes, in our chromosomes, before we were completely human. Someone's thought of this already. In the Pleistocene—"

"Someone's thought of this in the Pleistocene?"

"You're being obtuse. So, in the natural growth of our minds, we detached the fears and...symbolized them, and put them in our genes. But, Tracer, the point is, if we could do that, shouldn't we be able to remove them—"

"The same way?"

"Change the abstractions. And other things, too."

"Remove our deepest, most irrational fears—"

"Remove them."

Tracer leaned back and jiggled in her swivel, desk chair, "I don't quite see, but since I'm not a geneticist—"

"That's...not it...Oh, forget this, too. Lately I've been forced to follow all these foggy thoughts, any and all that come down the pike. Forget it. I wish I knew where Farzi's hiding. Everyone thinks it's a scheme and I'm in on it. When she calls, she sounds...terrified somehow. But she won't tell me why she can't come home. And, Tracer, Farzi won't come home." She pulled her heavy hair behind her ears, cooling them.

"It's got to be a Moslem thing." They mulled this over for awhile.

After Roberta left, Tracer went back to her cuttings, but caught her gaze slipping past the bones to find the sand painting. Suddenly it gave her a fright. Jolted out of her desk, the big, dark woman roughly pulled the sand painting off the wall and pushed it under a table. "Roberta," she whispered aloud for comfort, "you and your freaky ideas." She knew they were only words and shouldn't bother her like that.

Dorcus greeted Roberta in a limpy, jumpy, excited hop across the lab, "Just sent from White." He was holding out a well-preserved hominid jaw. Roberta took it from him, tipping it up and rotating it in her hands, looking at it from all angles.

"Wonderful, it's wonderful." First seeing a newly discovered fossil often overwhelmed her. There was always the promise of what each discovery might mean.

"While I waited for you, I got the Nbung skull back from the photo lab. I had this gut feeling," his excitement compressed her up to a long work table under a fluorescent light; he picked up the repaired skull. "Look." Slowly they fitted the jaw into the cranium. "Perfect, huh. It was found in the same general location. Near the grid where he found the skull, I guess, but deeper—"

"There's distortion." Feeling the depression with her fingers.

"Under a lot of debris. That's why. We'll see, but it looks good, so good. White's too cautious to talk. But he sent it back with Dapplier so we could start matching it. Peculiar, you know. He's had the skull for months without doing much with it. Then he sends it to me, and you almost ruin it. And now, now he finds the thing's jaw." He tossed his face up ponderously to meet his balding crew cut, "We've got so much to do here. Erectus, certainly, but look at these molars." Dorcus took the fossils from Roberta, lay them on the table, and hopped away.

Reaching out Roberta caressed the glassy cranium tracing her finger over the imaginary jaw line. She was not so sure as Dorcus that the jaw was a fit. Warm tears from her heated insides prickled her eyelids, "Why grinnest thou at me, thou hollow skull?" She felt a release, the giving way of a tightening loop at the circumference of her mind, "Save that thy brain, confused like mine, once sought bright day."

Dorcus returned lugging equipment, "Come on," he called to his assistant.

Dorcus had left her moments after admonishing her for the fourth time about the preservative, when she looked up at a noise half-expecting him back again with more nervous commands. But coming in the door was a husky man, square-faced, swarthy, bearded, his grizzled curly hair sticking out of a rose-colored head wrap.

"You are Roberta Branwaithe?"

"I...was just cleaning up to go home." She brushed past him, locking up the fossils and shoving papers into the drawer. He followed her silently, until she reached for her coat.

"I only want a moment, Madame Branwaithe, to deliver

a message. From Farzi Behroozi."

She stopped, realizing that despite the accent and intimidating look, this man had not come from Behroozi himself, sensing finally that he was not menacing her, but was as uncomfortable as she about this encounter.

"A message?"

"Further directions from her." He squinted in Roberta's face. "Farzi isn't able to call you at this time."

"Oh my God, is she all right?"

"Yes, safe."

"What in creation is going on?"

"Madame Branwaithe, I will tell you what I may. That's all. In order to help Farzi you must be in Manhattan on Friday. But you must tell no one that you are going." He handed her an airline ticket. "The business is running its course." Graciously he tilted his bonneted head and backed her out the door. "Good-bye, Madame."

"Wait, where do I go when I get there?"

"Farzi will call before you leave. Again, good-bye."

It was absurd. How would she get time off, with the new jaw and all? And her father, how could she desert him when he was being so maddeningly an invalid? Then what would her friends think since the messenger insisted that she tell no one she was going? Could she be sure he was from Farzi? Was she going to disappear, too?

The rain had passed leaving a watery yellow patina of shimmery evening light. Inside stalwart Persia Gallery which huddled amongst the taller, more dignified buildings of metallic glass, Denis and Tony argued not so much in anger as in frustration.

"We can't without Farzi's signature."

"But we haven't got that, Tony, and we don't know when—why did she do this, Tony? The accountant explained to me—the way he explained it to me, it's gotten past the given time, and if we don't get these papers to Hajinlian, he'll never be able to close the deal. We've had this thing going for months, the consignment's in escrow...wouldn't Farzi, our Farzi would not have dropped us like this."

"I don't know. I can't think what's what anymore. I tried to talk to Roberta, and if you're right, and she knows where Farzi is, she's putting on one consummate act. After the races I called Cam. He'd stayed on with her when we left, and I had hoped he'd gotten something out of her. But no. Cam's no help with Roberta. Any influence he once had...and he thinks, if you can believe this, that Roberta doesn't care, isn't interested in where Farzi is. That I don't get from her at all."

"Fine. In the meantime, Anthony, my friend and partner, what do we do about Farzi's signature?"

"We wait."

"And maybe lose the deal?" His face reddened like an excited baby's: quickly, from the neckline up.

Tony turned on Denis, feeling accused, "I'd forgotten about this fucking deal. I've been worried about Farzi."

"Better worry about the business."

"Can we get some kind of power of attorney?"

"No. Are you kidding? You should shake it out of Roberta where she is."

A scuffle at the door broke into their self-absorbed talk. The wide backend of a heavy-set man appeared: Terry pushing or rocking at something.

Tony shouted, "Hey, Terry." Then he saw MacBeth behind him. The moment fell dead still.

"I told you this was no good coming here, Bill."

Tony didn't want to get beaten up again (as much fun as the first time had been), this time by an irate Canadian. "MacBeth, hold up a minute." Horrified, he realized he was about to bolt as an almost ludicrous figure attacked him, slick hair and long mustache looking like the villain who tied the damsel to the track. He got up close to Tony's outstretched chin.

"I want to tell you face to face, Jerk, that you've destroyed my marriage, and you've done it not from any great passion which I just might have understood. But on lousy damn impulse. So, I will destroy something important to you. Angelique has it figured out what's happened to your fiancee. What's her name, Farzi? Well, Farzi's never going to marry you. You'll never see her again." In a cold burn like decaying neptunium, he got even closer in Tony's face. "As you know, I've got...political connections in Canada. Step one foot on our soil, and I'll have you jailed on real nasty charges that will keep you locked up for the rest of your despicable life." In swift, economic strides, he walked out of the gallery. Terry lumbered over to the speechless art purveyors.

"I told him not to come here. Hell...and his horse lost, too."

"What does he mean about Farzi?"

"I don't know. He's high strung. I've known him since we were kids, and he's always gone off on things so easy—"

"Terry for chrissake, what does he mean about Farzi?"

11

When one at last hears the truth,

or fragment of truth which one names the truth,

one senses it.

———

Roberta caught sight of Jon Martin part of a crowd about to board the bus in front of the Union. Pushing ahead she plopped into the empty seat next to him and poked him with her elbow, "Hey, where you off to?"

"To Wilhelmi delivering these proofs. And you? Where's your car?"

"Getting a new alternator. I'm meeting Jill downtown, and she'll take me to pick up the car. Roundabout way, huh? I don't see how you do it without driving. I feel vulnerable taking the bus—"

"Oh, but Roberta, I'm a poet."

"So you must ride the bus?" His compact little body settled in nicely next to hers. "Is this—"

"An article only. Dull. Nothing fun this time. But, but, I'm working on something. This here," he held up a manila envelope, "is about T.S. Elliot. Up here," he touched the jet black rim of his circlet of hair, "I have something brewing, which if I could just dig it out would, would rival Elliot.

I know I sound like a fool boasting, but if I could get it out... Maybe Elliot, or somebody, won't let me; jealousy forfends."

Roberta leaned back in her seat listening to his yeasty, mellow voice."

"Too bad you can't collar Elliot, Jon, or whoever, gather him up, hold him by his stuffed ruffled front, or his ripped tee shirt and say, 'Listen, you beanhead, get out of my love song.'"

"Berta, you've been working too long with dead bones."

"I have. And now we've got this mystifying new jaw—"

"I heard scuttlebutt today. Somebody from paleoanthropology was saying...who was that? Some big deal?"

"We just started looking at it. It's like an erectus jaw, but the molars are small."

"How exciting is that?"

When they parted at Roberta's stop, Jon turned himself halfway to wave from the window. She was smiling up at him receding along the lengthening pavement, and he thought how he'd forgotten to ask her about her artist friend. If she'd shown up again. He had no idea how much he had comforted her.

When she saw Roberta approaching, Jill at once began to talk being the kind who feels that a long pause indicates unfriendliness and far be it from her to be assigned hostile intentions.

"Thank God your car broke down and you needed a ride. I've been trying to get a hold of you for days."

"I haven't been home long enough for anyone to get me."

"Well thank God. And you wouldn't believe it but now

I'm truly worried about Farzi. You might be right after all. So, first, tell me where she is—"

"Look me in the eyes, Jill, and pay attention. I don't know."

"You don't?" She looked crestfallen.

"No." The two women ambled toward the car lot. "What is it? Why are you all of a sudden worried?"

"Don't be sarcastic. You know how I feel about Farzi. Between Farzi and Tracer I'd have to choose Tracer. You've mixed us up with the strangest people, Roberta, and we used to have such a nice group of friends. It's just that Farzi's selfish, out for herself, and I've never had much sympathy for people like that." Roberta waited for the well-intentioned woman to reappear and displace the stocky primitive now confronting her. "Roberta, are you hearing me?"

"Yes, of course. Somebody has to find your car. It's over here, come on." Jill waded in her word flowage over to the blue van, then was silent while she unlocked the door and buckled herself in, the procedure taking all her concentration. Deftly she pulled out of the lot.

"I'm actually scared, Roberta. This whole thing's bothered me so much I wake up in the middle of the night shaking. And I don't even like Farzi...Roberta?"

"Yes, I'm following you."

"Then why are you sitting there silent like a Buddha? I'm so upset."

"Start from the beginning, Jill. That would help." All she could muster was a weak detritus of interest. What could Jill know?

"I think Farzi actually is in trouble because of something important Angelique said. We were driving her and Bill to the airport when we got to talking about Farzi being there in New York. That's where Bill and Angelique were headed. You know how people talk. I said Farzi was getting ready for her wedding. You know."

"Yes." Punctuation, that's all. Think of it as that. She didn't want to rush Jill. She hardly wanted to hear her at all. She would really have liked to shut Jill up, but she didn't see how.

"Muslims. Angelique whispered something about Muslims when Terry asked about Farzi and Iran. But Bill said Angelique was talking about some Black Muslims she knew, and he said that Black Muslim isn't the same as Islamic Muslims, made fun of her kind of. But Angelique kept asking questions about Farzi and Tony. Then, I interrupted because I happen to know that Black Muslims are Islamic. And then Angelique said something like, 'It's a horrible sin...to my Muslim friends.'

'What?' I said.

And Angelique said, 'Muslim men may marry anyone, a Christian, a Jew. But Muslim women must marry only a Muslim man.'

I just stared at her, Roberta, and said, 'What?'

'Farzi Behroozi's not marrying a Muslim,' she says. Well, I told her that Farzi's not into all that Islam stuff. I tried to explain. It can't be that backward in Canada, can it? But you know what she said then, Roberta?"

Holding her breath Roberta merely shook her head, her sight pulled away from Jill's rapt expression.

"She said that she heard from this Muslim guy that Heshemi Behroozi had contracted for a Muslim husband for Farzi. Honest to God, could this be why Farzi's disappeared?"

Roberta felt a creeping terror curdle her stomach lining with panic: it should not be.

"Yes, Angelique's on to something. It's got to be something powerful we don't comprehend."

When one at last hears the truth, or fragment of truth which one names the truth, one senses it. Like the face of an old friend not seen in twenty years, it's not what we recall, but we recognize it anyway. Roberta controlled her fear and agreed that the danger to Farzi might be as unusual and oblique as Angelique's hint implied. She trusted Jill who was after all no fool and had told only Roberta about Angelique's revelation. Hadn't even talked to Terry about it, unsure why not.

"But I think Bill Macbeth knows, too. Terry came home yesterday from Persia Gallery with a story about how Bill threatened Tony. You heard about Tony and Angelique?"

"Yes, yes."

"Well, Bill's back in town, and yesterday he told off Tony. He said Farzi's wasn't ever coming back and wasn't ever going to marry him."

"I wonder if Angelique knows anything more, like where Farzi might be?"

"I don't think so. It was all almost an accident what she figured out...good God, Roberta, we're in Waukegan. Where is your car dealership anyway?" They struggled back to the commonplace relieved and amused.

If she was going to be leaving soon, she had to check

in on her father beforehand. But was it necessary? She was, after all, only going to be gone two days...It wasn't necessary, only seemed so. Couldn't tell anyone she was going anywhere. Dorcus had come to expect her to work weekends. It'd do him good if she didn't show up for once. She had promised Jill she'd keep her informed. But then, Jill wasn't ready for any of this. Although it was probable she'd be back before anyone knew she was gone, many conditions, provisos, had to be met with. It was complicated disappearing.

Earlier in the week she had consulted with her father's doctors. The psychiatrist had declared that her father was the sanest man he knew. Roberta didn't doubt it.

Chronically sane Adrian Branwaithe was dozing comfortably when his daughter arrived.

"Hello, Dad, feeling okay to talk? Sorry I came so late."

"You always do. Come under cover of night. Remember when I taught you some constellations? Andromache and Cepheus, and the Big Dipper?"

"And Orion...Orion was my favorite."

"Are they out tonight? Too early, for Orion."

"It's cloudy."

"Too early in the fall."

She sat uninvited as usual, envisioning her father dressed always in a dark suit, wrinkled white shirt yellowing a little, dropping an overstuffed briefcase at the doorway; he had traced the constellations for her as solemnly as he had looked into the gorilla's eyes."

"I was lucky, lucky getting Mom and you."

"Nice of you to say so."

"It's all so much luck."

"Did you bring me something to read?"

"Better than that. Good news. We're getting the house ready. You'll be able to move back in about a week."

"God damn it, I can't do it," he seemed lifted out of his chair by the sudden anger, awakened with a jar from his phantom stars. "I'm too ill to leave, can't you see? Ask the doctor—"

"This is his decision. He's told you that." Firm, patient determination, something she really hadn't tried with him before. She'd give it a shot, a long shot. "He released you from the hospital. You're well, you've recovered. You were well then, you're even better now. There's no reason for you to stay here any longer. You've regained your...Dad, you're not going to die from that stroke. He's told you—"

"Shut up your mouth, you lying bitch. You and that quack doctor don't know what you're talking about. Of course, I'm going to die. I'm dying right now, this minute."

"You're making a fuss over—"

"Shut up, I said. Let me die in peace. Why do people, does everything, want to go on and on? It's indecent really. Everything, everyone wanting to go on forever. I don't want to—"

"Dad, you don't have to yell—" Frightened, she moved over to him trying to quiet his flopping, trembly hands.

"Just let there be an end to it. Do what you can while you can. Then let it end." He sobbed, "Who or what would honestly want to go on forever..."

Roberta lifted her head. A nurse who'd heard the shouting had hurried in, "Come on, Doane, it's all right."

Together with the help of a tranquilizer, Roberta and the nurse, settled him. His anger spent, he turned aside and sullenly let them administer to him. The young woman aide asked no questions: old people flew off once in awhile. They were all losing it. Some were poor old souls. Roberta watched her giving instructions to the back of his head. He had all of his hair, still thick, now white. Old people, you either patronize and sentimentalize or ignore and pity. Her father had said that once. The young woman left the room.

"Dad?"

"Go home. I'm not going to apologize for yelling at you either. You provoked it. Anyway, you don't forgive."

"I'll see you—"

"Right here. I'm staying right here. No one is pushing me out."

"We don't...no one wants to push you—"

"Good."

Well, she had come to see him before she might have to disappear. And it did make the idea of disappearing a little easier for her.

At home in the evening packing, Roberta was brushing the cat away from curling up inside her suitcase; every time she'd turn her head, he'd be back, so she talked to him reassuringly, stroking his chin and the side of his head with her long fingers.

"I'm only going to be gone two days. My return ticket's for Sunday night. And I'll leave you plenty of food and water." She wasn't supposed to tell anyone she was leaving, so how in the world was she supposed to get someone to take care of the cat? Didn't Farzi realize that if you had a cat you couldn't just leave and tell no one? You can't disappear if you have a cat. Why in the world hadn't Farzi called to let her know where she should go when she got off the effing plane?

Then, near three in the morning, when Roberta had run to the ground over and over in her head what Jill had told her, worrying herself numb, Farzi called.

"It's vital that you don't interrupt when I talk right now, Roberta, just attend. My messenger arrived...isn't that right?"

"Yes."

"And you understand?"

"Yes."

"It's something you will do...what I ask?"

"Yes. Yes. But where do I —"

"Hush. And you'll find out for me if Tony has the Aristosos contract on file?"

"If he'll tell me—"

"Or ask Denis."

"He may not tell me either."

"Thirty seconds, I have thirty....Roberta, forgive me for getting you involved in this. Will you forgive me?"

"Why forgive, Farzi? I'll come, but...whatever you may think, there's got to be another way out of this—"

"Don't talk now, Berta."

"It could be a trap?"

The phone went dead. Roberta flung it over her shoulder onto the carpet in a melodramatic, but satisfying gesture. It honked obscenely into the thick pile. One moment a desperate attempt to get a grip as if with raw fingers pressed into the frayed edge of the window sill, hanging almost dead-weighted, flesh too much for you, and not enough, not nearly enough. Next moment monotonous, crude bellowing of more empty, meaningless noise. And she still had no idea where she should go. God damn you, Farzi, it's a goddamned trap.

One thing appeared certain, before she flew to New York the next day, she had to find out about this Aristosos contract. Did that contract have anything to do with this trip, or was Farzi taking a sudden interest in her business? She'd sounded strange as if she was being timed and monitored. A disjointed call...Farzi had sounded almost disappointed when Roberta hadn't interrupted. That would be ripe.

Denis met Roberta at the door of Persia Gallery his head bobbing puppet-like, shouting, "I'm leaving, Delores, I'm going to lunch. Roberta, come on. Come with me." He made to take her arm.

She said, "I came to talk to Tony," while being urged down the street.

"Yes, he's not here. Roberta, come on. We'll go to Frankie's. He'll give us one of those semi-private booths, and he said he'd keep a lookout for us."

"What's going on now, Denis?"

"Just like he did when that big Mafia guy was in town. He said he knew just how to do it. Keep still, please. You never know who might be...around."

"For chrissake."

Frankie was at the door of his strange establishment, part cabaret, part cafeteria, always glowing and well-populated even at four a.m. Expertly he led them to the semi-private booths, handed them menus, nodded meaningfully at the trembling, slender art dealer. "This should be okay." Roberta watched him slink away.

"All right, Denis, what is this?"

"I didn't want an upsetting word said around Delores. I don't want to frighten her any more than she already is. If we talk around Delores, she'll quit on us, and then where will we be? We can only trust our goddamn accountant because Delores knows in her head where every goddamned penny comes from and goes to." His head swagged, "Now this. So, what the hell do you want to talk to Tony about?" He put his hands flat against his cheeks, "Shit, Roberta, I don't know where he is. He didn't show up this morning. Last night I tried to get him until late, late, about this deal that's falling through because Farzi isn't here, and he wasn't in or he'd have answered. No one's seen him since he walked out of the gallery last night with Cam."

"Did you try Cameron?"

"Of course. Couldn't get him. It's just not like Tony. He never goes off except on business unless...Everything that's been going on lately's spooked me. Ever since Tony got beat up, I'm not thinking straight." He drank some of the coffee Frankie set before them.

"It's probably all right, Tony's probably with a woman—"

"He lets me know, it's the business...and he always comes in the morning."

"Denis, is the Aristosos contract on file?"

"Aristosos? What're you talking about?"

"Is it...the Aristosos contract? Is it on file?"

"What are you talking about?"

"Farzi called."

"She is messing us up big time."

"And she said could I find out for her if the Aristosos contract is on file. She said to ask Tony."

"Does she care we need her here? No."

"What could it mean?"

"How the hell do I know. We haven't got any Aristosos contract. I've got to go back to the gallery, find out where my partner is, my business—my livelihood's about to—Jesus Christ, Roberta, your goddamned mysteries don't interest me at all. I'm sick of them." Up he bolted.

"Wait, wait. I'll go with you." They raced back through the busy foot traffic. "Can't you just...doesn't Aristosos mean anything to you?"

"Nothing."

They were at the heavy, glass doors of the gallery, "Please, have Tony call me. No matter what time he gets back."

"If he gets back..."

Tony called her sometime after midnight.

"Denis said it's important, about Farzi."

"I'm glad you're safe, Tony."

"I've been a blasted fool, and I'm fucking finished with being Mr. Nice Guy.

"What happened?"

"Just as Cam and I left the gallery last night, a couple of men stop us. They say they're from Farzi, that they've got a message from her. They say Farzi wants me to go meet her, she needs me. I fucking thought it was on the fucking level. Honest to God, how could I have been so stupid? The men take off, and I said to Cam how can I go meet her when

I don't know where she is. Cam thought she must figure I would know where to go somehow. Cam thought these guys were on the level, too. And Cam's a smart guy. Yeah, real smart. Both of us really brilliant. So we figure out she must mean where she last told me she'd be—the Adirondacks with the Cassoffs. I never believed all that Switzerland stuff. I thought you were doing that to get me out of the way for some daft reason. So Cam took me to the airport. And when I get to Blue Mountain Lake, Farzi, of course, isn't there, only old man Behroozi with his thugs, pushes past me at the door scaring hell out of the Cassoffs who now think we're both lunatics and maybe we are. But at least that bastard— he set the whole thing up thinking I'd lead him to Farzi. He knows better now."

"What did you do—"

"I'm going to tell you what I told him. I am no longer everybody's patsy." His hoarsy voice showed the strain of an inner shouting, a deep, stressful, hidden scream. The sound stretched and scraped on Roberta's ear drums.

"I'm sorry, Tony—"

"I asked the madman why he was searching for her and you know what he said?"

"What?"

"That she has to get married. Can you believe that?"

"I'm beginning to."

"Not only does he want to stop her from marrying me, but he's going to make her to marry some Iranian he arranged for her when she was born. He says she has to for the sake of his inestimable honor. Can you believe it? He can't force her to marry someone she doesn't want to. I told him that."

"What'd he say?"

"He spat in my face. His two hoodlum creeps grabbed my arms, or I'd have ripped his head off."

"It's...absurd—"

"I'll get him. You wait. Farzi and I will get married, and I'll send him the announcement, wrapped 'round a bomb. You got to do something for me. When Farzi calls you again, tell her it's all out. That I understand why she ran away. She should come back because I understand. Not to be afraid...there's not a fucking thing he can do to stop us. Okay? Roberta?"

"Okay."

"I've got to go get some sleep."

"Yes, you sound awful. And no wonder. Can you tell me something? I wouldn't ask you now, but it's very important. When Farzi called me last time, she mentioned an Aristosos contract on file. She said to ask you about it."

"We don't list anybody like that."

"What could she mean?"

"There isn't a client, or art work, or anything by that name on the computer."

"Are you sure?"

"Oh, yes."

"Somebody Farzi knew—"

"Unless...yeah, Mrs. Aristosos, some old friend. I think she died last year. Farzi went to her funeral in Queens."

Tomorrow morning she would fly, and as yet Farzi Behroozi hadn't called. Where in the hell would she go when she landed? Queens? Forest Hill?

Eight a.m. Two hours before Roberta's plane was scheduled to take off, Farzi reached her. Roberta fumed.

"What did you expect me to do when I got there, if I had already left? Just answer me that."

"I knew I'd catch you. You never leave until the last minute. It's occasionally irritating traveling with you because of that quirk."

"Oh, shut up, Farzi, shut up—"

"I'm...I can't call you whenever I want, Sweetie. At least...not when no one is around."

"And no one's around now."

"Can't you tell?"

"I suppose so. And someone was there last time you called."

"Of course."

"That stuff about the Aristosos contract—"

"I can't always say what I want. I'm almost never left alone anymore."

"Why?"

"The people who think they're protecting me, watch me constantly. And they are helping. They are hiding me. Only I can't stay here much longer."

"Farzi, this chase is over. We know about your father and the Moslem marriage, and we know what's going on. You didn't have to run. You can get a restraining order from the police in case he tries to kidnap you—You see Farzi, I do know what you're up against. We're not minimizing or belittling the danger you're in. Tony's got the picture, too. He says come back, we'll work it out. We can get some kind of restraining order. Then after you marry Tony, what can—"

"Oh, Berta—"

"We've figured it out. There was no reason to hide it from us. It's out, and we can do something about it."

"You figured it out. And it's not going to help me one bit. Unless you can change it."

"I don't understand."

"I'd be killed, Berta, I would be killed...and it's dangerous for you to know these things. It's only partially out, Sweetie, and partially may be the most dangerous of all."

"What do you want me to do...when I get to New York?"

"Meet Mrs. Aristosos. Tonight at seven. At Rockefeller Center, right in front of Prometheus. She'll find you."

"You know, it's damn lucky you caught me. Tony told me Mrs. Aristosos was dead. I was going to look for her at Forest Hill."

"What on earth—"

"Tony said you went to her funeral in Queens."

"He's thinking of someone else. That's too good. I wanted to give you this information last time I called, then someone walked in. I had to pretend it was a business problem. So, I leave you a terrible clue. I sculpt a poor form here, not so?"

"You sculpt as usual, exquisitely."

"Benedicite..."

12

Always, everywhere, moving people trod back and forth amongst the plunging, exasperated automobiles, whose exhaust fumes were everyone's perfume.

———————

After walking Manhattan for hours in the drizzling rain, Roberta joined the crowd streaming past Rockefeller Plaza at dusk. She felt singularly bewildered by the pressure and constancy of the throng, the packed isolation, cold in the damp fall air, yet hot and contained. The city night beat here and then there, beside her and from the echoing distances, relentlessly. Always, everywhere, brilliantine slicked lights flashed blue lime green white, glossy red—dank, heated air from below the city streets hissing sewer vapor—wind smacking the city sound against the glassy, patchwork tunnel of skyscrapers. Always, everywhere, moving people trod back and forth amongst the plunging, exasperated automobiles, whose exhaust fumes were everyone's perfume.

Behind Roberta the gilded Prometheus posed in steadfast flight.

A woman had been standing next to her for some time, watching her shiver and sweat.

"Roberta Branwaithe? I am Mary Aristosos."

"You found me."

"Of course." She was a self-effacing, graying, frumpish woman in a camel's hair coat too heavy for the early fall weather. Everything about her seemed out of season. She had dark, rumpled eyebrows, brown, furrowed forehead, red coral cheeks, and deep-set, wide-spread, eyes of flecked gold and aquamarine.

Mrs. Aristosos suggested they find an empty bench to sit and "talk in private." Roberta was as dumbfounded at this particular emissary as she had been at the tiny lady who had collected Farzi's luggage: how on earth could these two unlikely conspirators be abetting Farzi Behroozi? Nevertheless, she sat as if hexed by Mrs. Aristosos in the circle of the glittering fire-bringer.

"I bet you're busting to find out why Farzi sent me here?" No answer. Roberta shied away from rhetorical language. "You're so antsy is why I asked."

"I'm...upset, Mrs. Aristosos, about all this. I'm worried about Farzi...you're here to—"

"Tell you what you gotta do next, what you think. But first I wanna say it: you and me are the only two people Farzi trusts right now. She told me. And me she trusts only a little bit. You, she trusts the whole hog. Is there anybody you trust like that?"

"No."

"Me neither. See what I mean?"

"I'm afraid not."

"Well think about it."

"Mrs. Aristosos, if—"

"I live on the top floor in the building next to Tattersall

Gallery where Farzi comes for years to deal. My husband and me, we ran a grocery store thirty years, a little one, 'round the corner from where we live. We get robbed once too often, he decides to sell it. Now, for months at a time, nothing happens. I'm bored to tears. Then the other day Farzi comes upstairs. She's always such a beauty, you know, so well dressed. Fancy, but not so's you notice, eh. I remember long time ago when I first seen her. She tells me she's a artist. A artist who sells art. It didn't matter one bit. We got to be friends. And now, she asks for my help. What should I do? I don't hesitate. She don't offer me a nickel for helping her. And you know what, I wouldn't put myself out if she did."

"Didn't offer me anything, either," Roberta grinned.

"Course not." Mrs. Aristosos' heavy brows dipped, disclaiming the inappropriate jest. "So, do you understand now?"

"About what? I'm sorry I'm so dense, Mrs. Aristosos."

"I'm sorry you are, too, because Farzi really needs you to be sharp."

"Then you're going to have to spell out what I'm supposed to do to help her. I'm getting cold."

"I don't think I'd trust you very far, Missy. You look too weak."

"Do I? What do you want me to do, carry the world on my back like Atlas?"

"Phooey," she flapped her hand. "Go to the Waldorf. Stay there. Be standing in the lobby tomorrow afternoon at exactly four o'clock."

"That's all?"

"Yeah. A reservation's there for you. I made it. Your name's Suzanne Feldstone."

"All right," Roberta sighed. "Mrs. Aristosos, thank you... for coming here."

"I don't wanna know what kinda trouble Farzi's in. She's a artist...a lovely, lovely artist."

The wealthy aura of the Waldorf ordered Roberta's tumbling doubts and soothed her sensibilities so that she slept amongst its munificent luxury in an animal stupor. When she awoke, she was determined to visit her daughter. There was time, and she would do it. It wouldn't be putting Margot in danger so far as she could conceive. And how could she come to New York even clandestinely and not see her own daughter? How better to bypass the telephone block she had been suffering? In the cold mid-morning sunshine, Roberta took a taxi to Riverside Drive where her in-laws kept her daughter for her.

Alice herself, long face highly rouged, answered the ring and seemed stunned to see Roberta at the door.

"My, my, what an unexpected pleasure." She spoke mid-Manhattan upper class.

"I'm only in the city for a couple of days...unscheduled trip came up. Is Margot here?"

Margot who had heard Roberta's voice, tore down the hall so that as Roberta asked for her, she appeared, looking almost overjoyed to see her mother. This was nothing like her usual easygoing greeting, and her lighted face touched Roberta mightily. She pulled Margot to her and almost wept, "Hello, Margie."

"Hey, what're you doing here? I'm so glad to see you."

"I had a hard time getting you on the phone."

"So you just show up, wow."

"Only for one or two days."

"Doing something for the professor?"

"Not exactly. Margot, I want to talk to you...about a new school, and other things."

"Well, I've decided I'll finish up at Dalton." She bent like a slender, tall reed toward her grandmother.

"Wait a minute. Have you thought about what I wrote...about coming to me—"

"Sit down, Roberta," interrupted the elegant older woman, "I'll get coffee, or do you want tea?" Alice ordered the housekeeper to make a brunch.

Sun invaded the breakfast room. Pink roses bought yesterday blinked on the mahogany table. Roberta kicked off her shoes, joked with her pretty daughter, ate eggs, hot muffins, sweet butter, everything within reach, feeling suddenly comfortable and lighthearted. For a moment it was as if the reason she'd come to New York had been to see Margot, not to do the bidding of her desperate friend.

"Are you serious about me living with you?" Margot herself returned to the sensitive topic.

"You bet I am."

"But where would I finish school?"

"There's a high school that services the university."

"A public school?"

"Yes."

"You think I can go there?"

"Not to worry, they'll let you in."

"Oh, very funny, Mother."

"What Margot means, Roberta, is will she be able to get the kind of instruction...the advantages she's used to?"

"Maybe. Probably not. What does it matter? Margot, you're full of preparation for any university...for whatever. There are other matters——"

"Oh, Roberta, she's certainly been exposed to the seamy side of life living in New York."

"There are other sums of the parts I want her to learn about. Things that I'd like you to see, Margie. With me. You could take some courses at the university if you feel that——"

"At the state college?"

"Jesus, Margot, I'm not condemning you to purgatory."

"Your daughter's used to the best. She's already been accepted to Harvard."

"Eventually, I want to study medicine."

Roberta stopped listening; she, of course, recognized the language they were speaking. She sat on in silent regret for having mentioned her little scheme. Margot's life was charmed. Her in-laws had done well by her. Roberta tried not to sulk, tried to be obliged and appeased. Taking leave on the steps of the brownstone, she said she'd stop by the next day before flying home. Alone after they had closed the door behind her, Roberta insisted she was gratified, was unreasonable to feel whiffy and oppressed. After all, Margot had been loving and happy. She'd been safe.

Walking on a bit, searching for a cab, her normal good humor returned to her. "Come on, Suzanne Feldstone, you ought to jog all the way back to the Waldorf after what you just ate." At the red traffic light she saw a lone taxi besieged by customers. She picked out a man, a what's called distinguished-looking type coming toward it laptop case slung over his shoulder. He wore a paisley cravat, and his mouth puckered as he approached the curb, his prominent eyes flicking up and down the street. Caught up in his desire, Roberta watched him lift one liquid, motile hand to hail the cab. Part of a tailored suitcoat sleeve crept out of the cashmere overcoat. An esteemed, imperious presence he compelled the taxi to slide forward at the green and let him be the one to enter. Bending over he grabbed the door handle. As he did so, Roberta saw a rheumatic Cro-Magnon reaching out to feed a cave fire; then a hungry Homo erectus competing with nipping hyenas for the saber-tooth's kill; a tiny-brained pre-human striding across the lava ash pausing momentarily to stare at a sudden movement; and so to some undefined commonalty, not quite bipedal, but sharp-eyed, digging with a stripped twig into a termite mound, sucking the clinging termites off the stick.

"Poor little ape."

Roberta put her head down against the rising wind and searched for another cab.

In subdued dread of four o'clock to come, Roberta Branwaithe crisscrossed the hotel's opulent lobby half-expecting to be whisked off with Farzi Behroozi on a magical flying carpet to Teheran. Afraid she was being too conspicuous, she searched for a vantage point at which to station herself. Several idle bellboys in low-keyed chatter, heads together, lounged near the bank of elevators. Desk clerks greeted a few, staggered newcomers. One clerk clipped together reservation and credit card slips in reproachful solemnity. Choosing a green, wing-backed chair set next to an enormous brass fireplace, she proceeded toward it. As she was about to reach the velvet chair, about to lean a hip against its lambent smoothness, the Waldorf lobby shifted, became a place of garish, senseless melodrama.

Heshemi Behroozi, fists upraised, burst into the room surrounded by an excited mob of squabbling people. Flanking the irate Iranian lunged his baggy-trousered thugs, and behind him flocked a muddle of babbling folk, a crew with wild gestures and supplicating postures, angry and terrified. Roberta, throat clenched about to cramp, spotted, within the pack, the tiny lady from the bank episode and the pink-turbaned man. She hesitated, just long enough for the mob to explode straight at her. But she didn't flinch. The uproar and incongruity of the weird scene hadn't registered beneath her cortex.

Roberta's inner mind rocked side to side in trembling disappointment. Words ricochetted: did you really think it would be Farzi? Did you think she would appear at the stroke of four? A terrorist with a herd of extras shows up instead, and here we go again.

Behroozi and his bunch had swung past a few alarmed, scurrying hotel employees. As he got to Roberta, Behroozi grabbed her shoulder, his eyes confused and furious. He'd been gulled.

Shouting orders security police tramped in through the side doors increasing the general level of hostile intent. Roberta's hand on the wing of green velvet softly stroked the finely powdered silk.

"Where is my daughter," screamed Behroozi, sinking his fingers into Roberta's shoulder blade. Several of his thugs began to scuffle with the hotel security. Then the N.Y.P.D. burst in, Behroozi gave a nod and all movement stopped.

Roberta tried to shake away from the man's pressing fingertips. "You tell me, Mr. Behroozi, you tell me where Farzi is. She was coming here—"

"All right, everybody, break this up," intoned a tall policeman, "Anyone not a guest here had better leave. No trouble, just get out." He was glaring in Roberta's direction.

"If he'd let go of me," she gave another shake. The policeman stared past her.

"I said, everybody not a guest, out. Right now, or we start making arrests." Behroozi and his watchdogs swaggered, chins out, toward the hotel entrance. Police poked with batons, smoldered, looked bored. Cosmopolitan guests and hotel employees proceeded with their business only mildly curious about what had been going on. Roberta followed in the wake of the entourage.

Outside on Park Avenue a cold drizzle had begun again. In several languages people were beseeching Behroozi. From what Roberta could make out, they were rabidly declaring their innocence.

One hawk-nosed, leathery, old man, determined to be understood, protested in and out of three languages. Roberta caught the English parts: "She told us she was in trouble because of a crooked dealer. We were hiding her from his wrath and the custom officials...unintelligible...what do you take me for? Would we have hidden her from her own father?...unintelligible..."

Behroozi moved toward Roberta, the old man following, "We became suspicious when we heard the rumors, those about the contracted marriage...unintelligible ...right after that we started to guard her. We never let her out of our sight, I swear to you. She was with us in the car." Behroozi looked up. Roberta met his gaze. "Your daughter told us to send for this woman here, to resolve the business problem. She told us today that you were in town—we had known that you were coming—to help her, and that she would join you, and this woman here. We would not have let your daughter go otherwise. But we heard you had come to New York, were with Yasid. Words move as the toiling sands in our community. And then here you were at the hotel..."

"Where is my daughter?" Behroozi rasped at Roberta. She treated it as a rhetorical question. The drizzle continued.

Behroozi shifted targets fixing his eyes on the old man in a bitter mockery. He flared, brought the back of his hand across the tough, lined cheek. Braced, the old man recoiled from the blow; the thugs pulled up onto the balls of their feet forcing the others back. Behroozi slugged him again, an open-hand punch to the other cheek.

"How," he fulminated, "did she get away between the car—she came out of your car—and the door of the hotel where we were waiting? Explain. At once. How?"

The old man broke down sobbing; the man in the pink turban stepped up for him, "How? How should we know? She was in sight of you, yourself, as well." A ruckus burst out—cawing, pecking, flapping, all words intelligible now.

Roberta fled away, back into the hotel, back to her room to pack. To fly, soon, home.

Where had Farzi escaped to? Where indeed?

Roberta left New York without seeing her daughter again, left with only a phone call message taken by the housekeeper: she would write when she got home. She sent Margot her love.

From the babble of a million signifiers, the sound of hundreds of voices, she fled. Leave your daughter in the clarity of one sane tongue, something of a thought, a vision, urged her. She tried to make believe she'd done so. But on the long flight home, her head pressured by engine drone, nose blocked by fetid recycled air, she stared out the oval window at the illusion of stasis, the joke of altitude, in the numbing claustrophobic non-ride, and felt the weight of all her losses drawing her ineluctably downward. Going back without Farzi, without Margot. Poor, poor little ape.

Roberta sought the sky out of the little oval, a piece of real sky cut out and pasted in front of her face. She caught her breath, "Benedicite, benedicite," as if she might not see Farzi for a long time. Then the sky bled.

There was Margot at six years old walking with her in the North woods, she pointing out buds, tracks in the sand, scat, tiny crimson wildflowers, stripped snake skins and peepers to the child. "Pretty," said Margot about an orange toadstool.

"That mushroom's poisonous," she cautioned. They walked on some ways, then Margot saying, "Don't step there, don't step on it, don't step there," in a higher voice, "There it is...there's another one," raised another pitch,

"Don't step on it!" Finally, finally sinking in, "Sweetie, because you don't want to smash them, huh, Margot, the orange mushrooms?" The child looking up accusingly; Roberta's mind clacks searching, "Margot, those mushrooms aren't poisonous to the touch, just if you eat them."

Partly relieved, "Oh, just if you eat them."

Roberta covered her eyes, leaned her weary head against the throbbing seat back, squeezed out reluctant tears.

The hungry cat squawlered as Roberta in guilt fed him more than necessary, whispered hurried apologies while heaping the bowl. "Let me be," she gritted at her ringing phone. Let me be. Let me be. She picked up the telephone more to stop the ringing than for any other reason.

"Oh, thank goodness you got home all right."

"Farzi," she rumbled tasting gall. "Why the hell did I go to New York?"

"My father followed you there."

"You wanted him to—"

"Yes. Everywhere I go, I get caught. You were right about its being a trap, but not how you meant it. These people who were helping me, helped me only conditionally. I had to use their help. I had to let them think they were aiding my father in doing so, not aiding me defy him. A lot of face has been lost. I've cut myself off from them forever."

"You cut yourself off—"

"But because of you I'm safe. I told them I was meeting my father...to thwart suspicion, and escape those who had become my prison guards, and for that I had to really produce my father. You brought him—"

"You knew he'd follow me, find me?" She hoped she didn't sound as aghast as she felt.

"Easily."

"Uh huh."

"Berta, I'm so tired right now."

"How did you disappear? Those friends of yours that hid you came bawling into the hotel practically fainting in front of your father. Then himself screaming at me, all this going on in about twenty different languages. They were trying to explain something, about hiding you, I guess. Your father was getting more and more furious, and they were looking more and more embarrassed. Hotel security barking at all of us, people walking around us gaping. Cops come. Your father is wrenching my shoulder, and I'm trying to point that out to the cop, and your father's shaking me and yelling, 'She came here to meet my daughter. You idiots let her get away,' that's in English. And your friends are trying to explain that you were right there, and poof, you disappeared between the car and the hotel. Okay, Farzi, how in creation did you do it?"

"...I set you up...I'll never forgive myself for that. You were in danger, and I knew you would be. But it was my only chance. Berta, I was in an agony of indecision, to let you walk into what could've been a terrible situation. Because...because I...I couldn't let myself be taken, stolen or killed. I told myself...I knew, well enough, that he wouldn't hurt you. But I couldn't be sure, in truth. So I used you, you too, Darling, to get away, and it won't be something I'll ever forgive myself—"

"That's nonsense. I, I decided—"

"You were coerced, emotionally coerced."

"No. I did decide...to go to New York...to try to help. You, the mad sculptor, you didn't make me do anything. I'm not a—you didn't liberate me from a block with a magic chisel or from a cloven pine, to do your bidding. I knew what I was doing. I knew there was a danger. And I made my...I chose my—I knew what I wanted to do, damn you. Now, tell me, how did you just poof, be gone?"

"I have an actor friend whose husband does stunts for the movies. It's his prop car. I was in that car all along...the one that was parked next to where we pulled up. But it never moved and they couldn't see me. When you do this trick it looks as if you step into...nothing."

"Right now where are you?"

"Safe. I'm in Switzerland. Safe from him. It's a safe place. He doesn't have much power here, or friends."

"So you won't be coming back right away?"

"He's getting old."

"But the business? Tony?"

"I can run part of the business from here. The imports I can do without connections. Maybe I can do my own work, huh? Tony can come here, someday, if he wants to."

"You'll be all alone."

"I'm relieved, not regretful."

"Farzi?"

"I owe you an enormous debt, Roberta."

"Dearly, my delicate Ariel."

"What?"

"Are you going to tell us this time exactly where

you are?"

"As soon as I get my nerves back. When I feel that he can't do me any harm. Yes. Tell Tony, and Denis. And...you know, the others."

"Farzi? Mrs. Aristosos—"

"Tell her, too."

A reflexive laugh, "She's a weird one."

"Isn't she, though. I'm going to set up power of attorney for you so that you can get my funds to me here. Tony and Denis and I will work out the business finances after I get settled someplace, and operating."

"Why don't you just give Tony and Denis power of—"

"Are you kidding?"

"All right. As long as all I'll have to do is send you your own money."

"And if my father continues to harass you, feel free to tell him I'm in Switzerland."

"You're not really in Switzerland, are you."

"I will be for a little while longer. Maybe a long while. I won't fool you, Berta."

"How come I'm still afraid?"

"Don't be...There are many other props we can use. If they get too close. Benedicite, I'm safe for now, Roberta, be praised."

13

Roberta was irritated, emotionally hung-over from her weekend romp, and struggled in flaccid over-civility.

In the musty laboratory Donald Dorcus, patting his lips, scrutinized the fossil jaw and newly reclaimed skull lying sided by side on the table. His handsome graduate assistant, Jeffrey, looked up when Roberta approached, then smiled awkwardly at her, "Professor Hawksley's in the office waiting for you."

"Get back here right away, Roberta, you've got to help us with this," Dorcus stewed. "It'll take months to do the thing properly." She heard him drone on as she moved down the hall. Trying to impress the new assistant.

Tracer was sprayed onto a cushioned office chair, her foot, in heavy field boot, on the edge of the metal trash basket—one of her masculine poses which despite her size and attitude always managed to make her look affected. Roberta was irritated, emotionally hung-over from her weekend romp, and struggled in flaccid over-civility.

"Hey, Tracer, you been here long? I'm late this morning." Leaned against the desktop, tried disarming banter,

"Dorcus has an ingenue he's cultivating in the lab."

"You look exhausted. Don't bother making apologies. Where've you been, Bertie? Tony, Cam, Jill—I've heard from them all. They're looking for you—"

"What could they want?"

"Spooked over this Farzi stuff."

"Yeah, well, I was in New York. I found Farzi...sort of. Then she disappeared."

"You saw her?"

"No. Almost. I almost saw her. But I spoke to her later. She had been there. The...I saw people who had been hiding her. I guess that's as close as I got..."

"You're not making any sense."

"I know. It's...baffling. But Farzi's safe. I think."

"Stop perseverating. Just fill me in. It isn't a secret anymore, is it?"

"No. I'm not sure how much it ever was." In fugal procession she retold her weekend in New York, and Farzi's legerdemain.

"So you want me to believe that Behroozi will kidnap her and even kill her to save his honor?"

"Absolutely, it's a cultural thing."

"It's an obscene thing. And it's obscene I'm in any way connected with it."

"That's a cruel, mocking thing to say."

"And you're not going to forgive me for it. Maybe it was—"

"What'd you mean by saying that?" She kicked Tracer's leg off the wastebasket, leaned into her space, angry. "I...that I won't...forgive you...for what you said? Am I not the forgiving type? I somehow don't forgive—"

"Bertie, I didn't imply that you're unforgiving—"

"Well, my father recently told me in no uncertain terms that I'm unforgiving, and it sounds like he's right. I never thought...I haven't always been like that—"

"Oh, you are forgiving. Certainly you are. Don't make me mad, Roberta. You've always been much too forgiving. Not me, though. I'm not going to pardon some things. Not at all."

"That's what scares me. I've been thinking that way, too, lately. It's terrifying."

"And I'm going to continue not to. Looking at the world the way I do, it's not possible to justify everything."

"But forgiveness is the first step in reconciliation, in redemption—"

"In acceptance."

"Yes, Tracer, that, too, forgiving and accepting...oneself and others. But I'm having trouble—Do you know that forgive is a synonym for condone?"

"The acceptance of the unforgivable act is destructive."

"Unforgivable act—"

"Would God forgive a repentant Lucifer? Or does He only forgive gnats?"

"Yes, yes Tracer, but, but you're not following me. I know forgiveness is good. What if I do something mean to you, to further my own purposes, and I repent it and ask your forgiveness, wouldn't you give it?"

"I might if it was a result of weakness."

"Well, then, what kind of unforgivable act are you talking about? What's unforgivable?"

"The misuse of power. Is never committed from weakness."

"Tracer, it's terrifying. But it's what I've been suspecting. Pardon of oppressive acts supports the oppressor. Not punishment, the act of pardoning. Forgiving just goes ahead and makes us self-destruct. We have to have something to forgive, so we go ahead and accept monstrous evil. We must forgive, or we can't have sin. As far as I'm concerned, evil acts serve no good purpose."

"Yeah, you got it. There are some things that must not be forgiven. And Bertie, don't worry about turning hard. Next to me, my nature—I'm a falcon—you're a dragonfly."

The light from the doorway blinked and the small, cluttered office was suddenly stuffed up with life as Jill's dumpling figure entered. "My God, Roberta, where did you go over the weekend? I told Terry, when I tried and tried and couldn't get you, she's off and disappeared now just like Farzi. I was about to call the police, but Terry said look how good they were about Farzi."

"I found Farzi. She's all right."

Tracer rose, "I think I'll leave. I don't need to hear this again." She widened her eyes and flattened her lips, spreading her nose in a Toltec smile. Breathing easier, Roberta watched Jill take the seat Tracer had vacated. Jill's round softness, plump as she was, inflated the space made small by Tracer's presence.

Recounting to Jill what happened in New York, Roberta was relieved to find herself dwelling on her visit with Margot.

"Jill, she's a beauty. She looks like Cam. I forget when I haven't seen her in months and remember her features in my mind like a ten-year-old's, only bigger. So I'm always awakened to her as a young woman, when I see her again. It's a shock when she's there, almost grown up, and I notice all over how lovely she's become."

"Cam'll be glad to hear you saw her."

"I suppose he will—"

"In a way what you did took guts..." shattering admission, after seventeen years of staunch disapproval.

"We had to give her stability, and we were splitting. I could see what might happen to her. She's so good, and smart, and happy. Lately, I've wanted her back..." She shook her head to free the acids settling in her throat. All the overwrought, soddened excitement she had sloughed through this last month sucked at the soles of her mental feet as she tried to carry on.

Jill contented herself with the mildly disapproving, "It looks like it's turned out okay." Then brightened, "Why don't you come have supper with Terry and me tonight."

"I've got to check on my dad."

"Well, Saturday then. Come to the races with us. Tony's going, too."

"I'll see, maybe, Jill."

Roberta hurried back to the lab curious to learn what Dorcus could be making of the new fossil jaw. Receding sunlight splotched the lab in late afternoon shadows. The two men had switched on overhead lights subjecting the newly discovered fossils, resurrected after hundreds of millennium, to a wicked glare. Dorcus pushed the jaw section up to her face, "What nonsense have you been telling Jeffrey? This was found not two hundred feet from the erectus skull."

Roberta moved away, picked up the skull, and shading it from the brightness, turned it over, searching the underside in the area of the lower jaw joint. Taking the mandible from Dorcus' hand, she hefted it, carefully fingering the jaw joint, rubbing the thin buttressing. She set both fossils together on the white sheet covering the work table.

"It isn't thick enough. I want to do some more measurements. I think it's younger—"

"Don't show your ignorance. You're missing the point. Jeffrey got it right away. He spotted the fit and saw the significance. We've got a spectacular find here, and you quibble."

"I think it's got some resemblance's to the Heidelberg mandible. And yes, it has some other interesting affinities. Which we've gone over. But to say that this particular jaw fits this particular skull...I have questions. We, you and I, reconstructed this skull. We've got to be careful what we surmise, because we put it together. We need some confirmation...more to compare it with. Look, if we had adjusted this piece here...a difference. I've done some drawings to scale, I want to show you. If we had, if the joint had been moved a smidgen, just here, the mandible wouldn't fit so nicely." She sighed, impossible. "When we repaired the damage, how do you know we got it right?"

He'd listened, tediously listened, to her arguments. "We've got an erectus with an archaic jaw. Maybe an early archaic."

"Yeah, sure. If we used enough cranial plaster."

"I don't like what you're insinuating." He limped a stiff pirouette showing her his backside. Not bothering to equivocate.

Deliberately she turned to the new proselyte, "What this means, Jeff, is that I know what we've got here, and he doesn't."

She might be pushing too hard, and Dorcus would find a way to get back at her, but he'd never fire her. Again she repeated to herself that she was valuable to him. So, speak out....Until you do go too far.

"You arbitrate, Jeff. For me, I know we have two very old bones here. I can study them and live with what they might be. For Professor Dorcus...he thinks he's wrenched their secret from them, or soon will conquer their design, expose them for what they are. Homo erectus archaic Homo, solved, two parts of one. He doesn't know, and he never will know." She began to tremble, had gone too far, "about what it means."

The young man with a half-smile took the mandible from the table. "You scientists always get so worked up about this stuff?"

"She is not a scientist. She's a lab assistant, just like you are." Satisfied, he watched her turn crimson, then face away from Jeffrey as if to confirm or put a price on the professor's mastery. "Let's go over the traits again, Jeffrey. What we have here shows mosaic evolutionary process."

Roberta left the lab early hoping to reach the nursing home while it still admitted visitors, stay only half an hour, and have some of her evening left for quiet thought. Quiet thought was what she needed as opposed to active thought, or quiescent non-thought. Quiet thought let one respire.

There was someone else in her father's room. She peered into the open doorway, leaned forward tentatively, her rounded hand up signaling she was going to knock.

"Roberta, is that you? Chrissake c'on in."

"Isn't someone in there with you?"

"No."

"I thought I saw a priest."

"Hell no. I'm not ready for one yet. Not quite. Sit down. I was waiting for you. I couldn't get a hold of you all weekend."

"I had to go to New York. I looked in on Margot."

"And she's doing terrific. I know, she writes me a lot." Roberta slumped into the chair next to the desk he was sitting at.

"Have you given any more thought to what I said... about going home?"

He gave a petulant toss of his hand, "I can't go home yet. I'm not well enough."

"I don't understand you, Father. I don't understand you one bit."

"I'm a sick man, Roberta. You just don't want to accept that."

"The doctor—"

"I've got a new doctor. He's a specialist—"

"So is—"

"And comes highly recommended. He's found this irregular heart beat."

"A heart specialist?"

"The stroke's weakened my heart. Here, I want you to call him, Doctor Pritchard. I'm taking a new medication, started just today. That other stuff Suharda had me on I was having a bad reaction to. I think I was allergic or something."

Roberta didn't speak; she was searching out a measured response. "Do you know how a fossil's created, Dad? What it's made of?"

"What's this got to do with my heart?"

"How it happens a fossil becomes one? When organic material doesn't decompose, but instead becomes changed—each molecule does—until what was once organic becomes stone, in the exact form of the original, but stone. No one knows, completely understands, how it happens."

"I don't care to hear all that twaddle right now, Roberta. I want you to call this doctor. He'll tell you a few things."

Roberta took the paper he shook at her, stared at it, "You're happy here, and I'll come visit you like you visited the gorilla in the zoo. Remember, Dad, how he smashed against the Plexiglas trying and trying to break out? I'll come visit you, Dad. Maybe I'll bring some fossils."

"For all you're my daughter, I've got to say you're crazy, daffy, loony." He brushed a hand through his stiff, white hair setting it on end.

"I'll bring a fossil cranium, and you can hold it up like Yorick's skull. And it won't mean anything more to you than it did to Hamlet...or Professor Dorcus for that matter. But you know what? It does mean something to me. Some ...thing."

"Leave me alone for chrissake, with your stupidity. You'll drive me nuts, too. Go call that doctor, Pritchard. I can't take any more of your drivel."

In the next week the patter and repetition of work in

the lab measuring, computing statistics, reviving arcane theories, absorbed Roberta giving her unlatched time in the evenings for the quiet thought she sought to reconcile her again to herself. Soothing things happen in a week: a scatological note from Jon Martin with a copy of the MLA article he wrote; visit with the old woman naturalist down the hall who loved bats ("There are more rabid cows than rabid bats"); all the violets bloomed simultaneously and the cat plopped smack in their midst as if he'd done the feat pretty; the newspaper girl went on vacation and neglected to get a sub. In addition Roberta had contacted Doctor Pritchard who seemed determined to diddle with her father's heart but wasn't alarming. She'd gotten a letter from Margot and written one back. No phone call came from Farzi. A week can pass when the earth rolled round in its diurnal course makes little difference.

Then on Friday evening, while waiting for the macaroni and cheese to finish baking and reworking again the reconstructed fossil drawings, Roberta was jolted by bangs on the door. Someone had gotten upstairs again without getting buzzed in.

"Father Charles."

"Good evening, Roberta." They stared at one another rigidly.

"Come in...you're in town?"

He took the place he'd blocked out for himself last time in the corduroy sofa, crossed his legs and leaned his head back, fine, hooked nose sniffing thoughtfully.

"On my way to the Franciscan Seminary...in Springstead ...these liturgical retreats are balm...for us ministering sorts.

And y'know I can't pass you by when I come this way, Roberta. So, I stopped to see how you are."

"Is Rosie still living with you?"

"Yes." He leaned forward and uncrossed his legs, took off his glasses, blew on the lenses and replaced them pedantically, one ear at a time. He parted his dry, whitish lips.

"In fact she's been behaving herself, attending school. Haven't seen any motorcycle fellows around. I've got the parish housekeeper looking after her this week."

"Did you ever...talk...get a chance to talk to Rosie's mother?"

"No. No, I've called her a couple of times. To let her know how Rosie's doing. My sister's not the type to...it's funny. We've so much gone our separate ways. But we were close once. Then in high school...She never got to finish. Got pregnant and married the guy." He triggered a half-smile, cocked one cheek, "When I was a boy, naturally, I had desires. But I had always wanted to be a priest. So...I was pulled apart, uh...two ways. I can recall coming home from little dates, so mixed-up. She'd be awake, I'd see her light. So, I'd go talk to her. How many times I ended up crying in her arms." Cupping a hand over his mouth, he shook his head, voice modulating, "Why d'you think she's let herself get so...coarse? She sounds like a beefy dock worker...like his woman, crude and elemental. Why'd she let herself...how could she do it to herself?"

"I don't know her—"

"Of course you don't. I'm not asking you for an analysis of Sandy's personality disorders. And only God can judge her."

It was a rhetorical question she'd been tricked into responding to. Roberta glared at the man, "I've got something baking." Left him to his bilious retrospection.

He had intruded, but she must temper her natural reaction to that because the man was acting like a fool. There were rules under rules, and so she must come out with the baking dish locked in hotpad gloves, and ask him if he wanted some supper. It all made for logical sequence. When she handed the casserole to him over the table, she began to have strong misgivings as his monologue droned on. And on.

Later he sprawled on the sofa, sinuously along its length. In one of his irksome digressions he had landed on dying in a state of grace. All evening Roberta had not said much, swallowing all provocative counters in hope he'd get bored and leave.

"Roberta?" She smiled at the inflection in his voice. He seemed about to finish. He lurched off the sofa but instead of making a move toward his coat, bent over her as she was getting up and took her hand, "I wonder if I could stay with you tonight?"

"I haven't got any room. I've only got one bedroom, this sofa is—"

"I mean, with you." There it was. In her bed, or maybe just with her arms around him while he wept out his frustration. "Of course I'm not talking about actually making love. But it would be such a comfort to me if you would stoke me...let me touch you. We wouldn't have to...consummate our desires...unless, perhaps, things got out of hand. But I don't see, that doesn't necessarily have to happen." Roberta must have looked stunned. "I have so many burdens. I don't want to sound poor spirited," he got a grip on himself, "But I don't know why I ever consented to take in Rosie. It wouldn't be making love, we would just, maybe just use our mouths. Is it asking too much—"

"Asking too much?"

"You're not going to worry about...the cloth. I know you're an agnostic, or awfully close to it. So, I don't think you'll care about my being a priest. Right? A man of God. The idea excites many women. But I'm not concerned about that with you."

"Yes, yes, don't concern yourself about that. I know you're only a man. You didn't come in as a shower of gold—"

"The comfort of it would be a release...from all my burdens. We're attracted to each other, Roberta. I'm burdened so. You do only see me as a man, mostly. And I'd appreciate—"

Roberta strode quickly to the door, jerked it open, "I think you should go right now."

Coming up to her, Father Charles seemed honestly puzzled, "You aren't offended, are you?"

"Offended? No, I wouldn't say offended. No, I'm not offended."

"After all, you're not a religious person. And... understand...what I'm asking isn't exactly sex."

"I guess with God anything's possible. Good bye, Father Charles."

She plunged the dirty dishes into the hot water sinking her hands in after them up to her wrists. Certainly not offended.

Three hours after Father Charles left, Farzi phoned.

"Berta?"

"Farzi. You sound...almost cheerful."

"I'm doing better here. There's much that's beautiful. And, so far, no one's followed me. Listen, Sweetie, I just finished talking with Tony. He'll set something up with our lawyers, so you'll get temporary—partial, some such shit— power of attorney for me. I'm going to need a large chunk of money soon. Also, sign the papers that Tony and Denis have, Lohquist contracts. I think you use my name, but you can check with the lawyers on that. Sign only the Lohquist papers.

"Uh huh."

"You're not getting all this, Berta."

"Yes I am."

"You're never paying attention on the phone when you say 'uh huh' like that."

"Well...I got it all."

"You sound a little flaky."

"That's because just a few hours ago I was propositioned by a priest."

"A Jesuit?"

"My God, Farzi, what difference does it make what kind?"

"For sex?"

"Not exactly sex," starting a low, wicked giggle.

"What? What for then?"

"Yes, yes, sex. He wasn't quite sure if it was sex he was asking for. But it was." Now she was chortling outright.

"Are you okay, Berta?"

"Yes...lots of waiting souls want bits of me."

"I...I've been asking a tremendous amount from you. Maybe, I've been the worst."

"No, not you. I didn't mean you."

"Of course you did."

"I don't mean you, Farzi. I don't know why, but I don't. You know what I can't figure out? Shouldn't he have been concerned about the sin on my soul if I went along with him?"

"Other things more pressing on his mind."

"Or maybe because, after I'd sinned with him, he could give me absolution. It fits what I've been figuring out. It's okay if he gets me to sin, he can forgive me then. I wonder which thing he'd have enjoyed more?"

Farzi was amused, "So it works like that?"

"I wish you were home."

"I do, too."

"I'm going to the races tomorrow."

"I though you didn't like them."

"Jill thinks it'll do me good."

"I'll give you a tip..."

"Yeah..."

"Bet on the horse...that never drinks water...but always drinks wine."

Their laughter together gave far more release than Roberta's earlier snickering alone.

In Persia Gallery with the sun at high noon Roberta met the lawyers who invested her with power of attorney for Farzi Behroozi. That done, she signed the Lohquist contracts, then sat drinking coffee with Denis and Tony awaiting their friends. Tony seemed relieved at how it had all turned out. "So, we'll have a Swiss bureau in a way, an inlet for art and, I guess, she'll set up an establishment somewhere, soon as she can. What I don't understand, damn it, is why she can't send her address? Why can't I go see her? If Switzerland's safe, why all this pussyfooting around?"

"Comparatively safe," put in Denis, "Isn't that right, Roberta?"

"Yes. There's still danger which she thinks might go away in time." She lifted one shoulder nodding her head, "After he dies..."

"What I can't believe," said Tony, "is that this is happening to people living in a civilized country."

Terry jettisoned his bulk through the open office doorway, Jill, his parachute, trailing behind him, "Hey, let's get going, huh. The ponies await."

They entered the track grounds by a grassy side aisle which led past the cool-down paddock and a few surrounding stalls. Everything sparkled blue-grass green and still white. At the end of the footpath, as a groom in bib overalls led a mahogany thoroughbred replete with bulging thews behind the fence, the big red horse swung his head around, snuffled, then ambled to the corner ignoring his handler's cluck, intent on reaching his long nose over the top rail to nuzzle Roberta's elbow.

Roberta, following her companions to the grandstand, felt the nudge at her arm, turned at the bidding, and yearned for a moment to stroke the stiff delicious mane and tender velvet spot between his flaring nostrils. Only an ephemeral greeting as the two creatures met for Roberta was passing by, traipsing behind the others, and the racehorse soon would be led to the gates. Nevertheless, a latent thrill ran through the woman, and the beast nickered and pawed its burnished hoof as if he, too, felt the experience. Felt it well met.

Later, in the stands as Roberta watched the horses and their jockeys in bright colored silks come flashing out the gates, she thought how electrifying when one has met a thoroughbred. How few had she met in her life?

The spectacle, horses flying a circle and then the race ends. And then again and again to the ends of other races, it seemed the same horses, the same winners, colors melded into a flat ribbon rainbow chopped sporadically by tossing hooves. People cheered and people dropped bits of paper in disgust. Once Terry's arms shot up and Jill grabbed him whispering, "Shut up or they'll mug us going out of the park." A horse race, thought Roberta, was one of the most spuriously heightened excitements she'd ever experienced. Yet there were thoroughbreds.

While her friends placed bets for still another race, Roberta left them to get a cup of coffee. She smiled apologetically as Jill asked where she'd be. Somewhere among the televisions flashing odds, the rushers to the windows, the simulcast results, she'd huddle down at a round, stained table and think a pleasant confusion of thoughts, the match up of Terry and Jill, their joy clashing with profound distress if the wrong horse clipped past the finish. Or Tony holding his bet stiffly while Terry flapped the tiny tickets about defying the fates.

A shadow crossed her musings. Glancing over her lifted

cup Roberta saw Heshemi Behroozi lower himself into the metal chair opposite her, his two hefty sidekicks behind him as ever. Behroozi stared at her opened-eyed. He literally did not blink. She was half-mesmerized by this immaculate self-control.

"You are thinking I follow you here. I have not." He blinked, twice, rapidly. "But I take this chance meeting as an omen. I tell you something, which will save me later trouble looking you up." Watching him put his palms flat upon the table top, Roberta swallowed the gulp of coffee she'd been holding in her mouth, pushed back her chair and got up. While he remained seated, eyes on his now flattened knuckles, she backed off.

"I'm going to place a bet."

"Stop. You, woman. You don't, I know this, woman, I know you don't know where Farzaneh is. But she use you as contact. My daughter a clever one. Tell her—"

Roberta moved off, "I won't. I will not carry your message to Farzi." He fumbled his way out of the chair and loped after her.

"You tell her, she come back, marry, and her father will overlook all. What kind of person are you who will not give such a message? I want to see—" he pushed past the crowding people as she wove among them ahead of him, pressing. He was determined she would hear, "She can be saved from a...unnatural and unholy action, a split, a dishonor. It must be stopped. Tell her."

Roberta nudged between two congealing groups, left him to fight around them as they melded, then ducked down the stairway and into the grandstand in search of Jill in the seats. That looked like Jill hailing her, pitched over what was Tony's head, her stomach bulge absorbing his brow and crown. "Here, Berta." The crowd arose to catch the horses down the last stretch, the people exhorting, roaring in unison, fixated eyes following the equine sweep. "What's the matter?" When Roberta finally reached her, "You look like you saw a ghost."

As the race ended, a moan thickened the air. Roberta dissipated her fear in the hot excitement surrounding her. She breathed deeply several times and held her breathe once for half a minute before expelling the air. "Behroozi came up to me in there. At the table."

"Behroozi, what did he do?"

"He just, uh, he saw me there. I think he frightened me."

Tony nuzzled past Terry half out of his seat, "What'd he want, that bastard?"

"Let me out, Tony, I got the place winner here." Tony slipped into the aisle squatting next to where Roberta had plopped down in the row in front of them when seats cleared as the flow of people went to the betting windows.

"So what'd the bastard want?"

In an unusual reflexive gesture, Roberta touched Tony's knee, "He wanted me to give Farzi a message."

"What? What was the message?"

Jill slid forward the better to hear, glowering in irritation as over the public address a voice began to announce the line up for the seventh race."

"Oh, shit," declared Roberta, "Oh, shit on them, shit on them all."

The loudspeaker voice quit.

"An Iranian curse," intoned Jill.

"That's my message," Roberta flared.

"Fine," Tony felt personally affronted and annoyed, "so what was his message?"

"I ran off. I didn't wait to get it." She would not carry his message, not even so far as this.

14

Roberta tried to control throwing
so much anger at so many people.
But there it was.

———————

A famous anthropologist was coming to the lab to see the skull and mandible. In preparation for his arrival, Roberta and Donald Dorcus were making casts of the fossils, while informing Jeffrey as they went along of the subtle procedure. Rattling around in a teeth drawer, Roberta found her father's house key.

"Holy cow."

Dorcus jerked up his head, "What is it, Roberta?"

"A key, that's been lost...mislaid for months."

"Oh, I thought you had...One never knows what might turn up...oh, never mind. It's just that...Remember that story of the green matrix and the fragments shipped all over the world? I thought maybe...but never mind. Nothing important could be lost in this lab."

Jeffrey piped up, "I know that story," pleased. "Hey, look, one of these teeth in this group isn't even hominid." Roberta walked over to him from where she'd been sorting bovid fossils.

"It's drypithesine."

Dorcus snorted. He was still irritated over her stubborn streak. The daffy girl refused to yield to his brilliant theory of a seductive new subspecies created from combining the fossil jaw and skull. So he was not astonished in that stuffy November afternoon—overwarmed by the heating plant and fooled by intense sun rays—when through the white light of the lab a policeman strolled. The officer's head rotated as he asked if he could speak to Miss Branwaithe. Hearing her name Roberta met him at the long, draped table which displayed the trim fossil rows waiting to be assessed by the paleoanthropological big shot.

"You want me?"

"You Roberta Branwaithe?"

"Yes."

"You know Father Charles Frankel?"

"Yes, I do."

"His niece, Rosie Marone, was found wandering incoherent last night along the interstate. She'd been hitchhiking and the guy in the car who picked her up beat her up pretty badly. Didn't molest her though. She said she fought him, and a trucker saw the struggle and pulled over. Scared the geek off. She ran away from the trucker so he reported to us. We located her little while later. When we ran a check, we found out she'd been brought in as a runaway couple months ago. We got this priest's name, and you as a local contact. Now see when we called the priest, someone staying there said the priest was on retreat. So, maybe you can help us?"

"Is Rosie all right?"

"I guess so. She was treated and released from the hospital. We got her in juvenile detention."

"Father Frankel is in Springstead. There must be a seminary or monastery or something where you could call."

"Oh, we got him okay. We found that out from the parish clerk. We called him, and he said he'll pick her after his retreat is over. On his way down."

"Oh great."

"Yeah, well, we got no reason to keep her, and no place to. Maybe you could?"

"I'll come get her. I can take her back to the housekeeper. If she'll go with me. She doesn't like me at all."

Dorcus had overheard enough to get the sense of the conversation, and to feel a deep satisfaction as Roberta followed the law out the door.

Not so surprisingly Rosie didn't complain about Roberta coming to take her home. She figured that going with Roberta was preferable to sitting in kiddy jail. On the whole—decided Roberta—as in Philadelphia. Roberta envisioned the two female primates as they tramped down the city streets to the car, the small one with bandaged head, patched cheek, black eyes, hobbling slightly. The tall one invisibly the same. A mess, thought Roberta, trying to moderate her anger which had been flourishing since she'd seen the girl led in by a policewoman whose eyes had met Roberta's conspiratorially. You have a beating coming or worse when you take rides from strangers said the wholesome eyes of the female policeman. Roberta tried to control throwing so much anger at so many people.

But there it was.

When they got in her car, Roberta was forced by that anger to ask, "Were they all right to you there?"

"In the jail? Yeah."

"That blonde cop who brought you out looked like a matron at Dachau."

"What?"

"Never mind."

"Yeah, well, she was 'toten a 'tude."

"What?"

"Never mind," the girl punched on the radio. She curled up in the seat corner sullenly, said little more. Roberta questioned her but got nothing except she'd run away from that nasty, nosy housekeeper and was headed back to her mother's when the bad ride happened. Bad ride like bad trip. Roberta let the radio scream and drove on in a miserable state of mind.

Rosie shouted over the radio, "You wanna tell me something?"

Roberta lowered the volume, "What?"

"There was this girl in the hospital room with me last night and all she could do was holler and say 'It's so soft it hurts. Soft hurts.'"

"What had happened to her?"

"I donno. She was weird like. Then she asked me if soft hurts. I told her she was nuts."

"Maybe she was, Rosie. Disturbed. Emotionally disturbed."

"Yeah, disturbed...but it made me think, you know, when she went like, 'Soft hurts' I thought...you know, I been in love, three or four times. You don't believe me, do yah?"

"No, I don't. Do you know what love is?"

"Do you?"

"It means something like you'd rather be dead than go on living without the person you love. No, I don't know what the word means."

"Hey, no shit? I woulda swore you was gonna talk about self-sacrifice and devotion."

"So?" She grinned and the girl turned to look out the window.

"Love aint sex."

"Found that out did you?"

"Shorty down."

"Rosie, I think when you know love, you know the truly good. Good finally makes sense."

"Nothin' makes sense." Rosie dragged her front teeth over her bottom lip, curled back against the door, and spun the radio volume up.

Roberta shouted, "Why'd you run away again?"

Irritated, "Uncle Chuck's a turd. That housekeeper sucks." When Roberta didn't answer, she got defensive, "You don't even like him. He thinks you do, but you don't."

"So, you don't either."

"Shut up, I do. I like him okay. So you're wrong. And I'll tell you, you're just a stupid old chick who aint nothin' to me, and I aint gonna say nothin' more."

"I'm taking you to your uncle's house for the second time. That's all I am, an old chick chauffeur."

"Wanna medal?" The radio blasted a beer commercial. The girl snickered and curled back up. "I suppose you'd like my mother better."

"I don't know her. I might."

"She's a slut."

Roberta gave a responsive shrug, "I still might."

"Yeah, well, maybe you're a slut, too, then. My uncle, he's an okay guy. And anyway he believes in God. And he said you don't. Which makes him a fuckin' lot better than you. And I believe in God, too. No matter what I do, I'll be saved."

"Oh, yes. And the people who do horrible things to you, too. They'll be forgiven."

"So what?'

"Only I won't forgive them."

Appalled and frightened Rosie slunk down and clung to the car door refusing to say anything more for the remainder of the trip only punching buttons when the wrong music played and cursing the stations. As they pulled up to the rectory, she tore out of the car and up to her room while Roberta explained to the housekeeper. Then she had a long, enclosed, soundless, disturbing drive home.

The telephone was ringing. Key still in the door, Roberta lunged forward, tripped over the small carpet the cat had kicked into a roll, picking up the receiver before it stopped.

"Roberta?"

"Yes."

"Why don't you get an answering machine? It's miserable trying to reach you."

"If people could reach me anytime they wanted to, I really would go mad."

"You were supposed to be here for dinner."

"Jill, I forgot. Well, really I mean something came up. I had to drive clear to the Chicago suburbs tonight. It made all other plans go right out of my head. I'm sorry—"

"This is what you're like, Roberta. A person just has to accept it, and overlook it. Come now. There's plenty of food, I cooked enough, and we'll wait dessert for you."

It wasn't possible, but rudely, to decline, "Okay."

"By the way, we have other guests, the MacBeths."

"They're reconciled?"

"Yes, temporarily. Come quick, it's been tense."

"How the hell am I going to help?"

"Just get over here. And talk only horses."

After eating what she could of Jill's cold dinner, Roberta felt, being the newcomer, that she should enter the conversation in some way. So she mentioned that she'd recently had her first track experience. As the MacBeths, dressed in impeccable European formality, focused on her, she blathered like an imbecile about the beauty of horses. Angelique, as usual, regally silent sat beside her royal consort, while Terry in new flannels, never formal, burst in impatient to ask Bill about his newest thoroughbred. On that subject MacBeth could talk almost exclusively to Terry.

"I wasn't about to let them slip one over on me, Terry. I got the bloodline."

Relieved Roberta closed out all horse-racing jargon, wandered wordlessly about in her mind, glanced at Jill who seemed to be taking in MacBeth's account, stole glimpses of Angelique as her dusky lids fell once, then once again over her turbid, yellow-black eyes.

When Jill went for the coffee, Roberta trotted after her. Barely had they made the kitchen, before Jill flooded over, "Seems strange as lord I don't know what. We get this call." She took a cracked cup in her hurry and vexation, "Roberta, reach me another cup." Roberta handed one back over her shoulder. "It was Angelique of all things. She says she and Bill were to be in town to talk to a stud man and wanted us to go out to dinner. I invited them here immediately. Last time we went out with them, it cost us two hundred dollars."

"Well, it's not unheard of. He must think Angelique is worth all the pain."

"Pain, oh come on. Come on, Roberta. You are so dense."

"All right, what am I missing?"

"Pain." Sarcastically.

"So what then?"

"That little affair of hers with Tony added spice to his pleasure."

"Tony's?"

"Good lord, Roberta, guys like Bill love to have their wives hot to trot—"

"Some men kill their wives if—"

"That's part of it, too."

"But that's like saying—"

"Didn't you ever wonder why I never married Terry Creighton Jones? Here take this stuff out, huh? And don't forget the sugar."

They all sat back, nothing more to say, sipping hot

coffee reflexively. Roberta, adjacent to Angelique, released a timid smile. Angelique no doubt was confused why Roberta had been invited.

"Roberta, I can't remember...have we met before?"

"At Jill and Terry's dinner party a couple of months ago."

"I've got a lousy memory for people's faces. Names, too. I'm sorry, I just..."

"It's all right."

"Wait a minute. At Persia Art Gallery. You're Farzi Behroozi's friend. Has she come back yet?"

"No. But she's not missing any longer."

"I guessed at why she ran away. The Moslem faith."

"Yes."

Angelique averted her head giving profile, elongated obsidian mask, tipped slightly upward. "It's too amazing. You know I was at an exhibit in New York at a very impressionable age when I first came across a sculpture by Farzi Behroozi. She was one of an exclusive group at Tin Pan Gallery. The brochure listed these new artists as the best of the best," she giggled, "like at a dog show. Farzi's main works that time were all busts of people. And right in front of me, I remember looking up from the brochure and there, right in my path, was the head of what seemed like the most beautiful man in the world. Sculpted by Farzi Behroozi, I saw on the card."

"Did you buy it?"

She smiled. "I wasn't married to Bill MacBeth at the time. Her pieces have always sold for lots of money. Sold very well, you know."

"I know."

"It's a shame she doesn't produce more..."

"She's thinking of—"

"I didn't get that gorgeous head. So it goes."

Was she, thought Roberta amused at Angelique's disenchantment, looking for the perfect skull, something like Dorcus' search? Into her coffee cup she laughed silently, and when she raised her eyes to Angelique again, there was lingering laughter in them. "Farzi did a figurine, of my daughter when she was about three," presented that fact as a gift to the supple-necked woman for having laughed so determinedly at her. "It, too, is graceful beyond reality."

"Oh, this is the head of a real man that I saw, and I'm sure I'll see him in the flesh someday. I think you're not at all like Farzi, for being her friend, I mean."

"Most people who know us think that. So you've deduced it correctly."

"Oh, I'm a good judge of character. And I don't give away how I do it. I can tell what people are like. I feel what's happened to Farzi is scary and strange, alarming," she drawled the last word, dripped it out the corner of her shapely mouth; then stiffened her motile features in annoyance when Roberta responded.

"I wish we truly understood what's happened to Farzi. If only it were strange. No, no it isn't unusual." She let her head wave back and forth haunted by her strong sense of being angry at this lovely woman. As if Angelique were obtuse to provoke her so.

"Angelique, Honey, I've been ready to leave. It's time we left. We have an early flight to catch tomorrow," MacBeth chanted as they wandered out the door.

Roberta rocked back clutched her knees, letting a last cup of coffee cool before heading home. She sketched one perspective, then another, Tony...looking for that osseous form...no, no, argillaceous, clump of clay, handled, distorted...manufactured by those strong, slender hands. Any wonder the head had been exquisite.

"I think I understand why Angelique made love with Tony."

Terry guffawed, "For the hell of it."

"She was flattered he wanted her," put in Jill. Terry wrinkled his pudgy nose, so she added, "All women are surprised when men want them; no matter how beautiful they are."

"But it wasn't that."

"Sex, Roberta, you've never caught on to sex."

Roberta bolted awake frightened by a wild buzzing, eerie and patterned, something electronic yet with the detritus of humanity floating about it. The phone, lordy if it wasn't the goddamned telephone. Four am, she noticed as she stumbled to the desk.

"Berta?...Is that you? Your voice sounds funny."

"Of course it does. Farzi what possible reason can you have for calling me at four o'clock in the morning? I mean, now you're safe in Switzerland—"

"Oh, the time difference. Oh, I'm sorry, Sweetie, I didn't calculate the time difference correctly. I must not have—"

"No." She sat trembling heavily on the sofa arm, "You didn't."

"Did you get everything arranged with the power

of attorney?"

"Yes, and signed only the Lohquist contract."

"All right. Now, I need some money, a good bit of money as a matter of fact. You're going to transfer this money into my account at the Swiss National Bank—"

"Into a Swiss bank account, how very exciting."

"Goofy, they don't do those kinds of secret accounts anymore. It's all open—"

"That makes sense, it's a better way of hiding them."

"Fifty thousand dollars into the branch in Montreau. Citibank will handle...Roberta, are you getting all this?"

"Yes."

"Are you aggravated with me, Berta?"

"No."

"Yes you are. Because you think I'm out of danger, and yet I'm still bossing you around."

"You're not out of danger."

"That I am not."

"Your father ran into me at the track."

"Sweet Jesus, what'd he say to you?"

"He was...blunt. He thinks I'm an idiot you're jerking around. He has a somewhat higher opinion of you. A higher opinion of his daughter than my father holds of me anyway."

"Did he threaten you again?"

Roberta would not deliver his message, a matter of principle by now. "No, not exactly. Nothing overt, his natural manner is abrasive...belligerent enough."

"Don't trust him."

"Of course not, Farzi."

"I'm easily scared still, right now. How would you say?"

"Skittish."

"I'll need the money by next Friday. Can you transfer it by next Friday?"

"I'll get on it tomorrow. I suppose it can be done, if you say so. Are you working on the business arrangement with Tony? He said you're opening an import-export component."

"Some art for Persia Gallery I can handle here. My Mideast sources are gone as you can imagine. But I'm seeing now about an establishment in Florence. Very small, very pristine. We'll see. Maybe I'll sell only my own work."

"Farzi, do you remember Angelique MacBeth?"

"Sure."

"I've met her."

"You're kidding. I used to see her in New York hanging around the local galleries. She wanted my Orpheus bust."

"Orpheus?"

"Oh, I did a mythological series when I was lots younger. They all had holes in certain places, like dotty take-offs of the Judgment of Paris. But not the heads. I never put holes in the heads." She was giggling.

"What's funny, Farzi?"

"Sorry, Roberta, I'm a self-amuser," giggled again.

"I think she was talking about that Orpheus bust just the other night."

"It was maybe ten years ago she wanted it so badly. I told her that years before I had sold it to some guy from Hawaii. He thought it looked sort of Polynesian. I wouldn't mind doing Angelique's splendid profile."

"She's like a daughter of the Nile.

"A little."

"Are you really as okay as you sound?"

"I'm surviving. I've learned from this...ordeal. Makes me a better person to learn to rise above my afflictions, and by God, I'm going to rise above the damn things—"

"Uh huh."

"And...maybe I've gotten stronger—"

"That's nonsense. All that absurd claptrap about suffering. People don't learn anything from suffering except how to suffer. Yes, that hardens them, but it's not anything good—"

"Berta—"

"Mixing up destruction and creation and the seed of one in the other. Rot. Do we mix them up because we want to validate cruely? Looking for a reason to destroy?"

"Berta. We need to find excuses for suffering, or we'd all be driven mad."

"No. That's not it. Are you really okay?"

"I go on fine. In time, I may be able to send you my address. I want to see Tony so bad and Denis and you. But nothing and no one else."

"I want you to come back here."

"Did you see my father at the races?"

"I know, I know.

"Get the money transferred for me, Sweetie. It's a down payment, so it can't wait."

Roberta started the transfer of money fretting sporadically about whether she had opened a trail to wherever Farzi was hiding. Doesn't matter, she assured herself as she climbed the smooth, swayback stairs to the fossil repository behind the lab. She's safe where she is.

Fairly safe. Fumbled with the key in the lock, whatever fairly safe means. Whatever. The door swung open into a darkened hall, a warehouse, really, without academic pretension. What the hell had Dorcus sent her after; glancing down at the sheet in her fist, she pulled her head up and scanned the rows of shelves and scrupulously labeled drawers and began to locate fossils. Strange, she could fathom no morbid thoughts about these scoured bones. Their interest for her was nothing like the fascination of Capulets' tomb. Did that make her off center? Was she laboring under some repressed thing horribly worse? Murder, mayhem, violence galore, chaos, nothingness. What worse? Ha! How we've been taken in. She located the requested samples, casts of three partial mandibles, a maxilla, cranial facial fragments, several teeth and post cranial bones. Arms and pockets full she ambled contentedly back to the lab.

Dorcus poked among the fossils, tossed a computer list across the table, "Get these articles for me, and Roberta, I can't find your notes for Klasies—"

"On my desk—"

"I looked there. They're not there."

"In the wire basket."

"Oh. Fetch them for me. But go get these articles here first." He tapped the sheet.

In the little office Roberta added her Klasies notes to the top of the stack of library material and was about to head back to the lab when Jon Martin walked in. He said he had to talk to her. It was important. Jiggling one leg on his knee, he sat on a rickety stool and accepted tea rather than coffee.

He groused over how bad his day had been, getting up his nerve.

Then Jon began huffing, "I probably shouldn't say anything...I saw Cameron yesterday at a committee meeting...But I was wondering, is it fair to you if I don't?"

"Well, what?"

"Say, how long have you two been divorced?"

"Cam and I? Longer than I care to remember. I guess, uh, let's see, fourteen years ago...Margot was three, everything was...in shambles. Cam had decided to be a grad assistant at Harvard, and I...was about to go on the first of several field expeditions in Africa...with the London University team. Why do you ask?"

"How did you both end up here?"

"Here's where we started. I don't know. I left the university, but stayed in London till my visa ran out. Came back here. When I got back, Cam was here, too. We both had friends, my family. Some of the same close friends. It's my home."

"I mean, do you think Cam...you're not...You two don't see each other much?"

"We've always kept in touch. Because of Margot mostly."

"Roberta, would Cam tell malicious lies about you?"

"I wouldn't have thought so." A weary laugh. "Maybe he would. What'd you hear?" She wasn't alarmed by what Jon might say; she was appalled by the fatigued disinterest with which she greeted his conspiratorial tone.

"Cam thinks you're losing it."

"Oh, I know that. I just...lose my temper around him. He drives me to it."

"He told me that you've gotten involved in some intrigue because of your friend Farzi, an international black-market cabal, I think he said. Something nefarious like that."

"Oh, lord, so I'm cracking up and Farzi's dragging me into a life of crime."

"From which Farzi's father is trying to rescue her."

"The hell, that's a lie outright. I wonder why he's saying these things?"

"That's what I wondered."

"To hear himself talk most likely."

"He said—Roberta, I don't like him talking this trash. And maybe I shouldn't be telling you."

"Oh, Jon, so what if you do. Cameron's a baby. Don't take seriously anything he said. Hey, I've got to get this material to Dorcus."

"Wait a minute. Your friend Farzi's boyfriend, he's a friend of Cam's?"

"Sure, Cam knows Tony well."

"Cam said that Tony told him you're getting big money out of Farzi and Persia Gallery now."

"Why is he saying all this shit in the middle of a committee meeting?"

"No, no. Cam and I went out for a drink after."

"I've got to leave. Dorcus is hopping up and down on his one good leg waiting for this stuff. It's what you guessed, Cameron is telling lies. I'm not going to get upset by—"

"Yes, don't. I didn't mean to disturb you. It's not what he's telling me. I know better, of course. But he might be telling other people."

"I'll discuss it with him." She leaned to get up, moving

him up with her. "I hope you defended me when he said all those nasty things."

The round small man shook his head indignantly, "I told him emphatically that you're not crazy."

"Can't say that, but I'm not a thief anyway."

"Roberta, I think this is serious business."

She ran Cam down at his evening seminar. As his students rushed out, she swam upstream in and accosted him. He was packing his lecture notes, snapping the pages, tamping them straight, and sliding them into his briefcase.

"Roberta. I've been meaning to call you. My mother said you'd been to New York on some business and seen Margot."

"Not business exactly. I was there smuggling art. Between that and double dealing, I've been making scads of money lately."

"What are you saying?"

"What've you been saying about me? I've heard a few stories you've been ad-libbing, and I want to know what the hell you're up to?"

"I haven't spoken—"

"To Jon Martin, haven't spoken to him?"

"I never said anything like that."

"Sheep manure, well-rotted."

"Listen. Tony told me you've got power of attorney for Farzi, and he mentioned there were some new European deals..."

"Illegal?"

"No, and I didn't imply they were, either. Martin must have got things mixed up. What do you take me for, Roberta?"

"What I've been asked by Farzi to do makes me uncomfortable. I don't need people gossiping about it."

"I can understand that. You in a hurry? Let's go get a drink, and you can fill me in about Margot. How's she looking? I'll be seeing her next month."

Roberta held her anger a moment longer imagining the artful exaggeration, the leading tone and back door semantics he'd used on Jon Martin to pepper his tale of the mad ex-wife involved in shady deals. Anything to make himself appear the spellbinding raconteur. Is there any truth in a good story? But she'd have to go with him now and defuse his interest in Farzi's business, to shut him up.

*"I'm not sure I ought to sign these papers.
Farzi hasn't called me about them."*

Trailing through the light snow which trickled and dissolved instantly on the hard cement, Roberta pulled farther into her coat and hurried across the car-plugged avenue to Persia Gallery. In the dark mornings of November she could believe in something called cold comfort. Last night Tony had arranged with her to come before business hours to sign more acquisition forms. She pounded on the heavy glass doors until Denis let her in.

"Freezing out there, Roberta."

"There's a purity about the cold, scrapping against the motor exhaust, clearing it up for people's breaths."

"Shut the door, huh. Tony's waiting in the office. We've got an important customer coming at eight, so we want to get this thing over with fast. *Vite, vite.*" He led her recklessly across the vermilion central medallion of the Kerman carpet.

"I'm not sure I ought to sign these papers. Farzi hasn't called me about them."

"She's not available for the business, that's why you

have power of attorney, she can't be here." On he plodded in a dribble of bleating.

They joined Tony who was leaning over a shiny parquet table.

"I haven't heard from Farzi recently, and I'm not sure I should sign anything more until I do," she informed Tony.

"Don't start anything, Roberta. I'm expecting a very important customer any minute. These are routine contracts."

"This is why Farzi gave you the power to sign transactions," Denis felt put upon to repeat, "So we can get on with the business while she's gone."

Tony fidgeted, "Roberta, it's a business deal. It needs Farzi's signature. It's going to make us money. I can't take time now to explain it to you."

"We'll explain later," coaxed Denis.

"Christ, I shouldn't have to," snapped Tony.

"Let's wait before I sign this one. It's been over a week since I last heard from Farzi. So she should be calling soon."

"Business doesn't work that way, Roberta."

Denis quivered, too, at Tony's manner, had to smooth over for him again, "This is nothing to bother about. It's a routine sales agreement. Well...we're putting in a bid, anyway, on some fabulous Islamic decorative art—"

"We haven't got time for long explanations. Just sign, Roberta. Damn it, here they are now. Did you leave the door unlocked, Denis?"

Roberta bolted up relieved, but halted as she saw a tall, stern, colorless man, a stooped, graven image, being conducted through the main gallery room by Jill and Terry. Denis looked back at Roberta while Tony raced out of the office doorway to greet the group.

"His name's Gerald Hanneman, friend of old Creighton Jones. He's got so much money, he could buy the Alhambra." Denis chased Roberta's flickering eyes, "Tony thinks we can swing a juicy deal for our Golden Lady." Then Denis, too, hastened into the gallery hall to lend a hand with the lucrative sale.

The back door needed a key to get out. However, in addition to the front entrance, the gallery had a rarely used side exit at the end of a low-lit corridor which was reached through the smaller left gallery room only accessible from the main hall. So, Roberta, of necessity, was creeping along the main gallery wall ignored by Tony and Denis, unnoticed by Terry and Hanneman, tacitly but pointedly acknowledged by a wide-eyed Jill, when into this curious tableau, crashed Heshemi Behroozi and his bullies.

Behroozi's head panned the scene. He located Roberta and pointed, "Get her."

His heavies wallowed over and snapped Roberta's arms against her sides. Shaking and twisting in their grip she jammed into the men, toward Behroozi, startling her captors who had expected her to jerk backwards. Struggling in pain, knotty fingers bruising her arms, she howled at Farzi's wild-eyed old man, "What do you want from me?" The question echoed half-muffled as Jill screamed, "Leave her alone, you—" being knocked against one thug's hard shoulder and dumped onto her rear-end, shrieking "bastards."

"I don't want to hurt you," Behroozi roared, "Be still."

"Then tell them to let go of me. What'd you think I'm going to do, run away?" He signaled and the heavies released her arms.

Crawling over onto her hands and knees like a painted box turtle, Jill watched Tony slide behind the round table and slap the security button. Police would arrive soon. Hopefully. She sank her head into her plump shoulders, tucked it into the dip there and wondered if she'd be called upon to bite someone in the calf if they didn't.

Both Terry and the staid Mr. Hanneman balanced on the balls of their feet aghast but ready if heroics were be needed. But they weren't apparently. Face darkened to red under her heavy bangs Roberta squared away defying this outlandish man. With indignation run amok Behroozi worked up a controlled rage.

"I go to our bank. They tell me about Farzaneh's singular withdrawal. Substantial amount, they say, and express appropriate concern. Another has authority, they tell me, to take funds of my daughter. You, they tell me, is other with such authority. Woman, I have no more patience. Give back my daughter's money. You have no authority. And you tell me where she is hiding, or I get you. I fix you for good."

"Mr. Behroozi, I transferred the funds at your daughter's request. She gave me the power to do this because she can't come back and do it herself. I don't know where she is. You can depend on that."

"Money goes to Montreau, Switzerland," he spat out.

"That's right."

The police burst in weapons dangling. Tony and Denis knew them well, a troop of duty cops moonlighting for area businesses. Tony tipped his head to the right. They grasped the situation, pointed their guns at Behroozi and down at his two hoods who'd fallen flat as soon as they'd seen armed men enter. Behroozi sputtered, lunged at the cops, and had to be cuffed.

After two policemen dragged off the shouting Iranians, Officer Taylor, his bronze skin glistening with exertion, took statements. Not the bungled robbery attempt he'd thought it was. What then? A half-dozen babbled versions later, he unscrambled what had happened and advised Roberta to press charges. As she wasn't clear exactly which, he suggested, assault and battery. The amazed Mr. Hanneman asked Terry to take him back to his hotel.

As she left with the cops, Roberta heard Tony screaming, "That jackass is ruining my business."

Tracer opened her door; above and around her robust figure the bright living room radiated Southwest: sorrel, chocolate, deerskin tan, dark green, deep red and welkin blue in enclosed rectangles on hangings and throws, pottery and rugs, paintings and a squat drum in the corner. Tracer moved aside and let Roberta in.

"What're you doing here?"

Roberta sank into a tapestry divan, wrapped a blanket filled with concentric yellow designs around her, and put her head back. Tracer lowered herself opposite onto an oak chest covered with a shawl imprinted with a zigzagged thunderbird. Roberta felt glazed over, remote. Tracer let her be.

Finding her own way, she swallowed tears and began to mutter, "There's an interesting resemblance...between these Indian figures and the motifs on Farzi's Persian carpets at the gallery. The Afshar rug's geometric forms...or even the Dashti behind Farzi's desk...the one with the hexagonals...stylized fox and camels..."

"Is there, now. Want a drink?"

"Orange juice or some kind of juice."

"Juice, Jesus, Bertie. Wait, I'll fix you a hot toddy. That'll help you relax. You look like shit."

"I know it." She kept herself intact thinking about the rugs, the patterns and shapes. When Tracer came back with drinks, she told her about Heshemi Behroozi's attack and arrest.

Tracer flicked around the ice floating in her scotch, "So he's in jail?"

"I doubt it. Posted bail. That's what the desk cop said he'd do. But I don't know if I want him locked up. What good would that do?"

"Stop him from hounding you—"

"I want him to stop harassing me...and threatening Farzi—"

"So lock him up—"

"That's what I'm saying, people go to jail, people get out—"

"I don't understand you," Tracer slugged the rest of her scotch. "You come here frightened out of your wits, and you don't want that stupid ass-hole put away—"

"They can put him away for the rest of his life for all I care. That's not the point. Something...has to stop. Look what's happened to Farzi. She's, she's...disappeared. He can make her do that."

"He thinks he can kill her—"

"He can make her disappear."

"Get him locked up, she comes back."

Roberta threw her head back in utter contempt. "She's disappeared. Locking him up is a fitting ending. That's all it is. That is all...it is."

"Drink some more of the toddy, Bertie. Take it easy."

"I'm all right."

"Yes, yes, I know. I know you are. Drink."

"What'd you put in here?"

"Little this, little that, few Indian herbs..."

"I'm getting sleepy."

"I didn't put anything like that in it."

"I can't go to sleep. I've got to go work. Important professor from Chicago coming to the lab on Monday. Tomorrow's Saturday already...Borrowed all these casts and Professor Romano from Penn. On our fossil the broken occipital bone left a gap...like the Steinheim calvaria, distorted, damaged..."

"Why don't you just stretch out there, right there on the couch, Bertie," helped arrange her feet, pulled the blanket with the concentric yellow rings up around her shoulders. "Just sleep for awhile, Bertie. Then you can get back to work."

"Tracer, whadja put in the drink?"

"Herbs, a very few...Indian medicine. Sleep."

"Isn't it funny...Trace... how that bank thought nothing of giving Farzi's personal financial information...to her father?"

Roberta awoke at the bang of cupboard doors. She moved, flexed stiff legs and back muscles, felt marvelous, healthy, clear-headed, alive. Sitting up stretching, teasing sinews to crack into place, deliciously, inwardly, she squeezed her body.

Tracer came out of the kitchen alcove, "Hey, let's get breakfast on the way to the university. I haven't a goddamn thing to eat in this place."

"So, Witch-doctor," Roberta headed to the bathroom, "what was that stuff in the toddy? Come on, give?"

"A relaxant, natural tryptophane, or something. The Hopi gave it to me. I didn't expect it to knock you out. Hurry up, I'm hungry."

"God, was I shaky. I don't know what happened yesterday."

In Pacho's Cafe Tracer worked on a three-egg, cheese omelet and hash brown potatoes while Roberta gratefully took in her morning coffee with an English muffin and strawberry jam. Ate quietly together until Tracer pointed her fork in Roberta's direction.

"I think you need to get away from this Farzi mess. At least until you get yourself under control. And you need to get away from Dorcus and the lab, too. And taking garbage from your old man, and doing Tony's business, and listening to Cam's shit. All that. Get out of here...go sift for Australophithecines under the hot, African sun."

"Not yet, something is...just beginning to make sense. I've been looking from the big end of the telescope—telos, the ultimate purpose."

"Sense, Bertie? This is just what I mean."

"Telos-cope. It's a word game, Tracer."

"What is?"

"I used to think everything. But that's the wrong end."

Tracer paused, alarmed a moment, then stuck a forkful

of potato into her mouth still managing to say, "You're talking philosophy. When we came in here, there were two guys from the road crew down the block sitting at that table by the window finishing up their coffee. On the way by them I heard one say to the other guy, 'Remind me to go to the john before we leave.'"

"Yeah, what does all that mean?"

"You're so fucked up with these mind games, you can't figure out when you need to take a piss."

"I have to strain for that analogy, Trace."

"I'm not drawing any analogy. You feel better now, right?"

"Much better."

"Start from here then. There must be someone going out in the field soon. Or come with me. I'm going out again in Spring. I'll put you to work."

"Finish your omelet." She tried to hide her distaste. "I hope you eat a lot of beans in New Mexico."

"Don't mother me, Bertie."

"Did you really hear those guys say that?"

Late afternoon at the lab Roberta completed work on the matrix surrounding the mandible fossil and walked upstairs to the department offices. Professor Dorcus was droning on behind his crescent desk about post-orbital waisting to Jeffrey and an unfamiliar young man. On the desktop cosseted in tissue paper the skull fossil—mute poser of question after question—lay isolated. She entered speaking.

"The jaw's all clean."

Dorcus popped his head up, "Are you leaving?"

"I've got to run see my father tonight. I'll be in very

early tomorrow, Donald." The two young men shifted about uneasily in their chairs.

"We're not quite done with this skull. It has to be finished tomorrow at the latest. I want to present the big boys with a *fait accompli*." Addressed this to her, but seemed to be talking still to the two young men.

"I have an idea about the occipital bone—"

"Well, we'll consider it tomorrow, Roberta, if you have to rush off."

Reaching the nursing home later than expected, Roberta hurried down the empty aseptic corridor. As she passed an open doorway, the home's usual stifling night silences were lashed by shrill jagged cries. Eerie wails of agony stretching the limits of the human larynx.

An aged emaciated woman wrinkled and disheveled tumbled head first toward Roberta from out the hollow room. Thin white hair floated over raw patches of red-yellow-flaked scalp. After her pounced a sturdy, pink nurse flanked by a slender, well-dressed woman in a black and white suit. Roberta inched close to the wall trying to get around them but was blocked by their erratic movements. She backed away as the two younger women struggled to control the old one, grappled at her nightgown exposing her mottled, puckered shoulders. The old woman batted at the nurse, then twitched in spasms to fight off the black and white woman with weak, ineffective swats. Her weird keen gave way to strangled sobs. Next moment she crumpled deflated, held up by one uniformed arm while a black and white sleeve caressed her.

"Mother? You're okay, Mother," the woman in black and

white cried out.

"Mrs. Devine?" The nurse juggled softly to keep her from slipping.

The old woman slid sideways in an attempt to release herself, tottered, slumping partly on Roberta's breast. Panicky she looked from one restraining figure to another. Then gaping at the black and white woman she ceased her struggle.

"Are you my daughter?" in a confused half-whispered.

The woman nodded wearily yes, nodded and nodded.

As the old woman faded into the darkness of her room, Roberta took two steps forward, but was stopped by the black and white woman's uncommonly bright, apologetic eyes.

"Never mind, never mind," Roberta moaned crept in retreat the rest of the way down the hall and into her father's room.

"My God, Dad." His lamp was lit, but he was sleeping. Sitting up in his chair sleeping. "Dad?"

"Oh, Roberta."

"How could you sleep through that noise?"

"There's always a racket of some kind going on here."

"But—"

"It doesn't bother me."

An awkwardness had buckled between them since the episode with Yorick's skull. Although she had spoken to him several times on the phone about his health and doctors, she hadn't come to visit him. And she hadn't tried again to convince him to go back home. Perhaps they could be calm with each other. They'd reached an impasse which favored her father, but was, however, a relief to Roberta.

"How you doing?"

"All right, I suppose. This new medicine makes me light in the head."

"I talked to your doctor Wednesday. He said you were doing well—"

"He's going to bring in a consultant. It's an interesting case, I guess...I am." He mused upon his own mortality pleasantly, kept it before him in fearful fascination, played with it, tossed it up and caught it watching its facets glitter in the lights. "By the way, Cameron stopped in yesterday. Picked up his books and left some other stuff. He's going to an APS meeting in Philadelphia in December. I guess he'll go spend Christmas with Margot in New York."

"He often does."

"Nice guy, Cam, most of the time. Good to talk to. What you going to do for Christmas?"

"Split a can of salmon with the cat." It was the least abrasive of the answers that had occurred to her.

"You think that's funny? Well, Cameron wasn't so bad. I never did understand why you—"

"I know."

"You didn't try hard enough. Neither one of the both of you."

"What did Cam leave this time?" She picked up a volume, "Martin Buber, and some political schlock."

"He's working on Jaimie Baren's congressional campaign. We discussed it. If I was healthier, I'd get into this fray, too. Cameron predicts that Baren can appeal to more voters because of the way he says things. His ideas just don't appear to be as good as they are."

"That's in his favor?"

"Yes. Nobody votes for one, single, sensible idea anymore."

"Well, people can vote for what they really want now. They used to be ashamed to."

He gave her his old, lately withheld, half-blink of approval. "Yes. Baren knows how to trick the voters good and proper."

"Cam didn't say that—"

"Of course not." He smirked. "He's a Jew, Baren. Which won't hurt him."

"Well, not anymore—"

"Because people won't know that. He's gone to the Methodist Church since he was twelve. A Methodist Jew. I like him."

"Dad, you are at heart, a true liberal."

"Yes, I am, proudly."

"We bought our first house when I was a little kid, from a Jewish family, remember?"

"Of course."

"You left their Mezuzah over the front door—"

"Naturally."

"As a good luck charm."

"Couldn't hurt."

She swallowed the tears of comfort and irritation, some sprig of joy powerfully threatening to overwhelm her and swamp the moment. They sat a while, she picking at the arm of the chair, he leafing through the campaign brochures.

"Since your mother died," he had let down his eternal guard, "it's been a long, slow process of learning to live in an empty world."

Roberta could only stare.

"So what of it, huh? It's not something you would understand."

"That's not what I was thinking. Please...let's get you out of here, Dad. Next week after this professor from Penn leaves..."

He seemed to have put himself in a reverie, "Even when you were a little girl, I thought you might end up a scientist. You were always looking to find things out. Discover what's hidden there."

"I want to discover what isn't hidden...what never was hidden." He looked through her from a long way away. He wouldn't hear her. The secrets, the mysteries, are infinitely banal. The puzzles are all. When one sets the thing going, that's the absolute, not when the thing is pried at purposely sealed, concealing itself to have one sicken with the desire to reveal what can only be believed because it is secreted. In that way, when it is wrenched open, nothing true is there. "What I was saying, Dad, is later next week, when all of this new fossil commotion is winding down, I'm going to talk to the doctor about getting you home—"

"Roberta, when you come again, stop by the house first, and in my filing cabinet are all the speeches I gave when I ran for Congress. See if you can find them and bring them here."

It was very late when Roberta passed the university on her way to her apartment, but the library and many of the campus buildings were still lit up like a field of yellow foxglove, the avenues and the hill still rampant with bundled and chilly scholars. So she hurried to the photo lab to check if Torrance had finished the shots he had promised her earlier. If so, she could take them home with her and study them tonight which would save her valuable time tomorrow morning. If her budding idea was near correct, the problem of the broken occipital bone could be resolved, and the answer to the skull puzzle would come one step closer.

Torrance had the photos for her. While whirling a scanned enlargement on screen, he pointed to the manila envelope and ignored her when she thanked him. On her way out the lab, she saw Tracer stepping up a stairwell from the basement storage room, seeming to rise out of a glowing hole.

"Hey, Bertie. What you doing here? Dorcus said you left hours ago."

"I came back to collect some endocranial photos from Torrance who never promises in vain."

"That *brujo*. Wait, Bertie. I've been hunting for you all day, and it appears I've been looking in the wrong places. You up for another hot toddy?"

"No thanks, I'm fine."

"I'll bet you haven't eaten anything all day."

"A little."

"Probably tuna soup. I'm breaking now. We can go get something nice to eat."

Pacho's, a gathering place for the various Native American students and staff, and exotic foreigners, lively and warm at all hours, drew them in. An outsider herself, clinging to her Mexican legacy, Tracer reveled in the cafe's variety of flamboyant patrons. Born Tracy Marie Hawksley, she nevertheless knotted herself a Toltec sign from the native blood of her mother's cherished ancestry. And Roberta respected the bond for it had made Tracer who she was, as well as who she would become, besides being one of the finest archeologists in the country.

While they sat eating, a large-boned, bronze Ojibway with chestnut colored, shoulder-length hair broke off from a boisterous group of students clustered around a big wooden table near the door, padded over to their booth, and sank down next to Tracer. He wore a Cubs baseball cap and was wielding a toothpick on his buccal molars. Jacob Poupart doted on Tracer, gossiped the campus talebearers. Roberta surmised he might be Tracer's now and then lover.

Staying out of their elliptical conversation, Roberta concentrated on her tomato soup and egg salad. For all the notice Jacob took, she wasn't there anyway. Hard not to long for this meal comfortably eaten at home with the cat, and maybe Farzi would call and let her know if she should sign any more of Tony's papers. She wondered idly if she hadn't better tell Farzi that she'd had her father arrested. Jacob griped on incessantly about a class he was failing, wanted Tracer's help—her intervention. Tracer's reluctance to get involved was palpable, and she had never learned to use tact. Amused, Roberta rolled the words Toltec tact around on her tongue. He wanted Tracer to discuss something with his sociology professor. Ah, Tracer would never do that...Bunched up in frustration Jacob Poupart strode off reducing Tracer's last words to something second-rate and small: that won't wash, Buster. Tracer plunged back into her meal finishing the large hamburger in record time. Then she flattened her nostrils and seemed about to pop.

"I thought that bastard had figured out a few things by now."

"Oh." Best be non-committal at this point.

"When did you figure it out?" Tracer breathed deeply in. "Probably by the time you were thirteen."

"Probably not. Figure what out?"

"I figured it out when I was seventeen, and my mother beat the crap outta me for staying out all night with the mechanic from my dad's service station. There are things you've got to learn yourself. You teach yourself, for crying out loud...and then, you know, you get it. I don't think Jacob's a stupid bastard...It hits you. That there's nothing new to learn from them. So you just start teaching yourself. Think I can convince him of that? I've tried, God knows how I've tried."

Roberta may not have been hooked to Tracer's train of thought, but she felt the trembling of the rails. Miles distant a feeling loomed before sight or sound. "I'm more angry, not that there's nothing new to learn from them, but at the lies."

"He takes lies in as if they were his meat."

"And it can't mean anything until later when you see it's wrong. Then it starts to have meaning."

"Maybe that's it, huh? Give him time? But what if the meat's poisoned?"

"Tracer, what are you—"

"Jacob poisoned...and no anodyne?" She pushed back from the table and hefted herself up. "Enough. I can't help that man anymore. I draw the line." She stretched over the table clanging aside dishes and getting her long vest messy with food droppings, to give Roberta a fast hug. "I'm sorry you got caught in the middle of this. You don't need one more poor slob dumping on you."

The big woman hustled out. Roberta sat, gnawed sandwich half-way to her open, dumbstruck mouth.

16

While she was deep in thought,
pencil buzzing over paper, a colliding, thwacking sound
of a scuffle or struggle in the outer hall disturbed her.

The completely reconstructed fossil skull and the newly acquired mandible lay shimmering together on a bombazine cloth covering a library table in the formal conference room of the paleoanthropology department. Most of the faculty along with the visiting professors hovered about the specimens, in serious discussion while never seeming to take their eyes from the display. Heavy, mottled, yellow draperies had been roped back from arched, leaded glass windows, but not much of the weak, winter sunshine was filtering in. Polished copper chandeliers swept artificial rays onto the mingling enclave.

It was a piece of reconstructive genius. Dorcus sighed with satisfaction. Moments before dawn had punctured the gloomy lab, he, Roberta, Jeffrey, and Fletcher, the newest graduate assistant, had made final readjustments climaxing in the skull's renascence. However, some obtuse questions had almost spoiled his mood. In addition to Roberta's stubbornness—those damned drawings to scale, cutouts for chrissake—there were her tell-tale curvatures overlapping on computer simulations, the use of high-dimensional plots. Doubtlessly it was her univariate analysis, not the damn sketches which had caused him to waver. Nevertheless, there was nothing conclusive in any of it. Seen one way the post-orbital waisting had tipped the balance in favor of Homo erectus. Seen another, toward archaic Homo sapiens—well, anyway, not an erectus. But no matter how the skull was reconstructed, inched apart, and constructed again, the fitting together of two fragments of broken occipital bone had left a fissure. There had been a telling gap where the two parts must connect, but they did not.

Then, when dawn broke Roberta had sprung upon them, almost at the last minute, an endocast on which she had located the line where the two sections connected, by recognizing the internal vascular markings. Dorcus was allowing her simple endocast trick because it couldn't disprove his theory. It took away some of the beauty... some of the clarity and parsimony, but nevertheless, destroyed nothing. He stuck with his first call.

Before the scientists were allowed to examine the fossils, Professor Dorcus welcomed his visitors and began to explicate the interesting features of the new finds. However, while hinting at their significance, he inadvertently flushed out a bevy of divergent indications. Scientists began talking over each other, straining to be heard, shouting. Calling them—indulgently, self-importantly—to order, Dorcus paused, waited, while voices trailed off, for questions directed at him.

In a fit of contrariety, Dr. Friedrichsen from the University of Chicago spoke first to Roberta. Dorcus had had, after all, to credit her with the fitting since only minutes before the visiting scientists had arrived, she had lugged in all those sketches and paraphernalia, and the mold she'd cast, and none of the other staff members had had a chance to learn the details of her procedure. Forget the fuss they're making, he consoled himself. It didn't matter a hoot if she'd concocted this representation, he was the man with the theories. She'd only done the hack work. Talented in some ways, she was, no doubt about it; but the endocast was a skillful rendering of something, she'd said it herself, that was too equivocal for definition. Let Roberta, with her overweening modesty stand for now at the center of attention. But just wait.

Listing forward Friedrichsen edged Roberta to the other end of the table where sat the famous Swanscombe casts lent from the University of Pennsylvania museum. The two in close conversation, Dorcus overheard, "Steinheim calvaria," several times, and ducked to intercept; yes, damaged and distorted, but from only 250,000 years ago, then far too young to encourage comparison.

As soon as Dorcus approached Friedrichsen, Roberta drifted toward the door. Let her go, the ungrateful—wench. He'd heard his teenaged son use that word the other night. How strange to hear a good Elizabethan epithet out of the surly mouths of today's youth. Yet Professor Dorcus approved any evidence that meaningful words of the past had survived into the modern world. So seeps into today the knowledge of long ago.

Roberta fled down the hall to escape the bickering

and blunderbuss back there, to create by returning to her own job steadiness and absorption once again. Inside the lab doors she took in two deep breaths of pungent odor, a stink to most people, fragrance to her grateful nose—she felt so glad to be back at work. Plunging into the fossil repository, she found several dental arcades she'd been measuring for a study of sexual dimorphism. When several anomalies surfaced, she had decided to remeasure the molars.

While she was deep in thought, pencil buzzing over paper, a colliding, thwacking sound of a scuffle or struggle in the outer hall disturbed her. Someone's finally throttling Dorcus? She looked up, tilted her head, faintly amused. Until the double lab doors smashed back against the cinder block walls, and Behroozi hurtled into the laboratory parting the air before him, his two minions heeling alongside.

Locating it, this time she gripped the scalpel purposefully, keeping it below the table, and spoke first.

"I'll have you arrested again if you come any nearer."

"I want to make a deal with you." He held his voice down willing his entire being to quiescence, "I do not cause hurt. I am...honorable man." Roberta didn't move a muscle, and certainly had nothing more to say. She was through, finished declaring idiotically what she did or didn't know. Let him vent, speak his mind, give hues and cries and chase all over the world after Farzi whom he'd turned into thin air, a voice—a reversal of Philomel, they'd ripped out her tongue—who was no more wraith than Farzi was now. And it was all the same to the lot of them. She would defend no more, nor deliver messages. And she would never make any deals.

Behroozi shrugged at her silence and paced the floor

of the lab skidding his rubber soles along its tacky surface sticky with bedacryl drippings. After a few more agitated laps past the long table, he curled around his disinterested body guards and halted suddenly between them chattering at Roberta once again.

"The deal is this. Farzi is in Montreaux, in Switzerland. You send money there. I find this out. I afterward must go myself to Montreaux, and by then she would be gone. As she was. I deal with you. Okay. The next time, when you find out where to send money, you tell me right away, before money is sent. That is a deal, you give me back my daughter, I reward you well. No price is too much, no deed undone as just reward. Reconciliation. You make me this with my daughter, it will be well for you. Reconciliation, you understand?"

"No. No deals...I've seen...all deals are inherently... unfair." No deals, none, ever. Not ever. Deals are superstition, superstition is making deals, deals with life, deals with death. There will be no more deals. She lowered her gaze to pick up the mandible piece moving the scalpel toward it.

He stormed at her, "Have you no soul, no womanly part? A fiend, before me stands such a one—"

Heavy footfalls cracked upon the lab floor. The thugs swung around; Behroozi in his furor hardly comprehended that others had entered the lab. In fact a line of people were coming through the laboratory doors: Dorcus holding aloft the fossil skull, Professor Friedrichsen followed by Tracer Hawksley and Jacob Poupart in his baseball cap. Roberta reluctantly set down the lower jaw fragment.

"Here she is, Professor, just as I thought—"

"I wasn't finished with our discussion of the cranium reconstruction, Ms. Branwaithe—"

"Wasn't that Farzi Behroozi's old man?" broke in Tracer close enough up to her now to nudge her as they watched him and his bodyguards exit. Probably he'd cursed her, she was sure he had, in a mixture of syllables pleasant sounding in themselves, before beating his retreat.

"What'd he want?" Tracer asked. The baseball-capped Indian flicked his tongue like a serpent to rid it of bits of tobacco ash. When that move didn't work, he picked at the fleshy bulb with his fingertip. Then, stuck the unlit, stubby cigarette between his lips.

"Roberta, we'd like you to return to the conference for a few minutes more if you wouldn't mind."

"Yes, please, Ms Branwaithe, I'm curious about the suborbital torus—"

"Bertie, meet us at Pacho's later, would you?."

The Indian sucked in his breath, the cigarette, obtruding at a forty-five degree angle above the lip line, bobbed up and down. Jacob, the cigar store Indian, how putrid of him, how intolerable that they all should have come gobbling in. Yet Heshemi Behroozi had been defused by their entrance.

Nevertheless, the effluence of fear had been stanched not by their intrusion, but earlier. Behroozi's discharge of venom this time had run harmlessly over her.

"Okay, Bertie? Jacob and I will—"

"Look, I agree with you about the bone weight, but what about—"

"Roberta, there're some further questions from some

other people—"

Farzi Behroozi's irate father had stormed the hell off again cursing enough to raise even these bones from the dead. Staring at nothing in particular, a spot over the doorway that looked as if something had hung there once, Roberta agreed to all their demands. A subtle and reverberating tune hummed within her, more triumphant than a Wagnerian march, and she sang *sotto voce* hearing the lyrics in her mind: "...was combing his auburn hair. The monkey he got drunk, and sat on the elephant's trunk...the elephant sneezed...and fell to his knees...and that was the end of the monk..."

A little after ten Roberta Branwaithe clipped into Pacho's, scientists' voices still squawking in her head but feeling generally elated. She joined Tracer and Jacob Poupart— head to baseball cap bill deep in talk at the round corner table—ordering coffee from a passing waitress who'd raised her eyebrows at her when she came in.

"Funny thing, you," began Tracer, "Can't you see that Dorcus is using you? Shamelessly?" The Indian smiled gracefully and raised his eyebrows. "I was just telling Jacob. Let you be an object lesson to him." Jacob excused himself and headed into the men's room.

"Doesn't Jacob ever talk?"

"He talks."

"You spoke to his sociology professor?"

"No. Jacob doesn't hold a grudge. Unfortunately, it's very Indian of him. A grudge can be helpful at times."

Roberta gulped hot coffee sputtering, "Dorcus's calveria

is not erectus. What an irony."

"Bertie, I heard a rumor, round about by way of Susan Alvarez at a theater benefit, that Cam's thinking of getting into politics."

"Is he seeing her?"

"What do you care?"

"Curiosity, I guess. I can be curious about who he dates can't I? After all these years, lordy, why would there be any jealousy left?"

"You said it."

"He's not easy to keep up with. Never stays with anyone very long. Lots of mood swings, I guess."

"She told me Cam's using this Baren campaign—he's been volunteering—to learn all he can. Afterwards, he'll run for an assembly seat himself."

"Why, when you say it like that, does it sound illegal? Or unethical?"

"So, you don't want to know. So, change of subject. The calvaria's not an erectus. Historians wonder how we archeologists can give a damn about people in prehistory. And I find it odd that you work up interest in the not-even-humans who lived so far back in the past they're no more than shadows. We must all be looking for something different after all." She was recalling the sand paintings in her office, "or..."

"Just sex maybe, maybe all we're searching for is a good fuck. Father Freud, Father Sartre, Father, Son and Holy Ghost." They began to laugh, a little hysterically.

As if invoked Jacob reappeared, slung his arm over Tracer's chair. The waitress refilled their coffee cups.

"Trace, I have this crazy thought about my father. Why he won't leave the nursing home. There are some very old, old people in that place. One woman's ninety-seven. She got frantic one day and...kept on talking on and on about how she thinks God forgot her. Forgot she was left here alive, forgot who she was. That gave me this crazy idea about my dad. Somehow he heard her, or somebody like her. So, he figures, believes in a way, that the nursing home is holding all the sick and loony old people who...God forgets to take. He'll hide there, then, among them. And fool God. And then maybe he won't die..."

"...Aw, Roberta..."

"I have to talk to Farzi again, soon. She hasn't called in over a week."

"Be careful. Behroozi plays rough."

"I'll just get my own bodyguard. Wanna lend me Jacob?" Jacob pushed his tongue between his incisors and tipped back his cap bill rakishly.

"So you don't know anything about Cam wanting to run for office?"

"Cam won't do. Not muscular enough."

"Bertie."

"I haven't heard much. He's asking my father for some campaigning advice; although, I thought he was humoring him. Taking his mind off his heart. What's the deal? If he is?"

"You and Cam have been my friends for years. I think he might be running with a bad crowd."

"Oh, politicos are all various degrees of power hungry—"

"Cam goes along. He'll get suckered in. Bertie, he's what the Navajo call a valuable man."

"I don't see how that means he shouldn't be political."

Tracer shook her head as if she had water in her ears, "Well, I've got a field expedition set for April."

Almost eight the next morning while rushing out of her apartment Roberta heard the phone. She pulled up at the door, grimaced, then decided on a whim to answer the ring. Mornings the phone never rang. Unless someone soliciting money called. Yet here she was swinging back into the room to pick up an insistent piece of plastic.

"Shock, Berta, here it is not the middle of the night, but it's me. Did you sleep well?"

"Farzi, where have you been?"

"Sweetie, you know I don't answer that—"

"I mean, why haven't you called in so long? Tony and Denis have tons of papers...to sign, want me to sign this and that, and should I?"

"Shit. I guess I'll have to phone Tony. It's difficult to do. He's become impossible to talk to."

"Doesn't listen?"

"That's you, Darling. Worse than that. He does listen. But he hears what he wants. What papers?"

"Contracts, I think."

"They're buying?...I'll call Tony—"

"Should I sign—"

"Don't sign anything more...till I give the word. This is a hell of a way to run a business."

"I imagine."

"Has there been any more trouble from my father?"

"A little, I mean, he showed up Monday uttering

imprecations."

"You said?"

"Cursing."

"Threatening you? Roberta, I don't want him to harass you—anymore. We have to do something about that. He's stopped bothering Tony?"

"Yes. Tony hasn't seen anything of him in weeks."

"Which makes sense because—well...it makes sense. He knows I do my business through you. I'll check out the new deals with Denis. That's the trick. Tony is so...ebullient."

"Good word."

"So you like it? But what if Heshemi keeps on bothering you, what then?"

"You're smirking."

"You can hear a smirk? Berta, there's an account at Federal Security I want you to close out. No wait, later I think. We'll send only a little of it to Florence now."

"If you're in Florence, your father will know. He gets the people at the banks to tell him where the money goes."

"Doesn't matter. He can't find me. Europe, Roberta, is lovely. And don't sign anything until you get the word. I'll talk to Denis...Berta? Heshem...if he bothers you again, I want you to say something to him—"

"I won't do that, Farzi. I can't carry any messages—"

"Yes. You have to get him off your back—"

"Farzi—"

"Listen. Tell him...write this down phonetically. I want you to—"

"No."

"Berta, this is not a message. It isn't. You're going to tell him something—"

"Farzi, what the hell do you think a message is?"

"Not this."

"Oh, sure. The trouble is you make me laugh, Farzi, that's what the trouble is."

"Put this down and say it:" Roberta copied furiously tongue stumbling in unfamiliar contortions.

"Persian?"

"Yes, Persian."

"And it means...do I really want to know what it means?"

"It's a quotation from Firdawsi. He'll recognize it: 'Despise not any foe however weak.'"

"This'll stop him?"

"It'll tell him what he should know by now, that bugging you will get him nowhere."

"Good, if it does. I don't see how. Maybe it says more in Persian. What do you mean, weak?"

"It does. It means much more in Persian. Weak, that's... something else. In some ways the English language is deprived."

"What if the languages all say the same thing, Farzi? He'll never give up."

"You're being obtuse, Sweetie. Stay calm. Benedicite."

Farzi had wasted no time. Roberta was in the lab no more than an hour when Jeffrey carried in with her office mail a note from Denis. Stop at Persia Gallery as soon as she could. Roberta, intent on some wavering dental statistics, thrust the mail in her handbag. She'd do the deed at lunch.

Beyond the Afshar rug covering like an illuminated manuscript Persia Gallery's central floor space, stood Denis, two gray-haired wealthy customers, and, pointing at a small, Luristan bronze, a vivacious Tony. Catching sight of Roberta Denis broke toward her and signaled peremptorily with his extended arm. Roberta thought how decisively Denis had shifted the tableau.

He rushed her in a hurried whisper, "Farzi called me. She wouldn't cooperate. We've got these contracts that have to be signed immediately. Our lawyers can't work it out right now any other way, except you signing. The thing is, are we going to stay in business? Listen...But if I just mention, a tiny bit, the problem to Tony, he howls. Listen to me. My God, Roberta, can't anyone talk sense to Farzi? We're going to lose the gallery."

"She wouldn't let that happen—"

"She's been out of it so long she doesn't know what's going on."

"Well, didn't you tell her? Didn't you just finish talking with her?"

"She doesn't understand..."

"Maybe you could explain it to me—"

"Oh, God—"

"All right then. I'd do what I could, Denis, but if she's asked me to wait—"

The customers with Tony were being distracted by the frantic, hushed dialogue across the carpeted space. Both Roberta and Denis drew up stilled a moment. Tony directed the couple into the glass office ignoring what was occurring in his main showroom. Once enclosed he picked up the phone all the while his eyes anxiously nailing his restive buyers. Denis and Roberta in static pose contemplate him until he turned his back to them, put the phone down, and huddled with the couple over his burdened desk.

Denis went limp, touching Roberta's arm. "I know there's nothing you can do but wait for directions. That's why Farzi gave you of all people the power of attorney. There isn't anything else you can do, Roberta—"

"It's not like I'm programmed; I have as much free will as anyone else—"

"That's nothing to get into right now—"

"Oh, shit. Let's say I signed your damned papers, Denis, let's say I did—"

"You wouldn't—"

"Hypothetically I could," she shouted, then modulated her response, "So, if I did, what does that mean?"

"We make a nice, tidy profit—"

"Yeah, okay, and..."

"And otherwise, we don't."

"There you are?'

"Yes."

"Well, you were right."

"What?'

"I can't."

"Jesus Christ, Roberta, get back here. Don't walk out like this—"

The office door clunked heavily shut as Tony raced out leaving his customers gawking fish-like through the glass partition.

"For chrissake, you two," he rasp-whispered, "I've got clients in there, clients. Denis, what the hell is going on?"

"I don't...want to get into it right now, Tony, not with

the Wigmores—" He puckered his lips limned with beads of sweat. Tiny droplets clung, also, to his hairline.

"Get into it right now, quietly and calmly."

"This isn't the time—Roberta, where're you going?"

"Back to work."

Tony stepped in front of her, his handsome, angular face congested with anxiety. "Hold on a bit. We've got an important contract needs your signature."

"You'd better tell him." Stopping midpace, she looked to Denis.

"Farzi called. She doesn't want us to proceed with the Wigmore and Associates base. Thing is, they've gotten into some trouble in Europe."

"We know that. It's limited to a demographic...oh, I get it. Roberta, you're not signing." If he could grab her, jar those iron gray eyes out from under the heavy flop of hair, he'd get her cooperation, rattle them lose from over those flat, wide cheekbones, make her sweat, he'd get her to sign. She kept looking at him, looking from under that dark mop, that stupid bitch..."I don't know how Farzi expects this to work. There's no partnership. The three of us can't discuss things anymore. She's half-way around the world. And we have to deal with—"

Denis motioned him silent, waving his opened palm at hip level. "Not now. We'll get the lawyers on this. Maybe you're right. Maybe you've been right all along. We'll get the partnership dissolved if we have to."

"It's all we can do. I can't run a business with this mess going on. Roberta, tell Farzi that. I've finally had fucking enough."

Denis set his salty lips together in agreement.

When Roberta, jittery and spooked—more from Denis' uncharacteristic decisiveness than Tony's ordinary tantrum—returned to the lab, she found Dorcus away, having left her a Neanderthal fossil for measuring. It was too difficult to concentrate; Tony and Denis were planning to wipe Farzi out of the gallery. She had withheld her signature as obligated, but what could Farzi do to squash this hostile takeover? Would her flamboyant maneuvers be enough to hold the men off?

Roberta surveyed the Neanderthal skull brought on loan from Pennsylvania by one of the guests come to study the ersatz erectus cranium. Trying to talk—trap of a mouth—gaping in the ubiquitous hollow grin. Would it speak, would it ever speak again?

"Back, huh, Roberta?"

"Oh, Jeffrey."

"Dorcus wants us to do the preliminaries on this dude. Uh, you can maybe get us going, huh?"

"What you have here, this staining— you don't see it on the cast, here though, on the fossil—this stain, and where the breccia matrix has been removed, this tells us that, in situ, the skull rested asymmetrically on its left side, not directly on its top..."

Jeffrey was gone, and still she worked on scratching into a crumpled, green notebook, in no hurry to reach the end of her description. Cameron startled her when he entered.

"You didn't get my note?"

"What note?"

"I put a note on your desk to call me. I need to talk to you." The office mail, shoved in her jacket pocket.

"I didn't see anything."

"Well, doesn't matter. You know I'm going to Philadelphia for the APS convention then on to New York—"

"I knew—"

"I'll be fetching Margot back with me for her holiday break. What I want is...the three of us can maybe do some dinners and things."

"Of course."

"That's about it," he was staring down distastefully at the Neanderthal, "and, by the way, you do know I drop in on your dad occasionally? He's doing better, huh? In fact, I got some useful pointers from him about conducting this political campaign I'm into."

"He was telling me—"

"Yeah, well, he's a sharp guy. You know, Roberta, you seem a little...preoccupied today." Hadn't wanted to say 'spacey;' he'd called her that once or twice in their short marital career. "Are you in a rush to get back to that brute—"

"Cam, I'm very willing to have dinner with you when Margot's here—"

"Very civilized of you."

"I'm trying."

While making supper for herself and the cat, Roberta kept her mind busy with odd fossil trivia; afterward ate contentedly, read a bit, and became drowsy finally dozing on the sofa, cat neatly curved above her head.

Someone buzzed the apartment. She slunk half-awake

to the intercom and answered.

"Robert Branwaithe?" Behroozi's gravelly monotone.

"Yes, Mr. Behroozi."

"I want to talk. I will not frighten you; this I can assure."

"No. No talk. Listen, listen to me. These words come straight from your daughter," she repeated the memorized Persian as Farzi had dictated it, then stood stooping to the intercom, a slight smile surrounding her large, square teeth. For a minute, no reply. It means nothing to him, she panicked, gobbledygook, or she'd smothered the meaning in godawful pronunciation. After all what could the Persian words do? When she stopped, Behroozi growled painfully, "Farzaneh gives you that to say?"

"Yes."

"Just like that?"

"As close as I can come."

His growl yawped, then deepened into a cavity of self-pitying rage, "I will find her soon now. It will not go on. Understand that, you. She uses you, a fool, to hide from me, and needs you no longer. You are finished, dirt, garbage. She throws you away like the useless fool you become. When I get Farzaneh, I will praise her for this. For nothing else." The intercom bleeped off. Shut off and gone because Roberta Branwaithe had untransubstantiated, turned evanescent, soon poof...in a twinkling of an eye...at the last trumpet. She wanted to giggle in relief but could not for fear of being forced to see the horror of it. He no longer knew her, since in that moment she had been played out. Roberta felt hope gush out her mouth and fear and corruption. What had been strangling her gave way in a rush of exaltation.

17

"Hitchhiking on the Interstate again.
She was struck by a merging automobile."

———————

"Ms. Branwaithe, Officer Talbot again."

When the cop stepped off the portico and approached Roberta on the wide cement steps of the Anthropology building, she couldn't decide whether the law wanted her because of Farzi's duplicity, Heshemi Behroozi's assaults, Tony's accusations, or because she'd consented to let Margot be raised by her rich in-laws. Probably just going to get arrested for the load of overdue library books sitting on the back seat of her car.

"Are you looking for me?" His face showed genial recognition. Wherever could he know her from? She had been mixing with the police all too often lately.

"I spoke to you a few weeks ago over a minor named Rose Marone. Remember, you helped us out with that little problem?"

"Rosie? What's happened to her?"

"Hitchhiking on the Interstate again. She was struck by a merging automobile."

"Oh, my God—"

"Some kids never learn."

"Is she all right? Oh, my God—"

"Pretty banged up, but she'll live. Nasty smashed elbow. Had surgery earlier this afternoon. We tried contacting the uncle, but his housekeeper said he's out somewheres, for a few days, and she can't reach him. Housekeeper said the kid's not living there with them anymore. She'd gone back to live with her mother. Housekeeper had no way to contact the mother, don't even know her name. The kid won't tell us anything. Means we gotta run down the mother and that takes awhile. This place is part of my beat so I thought I'd check with you. Maybe you might know the woman and save us some time and effort."

"Yes. I've got a number...back in my office. Oh, my God..."

After satisfying Officer Talbot Roberta took off for the hospital, then remembering Tracer, whom she was supposed to meet at Pacho's for lunch, she pulled abruptly into a parking place near the little cafe and bolted in.

"I'll go with you to the hospital," Tracer was eating a cheeseburger having given up expecting Roberta's arrival. She ate not bothering to take off her floppy felt hat. Roberta focused on her round, sorrel face somewhere under the rim of the hat and behind the dribbly, thick sandwich. A couple of Cherokees Tracer had introduced to her were pounding drums and chanting nearby, so Roberta had to lean forward to catch the words as well as to see anything of the woman.

"What? Why do you want to go with me?"

"This kid sounds like she's a mess."

"She is."

"So I'll go with you."

"Jesus, Tracer, she's not an animal in a zoo." Tracer took the rest of the cheeseburger along, getting grease all over the car seat.

Rosie was hooked up to an I.V. and sleeping uneasily when the two women walked into the room. Tracer held back from the bedside breathing heavily while Roberta stole over to view the injured girl. Rosie opened her eyes.

"Oh, no, you."

"Hey, I'm all you got. The police need...to call your mother—"

"I don't wanna see her," the voice was scratchy as if scraped by tiny bits of jagged glass.

"I know...I know."

"No you don't. You don't know nothing." The girl fought back dogged tears. Roberta lifted her hand out— toward one clenched fist which was hastily yanked away. She stretched the foolish, uplifted hand across her dry mouth.

"What were you doing on the expressway hitching again? Where were you going?"

"To my uncle's, I guess. Them cops aint even gonna find my old lady anyways. She got a snoot full and her and that prick, Leander, run off someplace. I don't intend to go no where with her. All she can do's bitch and rag on me."

Roberta moved around the bed to the window and peaked out at the flat hospital roof; Rosie shifted her focus to Tracer. "Who's that?"

Roberta turned her eyes toward the stolid, silent

woman, "This is my friend, Tracer Hawksley. She works at the university, too. She's an archeologist."

"Say what?"

"She studies prehistoric Indian people in the Southwest."

"Sounds stupid."

"What do you mean?" Often Tracer's first words, Roberta thought, to new people. Perhaps Tracer's first words as a baby.

"You guys're weird...I aint never coming near this dumpy town again. It's gotta jinx on me."

Roberta frowned at the bandaged waif seemingly pinned beneath slick, stark white, wrinkleless sheets, her livid bruises hiding dirt half-heartedly cleaned from her angry face. "You choose unusual places to run away to. Next time, try Switzerland."

"Outta your mind. I aint even gonna listen to you. And I aint going back to my old lady no matter what they do to me. You tell them cops to go find my Uncle Chuck. He'll come get me."

"They've also been trying to locate him. Mrs. Prinz said he's gone away. Maybe another retreat."

"Hey, kid," both pair of frazzled eyes swivelled to the impressive figure of Tracer who'd taken on the darkness of the room and seemed to speak from no where. "You've got to start doing it for yourself. No uncle, no mother. You've got to start right away." Rosie bit her bottom lip, unable to ignore the large woman's intensity.

Compelled, Roberta tried to translate, "Tracer's mother beat her up once, very badly, and—"

"Bertie, that was told to you in confidence," Tracer barked, and Rosie snickered.

"Right. You had confidence in me...I'd tell it only when I really needed to."

"That chickie's got an answer for everything, don't she?" rasped Rosie, and Tracer reared back to bray in appreciation.

At the lab in the early evening Roberta admired the newly created cast of the Neanderthal skull and whispered to Jeffrey, "Isn't he grand?"

The young man finished jotting in his notebook and snapped his head up, "You really think so?"

"It's a distinctive specimen, and we're fortunate to be allowed to copy it. Thanks to a loan from Professor Romano."

"Who?"

"Elderly man, the guy from Penn."

"Oh, yeah, him. I get them mixed up."

"You'd better not, if you want an academic career." She boxed in her palms the signature chignon, low-slung cranium which housed an even larger brain than a skull from its more favored modern progeny, or cousins. Scientists are wonderful, Roberta thought. At the turn of the twentieth century women weren't as smart as men because they had smaller brains; today, Neanderthals weren't as smart as moderns even though their brains are larger.

"Don't wait around Jeffrey, I'm going to close up in a few minutes anyway. Thanks, you did well."

He grunted and swaying slightly weaved a path amongst the fossil litter and out the door. Roberta locked the authentic Neanderthal skull in a metal cabinet but left the cast displayed on a shelf so that she could see it as soon as she walked into the lab in the morning.

The lights were off in Rosie's hospital room, and the girl was probably sleeping. Roberta halted on the threshold already suffocating in a swirl of odors: urine, soiled laundry, cleaning chemicals, and overheated, purified, circulated air.

Rosie saw a woman framed by the hall light in the doorway, squirmed, and shouted, "Hey, hey you. Turn some goddamn lights on. I can't see nothing in here."

Roberta flicked a switch as she entered. But the florescent glow didn't calm the antic, feverish girl who cried out in panic at her, and kept banging around in the bed, "I just told that nurse chick, I gotta quit this place. They won't let me go. I aint gonna die trapped here. If I gotta die, I'll die someplace else. Some hole, somewheres, under a tree maybe. Like when Richard's shepherd dog caught the rabbit. It got away finally, snuck under the fence, but we found it later, dead under the pine tree." The hot, sweaty girl bumped up in frantic lurches, tossed sideways twitching her arms, imperiling the I.V. liquid dripping into her vein.

Not daring to touch the girl, Roberta bent cautiously over the bed and spoke at her hot, overwrought eyes, "You are not going to die. Not here, not any place. You aren't that badly hurt." The girl suddenly quieted in rapt attention at the words. Roberta straightened up, embarrassed, "Didn't anyone tell you that?" Rosie shoved her jaw up, pushed out her lips and turning over, sank her flushed, glazed face into the pillow. "No one, huh? Jesus. Well, I suppose they didn't think it was necessary to. Who usually tells you you're going to be okay in the hospital, your family, your friends...Rosie, you've got a slight concussion, lots of cuts and contusions...

whatever, a couple cracked ribs, a bruised kidney, and a fractured ulna. That's the cast on your arm. You lost a lot of blood before they picked you up. You're running a fever, which is common in these cases, and...You are a bit in shock—"

"Fuck it—"

"Still, your spirits seem to be returning to normal."

"Leave off, okay?"

"None of those injuries are life threatening—"

"All right, okay. Don't go weird on me."

"Okay. You heard me?" Roberta backed to the window sill and looked over the hospital roof. Same ugliness creeping.

"Anyway, don't get me wrong. I wasn't scared to die. I would just go to heaven, that's all. That's where you aint going. You, you're godless. You are going to hell, Chickie. What do you godless geeks think anyway? Nothing aint there when you die?"

"I suppose. Maybe we just lose consciousness at death. But then again, maybe there is something else. I'm not saying there isn't, Rosie. I would never say that."

"Heaven."

"I don't know. But I surmise that the supreme whatever that is in charge, after we die will not accept all this as best. I mean, what it is we...people believe makes everything all right on earth, isn't going to be all right with...whatever is out there. No one is going to convince me that there's an...inevitability about everything that happens which makes it just or flawless. How can people be so sure?"

"Hey, chill, what do I care what you think? It's like, you're the only person I know who don't believe in God—"

"Your motorcycle friend?"

"Hey wait, that dude wears a cross all the time. Never takes it off."

"Impressive. Well, let me tell you, Rosie, getting to not believe in God means not letting Him beat you up."

Rosie expanded her big, onyx eyes engulfing the blasphemy, genuinely horrified.

"No big deal, kid," Roberta shook her head.

"You are loco. You screwy chickie. I'm out of here and don't gotta listen to no more badass talk."

"That's what I came to tell you, mostly. Your uncle's been notified, and the police say he's driving up tomorrow. As soon as you're better, you'll be released to him."

Rosie raised herself on her good elbow and almost rolled out of bed, "That's straight. Couldn't find my old lady, huh?"

"No."

"Yeah, so what, she cut out and is as good as gone."

The week was winding down, ultimately, at last. Friday morning Dorcus had put all his heads in a row: White's archaic Homo sapiens, perhaps, along side the erectus cranium that had been Dorcus' first and only find in Asia years ago; right beside them the Neanderthal cast, and ranging on nearby tables various cranium fragments comprising their entire permanent hominid collection.

On the corner table shoved amongst the mandibles and maxilla and teeth, out of the way, apparently, rested the erectus jaw. Hide it, by all means, show it up and hide it. It's significance lies in the clarity it presses upon the inner eye, the direction it foretells. By all means keep it invisible yet highlighted amid the confusion. Render it harmless.

Roberta pulled a sheet from the printer, a graphic showing midsagittal sections of various skulls, and brought it to Dorcus who waited beside Jeffrey.

"Here," she stretched the sheet out in from of them, "the angulated occipital bone, compares plainly with our skull where the occipital rises vertically—"

"Fine, fine, Roberta, but it should be obvious to you, I'll have to deal with that at a later time."

"We've got an anomaly, maybe even two species—"

"No, no. Cannot be. Give me that." He pulled the sheet over, "You've got to know how to view the specimen. Jeffrey, get me the density figures."

At the union lunch room Roberta greeted Jon Martin as she slid her broiled whitefish plate onto the table and fell into the booth seat. Repelled she avoided Jon's slimy, red, roast beef sandwich. Jon swallowed great gulps of it before speaking.

"So, Cam's gone to Philadelphia."

"Did he say any more nasty things about me before he left?"

"Nope." He gnawed on a hanging bit of floppy, pink flesh. "D'you get him straightened out?"

"One doesn't have to do much more than catch Cam at it to make him stop doing some things."

"Roberta, you're not still in love with him, are you?"

"You should be embarrassed to ask that."

"Why should I be? It's not like I'm talking about sex." He popped some horseradish on a bit of rubbery bread clinging to the mound of meat. "That would be embarrassing. Between the two of us, I mean. Sex talk, I mean...Roberta, haven't I asked you a dozen times in the last few years to sleep with me? What do I get? So you must be still in love with Cam. Although how you could be—"

"Because we've been friends for so long, I'm going to trust you with a discovery I've just made."

"Damn your ancient bones."

"This isn't about fossils, unless you mean my personal bones."

"I'm bored with discoveries. Unless this is about why you won't go to bed with me—"

She was stirring the remnants of her almondine sauce around the plate, "It's about food. Our species has effectively destroyed the sex act—"

"Spare me this—"

"Transformed, maybe I should say."

"Transformed, degraded, destroyed, I see possibilities in all of them."

"I'm saying, we've transformed the meaning of sex the way we've built weapons out of lead or uranium or wood, out of elementals—throw in a dash of human mind and poof—weapons. And out of the simple act of procreation—fool around a little bit, it makes you feel good—poof—we get modern sexuality in all its alarming and violent manifestations. And we're doing the same thing to food now. Radicalizing it, sanctifying it, making it into the enemy."

"And I thought I was simply enjoying this roast beef sandwich. Hate to tell you this, but what you've just said, indicates a rather shallow understanding of sex drives."

"I know it. In spite of all, I seem to understand the two extremes: sex as an innocent, the desire of love, and the other end, sex as control and domination. I don't ever get the middle area, what is really happening when people go out and look to get laid."

"The pleasure principle."

"The reality principle, if you grow up? Am I getting weird on you, as Rosie would say?"

He shrugged that off, "Did you know Cameron's going to New York after Philly?"

"Yes, and bringing Margot back with him."

"Uh huh, he told me she's coming here for a visit. I love the way your ex talks. He pronounces certain words as if he were giving you their etymologies. He wouldn't want you to mis-con-strue what he says. Berta, if I had published some really important book, like Cam has, instead of silly, sordid articles, you might have..." he caught her eyes, reached over and covered her left hand which lay against her raised forearm, right hand cradling her chin. She felt his warmth pass over her cheeks and brow, and his sudden, desperate ardor blotted the smile from her face. The mocking lightness no longer danced between them. "But a big book would have been dull work, insupportably dull."

She pinched his fingers and tried to bring the lightness back, "In-sup-port-a-bly dull." To which thrust he gave a slight, reflexive smile and went for more coffee.

Roberta couldn't believe it: Tracer was tagging along with her to visit Rosie again, ostensibly to give Rosie a book.

"Why do you follow me to this hospital?"

"What the kid needs is something to take her mind off her troubles. I think of those times I was going nuts...it's what I was trying to tell you about survival and Jacob. That bastard's not going to catch on until it's maybe too late."

"What's this?"

"A book about the Pueblo Indians."

"That'll wow her."

"Jacob stuffs prostitutes when he should be cramming for exams—"

"You have a mania about that man."

"Then he wants me to smooth things over for him. Like I could. Not the point."

Father Charles sped to the doorway almost embracing the women before they could enter Rosie's room. He didn't have the decency, thought Roberta as she stared him down, to be embarrassed by their last encounter.

"She has a badly bruised kidney, Roberta. They say she has to stay here while the kidney heals." The group backed into the tiny cell. Glancing up Rosie saw an invasionary force descending on her.

"Here, " spoke Tracer flinging the hefty book on the bed, "brought you something."

The priest cornered Roberta leaving Rosie to gawk at the colorful mesa of Tracer, thunderstruck.

"What do you think of all this? She was running away again."

"Maybe we should come back when...another time... Tracer?" Who had opened the tome and was thumbing through it.

"There, here's a section on the Zuni."

"Tracer, huh? We'll come back later?"

"No need to do that, Roberta," his fluid hand streamed toward her. "I'm not staying long, so you won't be disturbing us."

"But the Navajo are an Athapacean tribe. I stay with Navajo when I'm in the field."

Fearing treachery the girl studied Tracer's broad face, "You live in a teepee?"

"No, kid, they're hogans..."

Roberta inched her way around the foot of the bed, the priest sidling after her. They were blocked at the wall-edge of the window. Again Roberta caught herself staring at black asbestos slabs. The priest lowered his voice and dropped into staccato undertone.

"Roberta, Sandy's gone, left no trace. I think she's remarried or something. Roberta, these police interviewed her former landlady...Maybe Rosie shouldn't—she's not happy...been happy, my with sister, but Sandy has lead a rather...miserable time of it, too. Roberta, they have to understand, though, the rectory, a priest's home, is no place for a fourteen-year-old girl."

Roberta tore her eyes from the roof top—it was almost like a painting, all that fundament of expressive, black texture—focused on Rosie badgering Tracer from her prone infirmity. Father Charles motioned at nothing and took his wire rims off his hawk nose to wipe them on his sleeve. Rosie flipped to the pictures in the book with her good arm.

"They look like aliens in space helmets. Cool."

"Neat, huh? And this looks uncannily like

electromagnetic circuitry. They're called petroglyphs."

"What the hell's that a picture of? Hey," the girl was trying to catch Roberta's attention. Oblivious to any but his own meaning, the priest was piqued.

"Well, young lady, your language," he frowned.

"Hey...Chickie." Astonished, Roberta did a head fake jarring her hip on the iron bedstead. "This kinda Indian, 'Hopi,' look at 'im. Bet this is the kinda Indian smokes dope—"

"Peyote," put in Tracer, "for ceremonial pur—"

"That's enough, Rosie," blurted the priest, " You look for stuff like that. Everything with you has to have some nasty... interpretation, always an unwholesome interest."

"Hardly," drawled Tracer, "she's just right. Not sinister, accurate."

"Tracer, we should be going now."

"I don't think we ought to leave, Bertie. I think this guy should quit baiting the kid—"

"My niece is a troubled adolescent."

"So what—"

"Tracer—"

"That doesn't make her wrong here—"

Rosie was screaming, "Both you fucking bitches get the hell out of here. Here's your stupid book back. Leave my uncle alone..."

"Easy, kid,"

"Tracer, come on." Roberta felt like shielding her head with her arms and ducking as she squeezed toward the door.

"Better get outta here, Bitches."

"Rosie, this all isn't necessary," the priest had regained

his equilibrium, tossing off, "You see what I mean?"

Tracer hauling herself up to full six feet sought the priest's eyes, connected with them, then swiveled only her torso to include Rosie and somehow claim both their attentions at once, "Girl, this uncle of yours will eventually dump you on some disagreeable strangers. If you're not careful starting right away, this treatment will badly hinder your development. You aren't getting what I mean, kid—"

"This is none of your business."

"Uncle Chuck—"

"Don't shout at me, Rosie."

Tracer was implacable, "You're going to have to learn to be tough. Begin right this instant. And that does not mean what you think it does. Oh, all right, Bertie, let's go."

"I'll call you later, Roberta," Father Charles mouthed to her as the women left.

Ripping together down the acridly sanitized hallway, Roberta hissed, "Jesus Christ, Tracer."

"Why do you drag me into these things, Bertie?"

The telephone's shrill howl jarred Roberta who had been tapping on the computer trying to arrive at the elusive missing variables using a method that might not distort shape differences. Unproductive not to have disconnected the phone. Maybe she sought distraction finding the measurements too hypnotically enticing. Figures rolling past at a rapid, steady clip were absorbing, cleansing, pulsating in harness with Roberta's breath in long, comfortable vapor rhythms. Silence throbbed, followed by the phone's second shriek which her grappling hand hurriedly stifled. Farzi.

"Sweetie? You must have used superb pronunciation. Heshemi most definitely got your meaning."

"How do you know that?"

"Berta, I'm back here for a few days."

"Here, where?"

"In this country, close by, not—"

"Not that you'll tell me where. I'm not sure I want you to anymore."

"Some of my father's acquaintances have said they heard the word is, to let you be."

"Any tiny persons among them?"

"Since I'm where I am, I have to be very brief."

"Oh, yes."

"Are you alone, Berta?"

"Yes, I am. Farzi, is this risky? Your father's not going to get to you, is he? Aren't you taking a big risk coming...close by? God damn it, Farzi."

"No. Don't worry. No...Tomorrow, Denis and Tony complete a deal we've been working toward for three years. Tomorrow, finally and gloriously the papers are to be signed. We're selling the Valtat for a very agreeable price. Oh, by the way, I received my money, no hitches, nicely done."

"Nothing to it. Only thing they have problems with are the number of banks we're sending to."

"Rinky-dink, Berta, they're rinky-dink. Now this is my new request. At seven tomorrow night, you should take yourself over to the gallery and sign off the Valtat sale."

"All right. I'm to sign this one. Did they ever understand about the other?"

"Enough."

"So answer me, are you working...where ever you are?"

"Of course."

"I mean doing sculpture?"

"That's not what I can do right now."

"I'm beginning to imagine this incredible uselessness."

"Are you okay, Berta? You don't sound okay."

"I want you to come back here, to stay, so all this can end."

"My father's not going to harass you anymore."

"No, but you are."

"Don't do this to me. I can't talk anymore."

Roberta cut the connection.

An hour before sunset Roberta stood just inside the shimmering glass doorway of Persia Gallery accidentally catching a suggestive denouement being enacted in front of her. In abrasive shoe soles, it seemed to Roberta, irreverently crushing the indigo and cochineal runner gracing the dusky hallway, three men were completing a deal. Denis, yes, even so stunned, Roberta's senses coalesced Denis from the tenebrous air, Denis shaking the hand of a blunt, brown man, Heshemi Behroozi it was, being led out the side door under the obscuring shade, Behroozi with his hand under Tony's elbow, and yes, the swarmy, handsome head was Tony's, and the three men talked low together. Deliberately, Roberta slammed the glass door behind her making the stretched glass squeal. Behroozi was gone; only Tony's back wavered in the gloom as Denis clambered down the hallway to greet her. They confronted each other in silence for a moment.

Denis began, "We need him...to resolve some partnership problems." Roberta's ashen face recoiled from his limp words. They became the obelus she was awaiting.

"Resolve, Denis? Or are you finding a way to dissolve the partnership? Dissolve Farzi. What does Behroozi have to do with resolving anything?"

"He's been our main import source you know."

Tony appeared from the hallway, "None of this is any of your damn business, Roberta." He strode promptly into the office with Denis tailing him. Roberta sought out the Valtat on the cluttered wall. The men returned with Tony still in the lead, his extended hand clutching papers which he placed on a small, lacquer table, then a silver pen on top of them. "Sign these now, Roberta, and don't mess in any of our business. You don't know what's going on; you'll never know what's going on."

Roberta stood still, unheeding, unblinking, even composed, unmoved.

"Just hurry up. Sign where it says to, by the X. Farzi phoned here this morning and told us she had talk to you, so don't pull any bullshit stuff on us, Roberta." Still Roberta unspeaking, stood unmoved and unmoving.

"What's the matter with you, Roberta?" Denis piped in.

"Goddamit, Roberta—" Almost, she looked uplifted, but as if in a catatonic state, "Roberta?"

"No. I'm...not going to sign this right now...until I've talked to Farzi—"

"You did, you talked to her last night. I know so. She told you to sign about Valtat...Don't get any funny ideas. It won't matter to her one bit we're doing a little dealing with her old man. Believe me. Anything we can get from him."

"Maybe not." Her torpid mind forced her feet up, heavy ramming to prod the iron burden, like a horse weight pressing on her noggin, so she could advance her body out of the gallery. Pushing against gravity, she dragged past Denis and Tony who had slid in front of her.

"Farzi's not going to be very happy," Tony warned, "if you leave and don't sign this contract."

Again Roberta said, "Maybe not."

"Roberta, think about what you're doing."

As if in counterpoise the door to the gallery flew open. Angelique entered flourishing a cape, her long profile calm and equine, her oval eyes shining. "Hello, Tony." So beautiful thought each of those mortals in his or her own way. "Hello, all." Jill and Terry came in several paces behind her. Jill broke off and collared Roberta.

"I haven't seen you in weeks. Why don't you answer your phone?"

"Mostly I've been at the lab. We're in the midst of a fossil dispute."

"Look at them." She watched all three pawing men prance about Angelique and grunted.

"What's Angelique MacBeth doing here?"

"Doing? Doing Tony if you want the unwashed truth. She and Tony have been doing each other for the three weeks you've been too busy to answer your phone. After the reconciliation failed, she left MacBeth. But for some reason she's chosen to stay with us. Maybe so that Terry can do Bill the dubious favor of keeping an eye on her."

"I don't believe it."

"Believe it. Tony sniffing around all the time. I'm about to kick the whole bunch of them out. It's my house, you know."

"I know."

"Terry ran through the ton of money his father left him before he was twenty-five."

"I know that, too."

Tony sauntered over to Jill and Roberta, "I got an idea," spreading his arms, "Let's all go to dinner." He slipped the contract inside his concealed suitcoat pocket. "Then we'll finish this business later, huh, Roberta? Meantime you think about what I said."

"Come with us, Roberta, don't be such a hermit," Jill escorted her out of the gallery.

They were led to a round table Tony strategically seating himself between Angelique and Roberta. He fussed with the silverware, griped at the waiter, gave suggestions of what everyone should order, while touching Angelique on her arm, shoulder, neck. Table talk never went further than horse racing and politics. Angelique kept silent except to answer Tony's softly spoke innuendo-filled words meant only for her ear. Then she might answer silkily in return. Jill and Roberta said almost nothing.

While dinner was being eaten, Tony had been overly polite to Roberta posing as the reasonable man who would win her acquiescence in a while. Polite, if dismissive, until, when insisting that everyone have the superb strawberry cheesecake which only Roberta declined, he announced, "You've always got to have things your own way, don't you Roberta?"

"That's because she's smart," Jill shook herself awake.

"Hey, let's get that waiter and order the cheesecake," suggested Terry.

Tony pulled the contract out of his jacket pocket, "If she's so damned smart why can't she understand that if Farzi tells her to sign this, then she's required by law to do it."

"I didn't say I wouldn't sign that paper—"

"Well then here it is. Do it then. Here."

"I think...something might have changed. I've got to talk to Farzi first—"

"I told you, she won't care if we're dealing with her oily old man. And you can't tell when she'll call you again. If we have to wait even until tomorrow, it will blow the whole deal. Damn it, you are the most stiff-necked woman."

Jill and Terry exchanged glances; he moved his hand sideways an inch, a signal for her to be quiet.

"Yeah, wait Tony, let's have dessert first and then—."

"Shut up, Denis."

Angelique, who had been gazing for some minutes into the dim-lit spaces around them, had brought her attention back to the gathering at the mention of Farzi's name. Seductively, she played her long fingers over Tony's clutched hand, "I hear Farzi Behroozi's in Europe."

"Yes, and I need Roberta to sign this contract for Farzi as she was told, by Farzi, to do."

Angelique accosted Roberta's escaping, grey eyes. "What's this for?" she asked her.

"I'm her intermediary—"

"It's a simple business deal which Roberta hasn't the ability to comprehend the importance of," he pushed the papers in front of her.

"Not so simple, Tony," Roberta felt deadened by Angelique's long, articulated fingers still stroking Tony's fist. "I have to know whether Farzi has all the information about what her partners have been concocting. Maybe she does." She lashed her eyes off the copulating metacarpi to Tony's sulky face. "But the thing is, Tony, where do we go...where do we...go? Isn't that the question? Where do we go... from here?"

You don't know business, Roberta, and you've been criminally obstinate. Will you sign this now?"

"No, I don't think I ought to."

Tony jumped up, "All right, you smart-ass stupid bitch. I couldn't believe Farzi would be fool enough to entrust you with this power, and now, as I expected, you misuse it. You got so damn much of Farzi's money, you pay the bill. Come on, Denis, Terry," he began to pull Angelique's chair backward so she could stand; however, she sat solidly in it, tilted up her finely-tapered head and said she'd be along in a minute. Furious, Tony stamped out, Denis, funereal, skulked after him, Terry lumbering behind.

Jill trembled to her feet, "I've had it, Angelique. Get yourself a hotel room. I'm sick to death of all of this." Then she, too, departed.

The waiter appeared to clear the table. "No dessert," Roberta said.

"Bring coffee," said Angelique. "What's so disturbing in it that you won't sign Tony's paper?"

"I think there's been an unknown factor inserted which alters the situation now, from when I talked to Farzi and she told me to go ahead and sign off the Valtat."

"You're protecting her?"

"I'm not sure. Maybe I'm ruining her." Their coffee arrived blessedly hot and strong.

"Are you wondering at all why I've come back to your town? Are you?"

"Tony?"

"Yes." Robert's eyes wandered from the textureless skin colored like the hot coffee she was warily sipping. "Time goes so slow. I was with Bill for twelve years. I want to eat again, sleep again, make love again in quickness while time is flying by. It's awful. I'm constantly dissatisfied with whatever's happening this minute, at the same time as I'm in dreaded fear of what might happen tomorrow...Why is Farzi hiding? Is it a secret?"

"There wasn't ever any secret."

"I know about her father, to cleanse the family honor—"

"He is determined to find her, and she's in danger and must hide. But, I think, that isn't the only reason anymore."

"Will she come back?"

"Why should she?"

Across the table's length, embedded in features changed in an instant to unblemished obsidian crept a deep smile.

Roberta answered the phone aware by the light that she'd spent all night awake and that it must be nearly dawn. And knowing that it must be Farzi.

"Roberta, were you sleeping?"

"Funny thing, I wasn't. Do you know what's happened?"

"No. Did the negotiations fall through?"

"I went to the gallery a little early. Your father was there...making some pact with Tony and Denis. Denis said, before Tony shut him up, that your father was helping them resolve some import difficulties. So...I refused to sign the contract until I asked you about this new development—"

"You didn't!"

"And Tony went bonkers, just flipped out. He gets angry, Farzi, but I've never seen him this irate. Farzi?"

"Yes."

"Do you want me to...to sign the papers tomorrow?"

"You had to sign them yesterday, or we lost the deal."

"I was afraid of...that was what Tony said...but, without telling you...What if Tony and Denis were in league with your father to find you? Catch you? Are you there?"

"Berta, a considerable amount of money was lost."

"What can I say...I figured I had better not sign, under the new...circumstances. I made a mistake..."

"I've got to do some real thinking immediately—"

"I'm sorry, Farzi. I couldn't risk it, I thought if—"

"Sorry? The only problem Heshemi can resolve with Tony is me. Sorry? Of course they were selling me, my freedom, my life. I'll call you on Wednesday, Sweetie, no time now. Benedicite."

18

". . . I should have done . . . the primate thing, gone where I wanted, done what fascinated me, and carried you around slung to my belly."

———————

The old man snored leaning back in his chair, his feet resting on the bed, his outstretched body furry with political pamphlets and clippings. Head lolling forward, he growled and wheezed in heavy slumber. Nevertheless, as Roberta entered, he awoke, straightened his eyeglasses, and hurriedly gathered up the scattered papers.

"I'm all dragged out," he squinted at his daughter. "Cam and Margot were here. Took me out to lunch. I can't stand too much of that sort of thing, with this ticker."

"How're you doing?"

"Tired, didn't you hear me? You had a fine time last night at the big New Year's party, drank too much—"

"What? I drank nothing at all—"

"So...Cam said you were harping about Margo coming to live with you. After all these years. You must've been drunk."

"Oh, Dad, you...never forget an injury. I never forgive, and you never forget. Nice family motto we'd display." She banged into the stiff, sharkskin chair adjacent to the bedside table.

"So, you're planning to regain your daughter. She'll never go for it."

"I'll give it a shot, Dad, might work. You've regained yours several times—"

"What the hell does that crack mean?"

"Want to go to dinner tomorrow with Margot and me?"

"No, I don't think so. I've had as much gadding about as I can take."

"So you're not ready to check out of here yet? Even with the ersatz Methodist's campaign about to take off—"

"I'll just bet you haven't talked to one of my doctors in weeks."

"I haven't. Give it up, Dad, and go home."

"Damn it, I'm too worn out and ill for your senseless nagging." He shivered, "I've got things to do. Gotta get these papers sorted. Cam's coming back in the morning. And I have to locate those voter demographics to show him. You could help me with the chronology."

Later as she skulked out down the mined hallway, she speculated on possible benefits he might derive from enfeebling himself. He didn't fit any of the cases of those wanting to die, or to grow into an unhealthy decrepitude. Instead of seeking the aging ideal—slow while maintaining a certain dignity—he was caving in to dotage. He weakened himself, his picture of himself, perceptively each day hoping...hoping what? Gaining what? Was it true what she had told Tracer, that he was daring God to find him? Or perhaps...Maybe that might be the answer. Was he expecting one day to be revenged by beating old age to all its horrors? And laughing at it's devious approach, grim, shadowy-

spectral, ravening? I have bested you old man, he could proclaim, I have beaten you there. Her large eyes floated with tears unspilled.

Margot insisted on a bottle of sparkling Burgundy dawdling over the glass, refilling it after only a few sips, and giggling. The shrimp de jonge smelled too garlicky, the lighting too obtrusive, the waiter obsequious, and the silverware spotted. Roberta, who had chosen the restaurant with scrupulous care, feared that nothing she could do would suit her discriminating daughter. Maybe Margot might be finding her painstakingly chosen, paisley silk dress disagreeable—too unsubtle.

"Be reasonable, Mother, I can't come here now. I've only a semester left at Dalton, and I like it there."

"Okay, yeah, but afterwards, perhaps the University of Chicago."

"I've already been accepted at Radcliff and Smith."

"So get accepted at Chicago."

"I don't want to go there."

"I'd just like you...to be closer to me."

"Oh, come on now," extravagant toss of luxurious hair, thick like hers and the color of Cam's. "You haven't ever worried about that before. Hey, don't, I didn't mean..."

Roberta's heart stopped beating, panic dipped her in plasma deep-freeze. "I'd like, someday, to clarify our decision. I've feared, since we did it, how we hurt you."

"I used to feel hurt when I was really small about not living with you or Cam. But now, to be honest, even then, I never really felt deprived. Grandmere and Pops, I got everything taken care of by them. Sometimes, I'd have days when I'd wonder why I wasn't living with one of you, and I'd get all hurt and furious and tell the counselors about my feelings of rejection. But, it's like, you gotta believe, I could always tell you two loved me." Forthright girl, used the word without embarrassment.

"Oh, Margot, I..." She twisted her napkin, twisted and twisted it in her lap. Her voice left her when the moment to talk had finally arrived. She could only feel devastated and stare blindly at the young woman across from her who, mysteriously, was her daughter.

"I'm gonna tell you something else, Mom. I always knew you were my mother. And I never, ever, called you when you didn't come."

"Except the time I was in Tanzania and you had the chicken pox."

"I cried my eyes out about that, but Grandmere turned out to be an okay second choice. I never, well, so many of my friends were afraid. But I knew if I waited awhile, you'd show up. That's a very valuable trust I got early, and completely. I never got shat on like lots of the others. Their parents dumped them off at school, and felt virtuous. Gave them hardly any honest consideration. Rude, very rude. Other kids, their parents kept bugging them way too much. They despised them for that. Lots of times they did. Wished they were dead. Sure, I missed you. I won't say...But you were around and taking me with you whenever you could. And when you were around, you were really around." She dipped her pointer finger in the wine, stirred with it and stuck it in her mouth. "So don't use the mother thing on me, huh. I'm not resentful now, and...I've thought about it scads—I only used to feel bad because my situation was different from the other kids. I'd kinda felt out of it when the other kids hated their mothers. I never hated you. Weird huh?" She giggled, silly again. "I was only a little kid when you all set up this elaborate arrangement, so it really seemed kinda natural to me. It all seemed natural, you know."

"I convinced myself that I'd have made a lousy full-time mother. That...you were better off...without me."

"I had you. I have you now. I can love you without ever having had to hate you. Now you say you want me around all the time for some mother thing."

"Guilt thing? You think it's a guilt thing?"

"I guess I do. But I'm saying you don't have to feel bad. You all have given me...What didn't I have?." She tossed about on her chair. This was much too hard to handle. "Don't be a nerd."

"Margot...I think it's time you stay around because...I've got this crazy idea, it would be better for you. It'd be good for you, you hear? You might like what you see if you come with me. Don't shake your head like that, just like Cameron does, and don't be thinking it's too late. This raising you arrangement, I would never do it again. I thought I had two choices, actually I had three, but I knew each one, no matter how many, were bad. Do ordinary work, get a sitter, stay home, do what I didn't want to do at work for twenty years. Or pretend I had your best interest at heart when I only was afraid of what people would say. But I was wrong, all wrong. I should have done the authentic thing, the primate thing, gone where I wanted, done what fascinated me, and carried you around slung to my belly. And yes, when all your options are lousy you make a bad choice, one you deeply regret. But I wouldn't do it again. I would keep you with me like a gorilla or a chimp—" She slid over, reached out for her lovely daughter, "Hold on, maybe it's not too late," and held her tight. "It's time for you to come back here. The right time."

Margot released her mother with tender awe, then picked up a shrimp and plunked it into the full wine glass watching it founder and sink, "I'm telling you, I like us the way we are."

When Cameron joined them for dessert, both women had shaken off their difficult conversation. Margo, believing she'd carried her point, gave her mother a crooked wink as Cam squeezed her hand. Roberta left the match soul-weary and sorely ignoble.

As usual Cameron took over the conversation, "Your father is helping me considerably with the campaign. He appears to me to be just fine. What's keeping him in that sick room? Except for a little stiffness in one arm, he's mostly recovered from the stroke."

"Heart trouble." Talk continued to orbit Cam, spin in retrograde to contain Margot's activities; occasionally Roberta interjected something about her fossils to forestall boredom. But she couldn't rest content under the burden of her thwarted request. One so essential to her continued apperception.

"You don't head back East until Saturday, right, Margot?"

"Yeah, why?" A ripe giggle at her father's mugging.

"Why don't you go down to the University of Chicago with me on Friday and meet some friends I have there?"

"She's at it again, eh, Margot?"

"Why can't I convince you, Mom? I'm all set for next year, either Radcliff or Smith."

"I like Smith, myself."

"Bug off, Cam. What would it hurt to go down to Chicago with me and look, meet some people?"

A little petulant, "Oh, all right, I'll go." Brightening, "We can do some shopping. But don't count on anything. I won't change my mind."

With her humor improved Roberta went to the lab next morning to work, uninterrupted by Dorcus who never came in Thursdays until late. Why that was, she had never been curious enough to ask. At noon Dorcus presented himself in front of Jeffrey quizzing him on craniofacial architecture. Later he swung past Roberta the moment she looked up from studying the Neandertal cast.

Something irritated him, "Aren't you finished with that Neandertal evaluation?"

"Yes, but...Have you ever glimpsed out of the corner of your eye almost in passing, glanced at this cast as it sat here right next to the Archaic skull?"

"Why would I do that?"

"You can't look at them straight on, or you lose it. If you catch them both in the periphery of your vision, you notice, it strikes you...how infinitesimal, unlocatable the transition points are. Just a kind of visual connection, I don't know..."

"What are you running on about? Why are you messing everything up with inconsequential matters? You've refused to see the new skull as a link."

"Of course it's a link of sorts—"

"It's not a Neandertal."

"I know that. It isn't simple. That reconstruction we did throws me. An anomaly here—in the shape of the occipital region, here and here. Changes the vault form and expands the parietal—"

"Just tell me, are the measurements done?"

"We interrupting?" Descending on them, swooping like a goshawk chased by a sparrow, Father Charles landed at the fossil table, close behind him Rosie, drawn and pale, arm in a hot pink cast and forehead pasted up with white dressing. As usual she couldn't smile; Father Charles fairly beamed.

"Rosie's been released this morning. We didn't want to leave without saying good-bye."

Roberta appraised the scrubby, banged-up urchin-woman, "So you're out of that hospital at last. That's a relief." The girl scowled, passed behind her uncle to approach the fossils at an angle.

"Will you look at all them dead bones. What is this place?" She rolled her head taking in the entire environment.

"A laboratory. We find things out here, sort of."

"You find things out about dead bones?"

The priest's sharp face puckered, smile faded like weathered colors, "Roberta, I thought if you could get away, we might have lunch before Rosie and I start for home."

"These are special bones, very old, thousands of years old, some millions, even."

"Roberta, will you join us?"

"That big Indian chickie work here, too?"

"No. Tracer's in archeology, another area."

Rosie stroked the Neandertal cast in abstracted compulsion, dumbfounded, "Fuck, look at the way this skull looks. What fucking happened to it?"

At a final, breaking point of patience, almost unaware of his action, Father Charles' hand snaked out and pinched the back of his niece's neck. Tightening his squeeze he hissed, "Watch your mouth, young lady. I warned you about just this sort of outburst." Rearing her head back violently, in pain Rosie ripped away from him.

She screeched, "Don't you touch me. Keep your goddamn hands off a me—" Father Charles detonated from a gravity well within him, a singularity he'd never denied and never learned to control. With clenched fist he punched the girl, jammed a solid blow against her heat-splotched face. Blood spurted from her split lip stealing down her chin, dark red flux grotesquely fitting with the stained bandages and yellow bruises. Rosie's head flew up, eyes startled into unconcealed bewilderment as if no one before him had ever hit her.

The priest backed off severely shaken, "I think you had that coming, Rosie," trying to reestablish his prerogative.

Rosie whipped around bloody spittle riding her words, "God damn you. God damn all of it." With a sudden concentrated defiance she picked up the Neandertal cast and hurtled it across the room. It smashed upon the sticky floor—shattering.

Both Dorcus and Jeffrey ran for the girl, Dorcus shouting, "You little maniac, do you realize what you've done?" Father Charles stepped backward after all reluctant to interfere, echoed, "Rosie, what have you done, Rosie?"

The girl was enraged.

"I hate..." she spat out, "you."

Amidst the hubbub, Robert's insistent voice was finally heard. Rosie turned to her.

"Come on, let's go wash your face."

Dorcus, incensed, continued to rail as he bent stiffly to pick up the shards, "Get that brat out of my sight. Don't just stand there like an idiot. Jeffrey, help me with this." Stunned Father Charles bent over with Jeffrey to pluck shards from the gummy wooden planks.

Rosie sprinted for the door, Roberta after her. In the hallway Roberta expected a chase, but Rosie was right there trembling, enfolded within herself, leaning doubled over against the wall.

"Where am I gonna go now? I aint got no place to stay at." She was sobbing.

"That was a mistake, to do that with your anger," Roberta cradled the girl against her chest.

From the kitchen while putting together some soup and sandwiches Roberta heard Tracer's drone, "We'll live right on the reservation. Every year I take several grad students, and you'll be along to give us all a hand. It'll be a lot of work. Can you work hard, Rosie?"

"I aint never done no work."

"You willing to try?"

"Yeah, yeah, I will."

"We'll work for a couple months here getting ready before we can leave. Gotta wait till the snow melts. But we'll get you into our University High School. Then you can come to school to us in archeology. And you'll live with me and the others in the hogan."

"The cops okayed this?"

"Yup. Well, your uncle did. Same difference."

"You aint my foster mother or nothing?"

"Hell, no. No relation at all. No claim on you at all. You're my associate. I'll show you how."

Roberta joined them, fed them, listened to their prattle until the telephone rang. Knowing whom it must be, she hustled into the kitchen, for privacy.

"Roberta, are you alone?"

"Farzi, it's been two weeks. I've gotten more and more worried. Are you still safe?"

"Yes, I changed some addresses and now I am. There's something monumental and rather...odd, an odd favor I have ask you to do, this time."

"Ask me to do something odd? What could you be thinking? Wait a minute. Not so fast, you haven't filled me in...and, of course I can't go near the gallery. Did you settle up—"

"Yes, my father, Tony, and Denis—there's a wraith if I ever saw one—they'll make a glassy triptych. Yes, I'm out, and just by the—how you say—skin off my teeth. Thanks to...brave friend, to you. However, I will have to live very cheaply from now on."

"You know, I'd be thrilled to be able to think of you without panicking."

"Then, you probably won't mind doing me this little, odd favor if that would help to alleviate my situation and your concern?"

"Ah, yes. Have I not 'done thee worthy service, Told thee no lies, made thee no mistakings, served without or grudge or grumblings'"?

"Such pretty words, Berta. Of course you have...but there's more work. Remember the Prospero bust in my classical series? Now this is vitally important. Because I am no longer in the business, I'm going to have to sneak the rest of my money, in cash, out of the country on my own person."

"Are you out of your mind?"

"You must withdraw everything out of all my banks, all of it, every cent tomorrow, and bring it to the Civic Opera House in Chicago, Verdi at the Lyric Opera Friday night."

"I'll be followed, you'll be caught. Oh, God."

"Better get big bills—"

"Friday. I am taking Margot to the University of Chicago Friday."

"Wonderful. That'll be a good cover. You won't be followed. Heshemi despises you. He's changed tactics."

"Won't the banks inform your father—"

"I've taken care of that with a little threat of litigation. Barbarians. The opera tickets will be on reserve at the call window, under the name Aristosos. I'll get one for Margot, too, of course. Perfect."

"Who do I give the money to, a tiny lady? Or throw it in the window of a trained, performing automobile?"

"You'll be contacted. As usual."

"Yeah, well, I get very nervous. I won't even ask how much money I'm supposed to turn over to a complete strange—"

"Have some faith, Sweetie." End of conversation.

Roberta walked slowly back into the living room. Tracer sat, a book in hand, in front of the honking television. Rosie's battered little body had eased into sleep. Sliding onto one end of the sofa, Roberta stroked the stretched, limp cat.

"Who was that?"

"Farzi."

"No kidding? Is she coming home?"

"No. No, she's not."

Friday morning when Roberta arrived at Cameron's sprawling Victorian house to collect Margot for the trip to Chicago, he seemed thrilled to see her.

"Come in, sit down a minute. Margot's gone to buy some bottled water she can't travel without. I want to talk to you." Roberta balanced on the edge of his prized musnud not wanting to waste much time here. Having all Farzi's money, in cash, taped to her skin under layers of clothing— thousands of dollars—made her anxiety-ridden, overheated, and skittish. Even a little paranoid— she avoided his eyes. Maybe he could guess her unspeakable errand.

Eventually some of his words penetrated her abstracted discomfort. "So I decided I'd go ahead and say it baldly. It isn't a good idea for you to go on this way."

"What way?"

"Are you listening to me or to the harmony of the spheres?"

"I'm sorry, Cam, I was being a mooncalf..."

"Well...frankly, " He puffed, put off a little, "I was saying I don't believe it's wise to push too hard about this U. of Chicago thing."

"I don't intend to."

"You've already done a lot of pushing. Let the girl make up her own mind. She's made remarkable choices so far. I trust her to use sound judgment about colleges, too."

"Cam, I'm not pushing her."

"It appears to both of us that you are. Margot asked me to cool you down about this returning to you business. Don't overdo it, or it'll all come off phony to her—"

A sink line plummeted through Roberta's unconscious mind bringing an awareness, a flashing alert, an implosion of clarity. She straightened her spine and lifted off the cushion disrupting the arrangement of the seat.

"I think I understand what you're telling me even though you're obfuscating. Don't concern yourself. It's not in my plans anymore that Margot will want to stay here. She's a lovely, charming, bright young woman—already accepted by Smith and Radcliff—looking forward to a sophisticated career and that includes a worthy husband, but...Rosie is now my daughter."

"Good God how can you say that? How can you stand there and say that? You claim some half-wit slut of a— What is it? You must have some kind of kinky thing going for that priest."

"Shut up for once, Cam. I don't listen wide-eyed anymore to any of you second-rate, painted gurus." A temperate response which salved the membranes afire in her mouth.

He arched his sloping shoulders infuriated at her manner, "You've insulted your daughter, you've insulted me. How will you ever forgive yourself for that asinine declaration? How, Roberta? It'll end up haunting you forever."

"Forgive myself? I have given birth twice. The second

time with my eyes open. What I have wrenched from the ordeal of the last year...goes well beyond forgiving myself. And it's a hell of a lot harder to bear."

Margot tottered into the room balancing half a dozen bottles of spring water in her arms. "Let's get hopping, Mom. Cam, don't forget, I'm staying with Mother. We'll be getting home late. We're going to the opera tonight."

The huge hall darkened. The overture struck with a mighty chord and blew fury through the packed audience. Roberta forced herself to follow the music with her mind: tempo changes, movements, motifs, great melodic daubs on an elaborate mathematical canvas far beyond her grasp. She shook with the thrill of trumpets living purely on another plane. Then, as expected, her concentration began to drift, thoughts sneaked in to cross up the music, interfering as uninvited, obtrusive, tagalongs on a heavenly field trip. She began to lose the music as syllables formed, memory, images. Word followed intrusive word until the orchestra played an evocative melody as background to her pounding sentences; and Roberta stopped listening, gave in to the barrage of words.

Why could she never listen to music as other people seemed to do? With songs, even, her own words popped up alongside the lyrics making them mushy, sometimes meaningless. Always if there were no lyrics, the notes, the instruments' voices, the rhythmic tensions alarmingly beautiful, would synergize behind her consciousness and create a host of emotions. Reducible into words.

Sitting through the overture she became prey to a

mirage—the allusive music jumbled syntax in her mind. Words blemished the sound of instruments, wilting any pleasure for her. She kept calling her mind back to the music, exhorting it to ignore her own thoughts.

But Roberta had never before been to an opera. When the overture ended, she glanced at Margot sitting alertly beside her in the aisle seat. The girl felt eyes on her, turned to Roberta and gave a satisfied smile. She had detested the University of Chicago, but she loved her silly ol' mother, and tomorrow she was flying home. All was well. Perhaps that was what the overture had spoken to her.

Gorgeously costumed opera singers positioned themselves on the stage and human voices soared in breathtaking, long vowels, inflating blood pressure, describing inexpressible aural beauty. Italian—Roberta knew no Italian—flowed, burst, descended from all sides. She strained desperately to interpret what they were saying. These words she knew no meaning for were one with the impassioned music. Her own vapid words, those she'd fought to suppress unsuccessfully during the overture, had dissipated. They had been replaced with these unknown, blessed words, blessedly unknown. Her belligerent mind tried to catch some significant sounds to fit them into her knowing system. But they would not fit, would not budge from their meaninglessness.

How emotive the unknown words struck her. She was riveted by separate sounds, awed, released; ego punctured by the music, she was taken beyond her daily dreams. The music's beauty set a counterpoise to the unknown words and together in synergistic energy created what she could only see as a meaningful meaninglessness.

Roberta's logical mind tried to piece out individual phonemes. *"Ieo miseray"* sang the baritone, and when Roberta thought she recognized an English sound, a chill depressed her, this wrongheaded scramble to make contact with a cognate. Immediately, she rejected the need to understand becoming instantly buoyed and comforted. What was this insight, if such it was? Do only the words one doesn't understand hold meaning? Reaching out in the dark glow from the lighting over the stage, Roberta squeezed Margot's arm against her ribs. Meaning...less words, or degraded words for which we need to create new meaning. Either that or throw the bums out and start again.

Lights began to come up, people enthusiastically applauding, struggling up, sifting out. An intermission. Margot left to drink orange juice in the vestibule.

Silently Farzi Behroozi slipped into Margot's empty seat beside Roberta. She poked her friend and grinned.

"Oh, m'god," Roberta called out. The earth turned right side up.

"Hello, Sweetie." They gripped hands. Farzi's hazel eyes glittered like new stars at dusk. "After the intermission, wait a few minutes, then come to the women's bathroom behind the third floor balcony."

"You...you'll be there?"

"Yes, of course." Vacated the seat before Margot returned.

In an undiscovered bathroom among ancient blue ceramic tiles and chipped porcelain fixtures, the stained and creaky stalls stood empty. An outer, carpeted lounge provided a saggy, floral patterned sofa, torn, overstuffed chairs, and the privacy needed for the women to conclude the money transfer.

Roberta waited until Farzi arrived before she began to loosen her clothing and peel the taped money from her skin.

"Roberta, you're ridiculous."

"You putting all that dough in your purse? I recommend this procedure, painful but effective."

"I'll just carry it the regular way, thank you, and trust to luck."

They sat for a few moments quietly on the ash-pocked and soiled sofa, Farzi eyes seeking out what was artistic: cornice pieces, decorative moldings.

"You're going back now..."

"To Switzerland for a little, then to Florence, and I'll let you know from there."

"You must never come back here again."

Farzi gave a shake of her head, amazed. "You realize that now, do you? I thought I'd never be able to make you understand. It worried me, what you would think."

"When we meet again, where ever...you'll have to teach me even more..." She outlined her friend's strong jawline with her fingertip, "Isis, the original, primeval, Egyptian proto-goddess, of whom I've read that words of great and compelling power were hers. And sculpture, some say music, opera...Farzi—"

"Berta, I never taught you anything."

"First I thought I was crazy...then I thought you were. I didn't think anything would bring you back, not love, not anything."

"Depends on what you mean by love. To me love needs to be something I can touch."

"Money?"

"Are you joking? "

"You don't believe in anything you can't see?"

"Think, Berta, what you can see."

"The track of a subatomic particle, the detritus of the subconscious—" she leaned back into the dirty sofa and put her hands on the top of her head.

"For me, it's effort, and the effort isn't for anything it gives you back. The work of art, the fossil, the butterfly you name doesn't love you. But it's something you can touch as love."

"It's not enough."

"Oh, it is for me."

"But you do love, Farzi, you love me. I can't say if you love Tony...or Mrs. Aristosos, or anyone else, but I sense you do love me."

"Not for anything you give me."

"I ripped tape off my body for you—"

"Yes, but that isn't why I love you. It's an effort—"

"Farzi—"

"Like molding clay. It's what I feel for art alone and for you, and Mrs. Aristosos. It's very much the same. Listen, Darling, I can not give you a definition."

"But I eventually will approach one," she whispered, "I have to, for Rosie, for Margot...Hey, Margot. She must be wondering why I'm taking so long. I better get back."

The two women hugged fiercely. Farzi dropped her arms to her sides, "You go first. I've got to use the toilet.

Listen, I'll be out of the country before you get home tonight, and I'll call you from Switzerland as soon as I can. Go now."

Roberta pushed the scarred, outer door open and looked back at her still immobile friend, "Be careful."

"Go, Berta...get going."

Roberta loped down the balcony steps humming, *"Teo miseray"* and "Fare...well" floating freely in joyous evanescence.

Cam caught up to her as Roberta crushed through the lab door.

"Roberta, you've got to help me out. Something's come up."

"I'm in a big hurry."

"I've got a meeting, very important, this afternoon with the chancellor. I've got to be there. Can you drive Margot to the airport? Her plane leaves at three-forty-nine."

"Of course, but my car's in the shop again—"

"Well, get somebody's car or something, can't you?"

"Yes, I...of course. Don't let it bother you. I'll come get her at half past one." What did he think?

Since Rosie smashed the Neanderthal cast, the days working in the lab had been tedious. Dorcus could barely be civil. He ordered people about and carped without mercy at them over any supposed error. Now he had Jeffrey, pinned and wiggling, while he labeled parts of a fossil. Leaning over the seated graduate student Dorcus intoned while Jeffrey scribbled what looked like an auricular confession into the log: "frontal breath...frontal chord...frontal fraction and subtense...browridge thickness..."

Roberta hesitated, "Professor Dorcus, I'd like to speak to you for a moment, privately."

"Can't you see I'm busy?"

"I just wanted to tell you I'm joining Professor Friedrichsen's field team going to East Africa."

He pounced, puffed, accused and denounced so audacious the news struck him. But there was nothing he could do about it.

On the short drive to the airport Margot chirped happily sitting up like a lovely cedar waxwing while Roberta and Jill sporadically let drop casual or cryptic remarks between themselves.

"Well, you know, Mother, I didn't want to live here , but I certainly wouldn't mind joining you in Kenya for awhile. Africa would be excellent."

"Might be an appropriate graduation present, Margot."

"Africa, Roberta?"

"With Friedrichsen, for the field season."

"You decided on that out of the blue."

"I was going to ask, could you take care of my cat?"

"Yes. But what about Dorcus? Your job?"

"I'll get a leave or quit."

"Listen, Mother, Africa would be too awesome. You've got to arrange it with Grandmere and Pops."

The airport exit dropped them at the departures terminal. Margot insisted on saying good-bye before the security screening and waiting for takeoff alone. She didn't want to be a child.

On the drive back from the airport Jill broke the silence frequently with short anecdotes about Terry, Bill MacBeth, Tony; Roberta tried not to follow her line of thinking too closely.

"Terry said things'll never be the same between him and Tony because of Tony messing with Angelique. He knows how Bill feels, he says. I don't know how he could, since I've never slept with Tony. Never cheated on him at all, Terry, I mean. Terry says women ruin everything."

"Jill, did you ever wonder why, in men's minds, only the so-called bad women count for much?"

"Is this a trick question?"

"Yeah."

"Shut up, Roberta, will you?"

"Jill—"

"You always get me confused."

"Yeah, blessedly confused. I'm going to hate leaving my cat. You'd better take good care of him...probably four months."

"Oh, I will. Anyway, listen to this. Terry complained to me all last night, and then this morning Tony calls. Angelique's left town for good. Terry forgives Tony for his bad behavior toward Bill. So, I guess that means it was Angelique's fault. They're going to the races tomorrow."

"Did Angelique go home to Canada?"

"Not back to Bill, anyway, if she did. I don't think they know where she is. Honestly, Terry's been hard to live with ever since those two started screwing around. I hope they have luck at the track. The guys have all been running around so mad at each other." And on and on. Roberta punched at the radio button and curled herself against the door handle, like Rosie.

Having gone to bed early Saturday, Roberta, in the darkest part of the night, awoke abruptly to listen to a pause waiting for the next ring of the phone. She was sure that's what had awakened her. Nothing. No, it wasn't the telephone. She concentrated on listening again. Nothing. What was it anyway? She tried to drift off to sleep but felt restless and alert; her stomach complained. Clambering out of bed she sought the time. Eleven. Still possible to get something to eat at Pacho's.

At a back table Tracer sat arguing with a group of university people, Rosie, still bandaged but mending, to one side of her eating enchiladas clumsily, her left hand balancing them on a fork. Ordering rice and beans, Roberta squashed in at their table. Other people wound about the group some coming, some going, until Tracer, Rosie and Roberta, food consumed, sat alone nestled in the corner of the big table discussing Jacob who had just walked away.

"So then he finally got the pass. If he can let well enough alone for awhile. But does anyone follow my advice?"

"I did. I'm going back into the field. Africa. With Friedrichsen—"

"I'm overwhelmed. Let's celebrate. I'm ordering margaritas. No, Rosie, your underage drinking days are over." She called a waiter.

Rosie wrinkled her lip at Roberta almost as if noticing her for the first time.

"Well, Rosie, what's it like meeting Tracer's friends?"

"That Jacob's butt-ugly—"

"Isn't there anyone...no I suppose there isn't. What about Tracer? You approve of Tracer?"

"She's okay, I guess. The rest of the world is jerks."

Sipping the margarita Roberta described to Tracer how she'd smuggled her money to Farzi. Rosie seemed lost in contemplating the swirling people, oblivious to their conversation. When Jacob came back to announce he was leaving, Tracer joined him to exchange a few last words as he walked toward the door.

"Hey," Rosie began.

"My name's Roberta."

"I know."

"Can't you use it?"

Rosie watched Tracer end her conversation with Jacob and start out for their table getting stopped by a laughing couple half-way back. "We're gonna dig in New Mexico." Tracer guffawed, threw her head back, grabbed the man's hand. "Nobody beats up that big chickie," stated Rosie.

Roberta shook herself to upright, "That's straight."

"Hey...Roberta, you know what a teocallis is? We're gonna hop over to Mexico when we're down there and look at one."

Two days later clear ringing did arouse Roberta at five in the morning. She staggered, phone in hand, out of bed to the living room to properly wake up before speaking.

"Good morning."

"On your second cup of coffee?"

"I thought it might be you."

"Safe. Back in Europe."

"I'm going to be in Kenya for a few months. While I'm in the field, I want you to do a sculpture for me and deliver it to me in Nairobi."

"You couldn't afford one—"

"Never mind that."

Farzi pretended to cough, "What kind of piece do you want done?"

"Figures. A man and a woman. Locked in a love embrace."

"Ha." Farzi pitched her low, exotic laugh, "Old hat—"

"No, no hats at all. No clothes on. Stark naked."

"For you, Sweetie, I will cover their nude bodies all over with Neanderthal hair."

"Yes."